MOTHERS

MEMORIES, DREAMS AND REFLECTIONS
BY LITERARY DAUGHTERS

EDITED BY
SUSAN CAHILL

A MERIDIAN BOOK

NEW AMERICAN LIBRARY

NEW YORK AND SCARBOROUGH, ONTARIO

Acknowledgments

From *Womenfolks: Growing Up Down South* by Shirley Abbott. Copyright © 1983 by Shirley Abbott. Reprinted by permission of Ticknor & Fields, a Houghton Mifflin company.

From *A Very Easy Death* by Simone de Beauvoir, translated by Patrick O'Brian. Translation copyright © 1965 by Andre Deutsch Ltd., George Weidenfeld and Nicolson Ltd. and G. P. Putnam's Sons. Reprinted by permission of Pantheon Books, a division of Random House, Inc.

From *Seven Winters* by Elizabeth Bowen. Copyright © 1943 by Elizabeth Bowen. Reprinted by permission of Curtis Brown Ltd., London, and the Virago Press Ltd.

From *In My Mother's House: A Daughter's Story* by Kim Chernin. Copyright © 1983 by Kim Chernin. Reprinted by permission of Ticknor & Fields, a Houghton Mifflin company.

"Sido" from *Earthly Paradise* by Colette. Copyright © 1966 by Farrar, Straus and Giroux, Inc. Reprinted by permission of Farrar, Straus and Giroux, Inc.

From *An Unfinished Woman: A Memoir* by Lillian Hellman. Copyright © 1970 by Lillian Hellman. Reprinted by permission of Little, Brown and Company.

From *Facts of Life* by Maureen Howard. Copyright © 1975, 1978 by Maureen Howard. Reprinted by permission of Little, Brown and Company.

"My Wild Irish Mother" by Jean Kerr from *How I Got to Be Perfect*, copyright © 1978 by Collins Productions, Inc. Reprinted by permission of Doubleday & Company, Inc.

Selections from *The Summer of the Great-Grandmother* by Madeleine L'Engle. Copyright © 1974 by Crosswicks, Ltd. Reprinted by permission of Farrar, Straus and Giroux, Inc.

From *Bring Me a Unicorn*, copyright © 1971, 1972 by Anne Morrow Lindbergh. Reprinted by permission of Harcourt, Brace Jovanovich, Inc.

(The following page constitutes an extension of the copyright page.)

MENTOR TRADEMARK REG. U.S. PAT. OFF. AND FOREIGN COUNTRIES
REGISTERED TRADEMARK—MARCA REGISTRADA
HECHO EN CHICAGO, U.S.A.

SIGNET, SIGNET CLASSIC, MENTOR, ONYX, PLUME, MERIDIAN and NAL BOOKS are published *in the United States* by NAL PENGUIN INC., 1633 Broadway, New York, New York 10019, *in Canada* by The New American Library of Canada Limited, 81 Mack Avenue, Scarborough, Ontario M1L 1M8

Library of Congress Catalog Card Number: 87–62465

First Printing, April, 1988

1 2 3 4 5 6 7 8 9

PRINTED IN THE UNITED STATES OF AMERICA

In memory of my mother,
Florence Splain Neunzig

CONTENTS

INTRODUCTION

"A woman writing thinks back through her mothers," wrote Virginia Woolf in *A Room of One's Own* in 1929. Since then there has been an abundance and wide variety of literature written by women on the subject of the mother-daughter bond. Psychological accounts such as Nancy Friday's *My Mother/My Self* continue to interest a popular audience as do other nonfictional works (journals and diaries) on the order of *Between Ourselves: Letters of Mothers and Daughters*, which was first published in England. Several recent novels, all of astounding power and talent, constitute at least a semester's reading on the theme of the mother's presence in the writing daughter's consciousness and affections. In fictions as different in tone as Susan Kenney's *In Another Country*, Sue Miller's *The Good Mother*, Ellen Currie's *Available Light*, and Susan Minot's *Monkeys*, 'writing women think back through their mothers.' The critical mind working in *A Room of One's Own* does not date.

This book, *Mothers: Memories, Dreams and Reflections by Literary Daughters* is a collection of nonfiction (essays, memoirs, letters, excerpts from autobiographies) by well-known women writers on the subject of their mothers. In positive tones and vivid colors these writers remember the particulars of their mothers' influence: what they looked and smelled and sounded like, what they said and did, how they thought as mothers and neighbors and citizens, who they were as people, and what difference it all made to their daughters' unfolding.

Through the daughter's remembering eyes we see Eudora Welty's mother challenging the rules of the local librarian in Jackson, Mississippi, on her young daughter's behalf. We see Colette's beloved Sido simultaneously tending her Burgundian garden and her daughter's fertile sensibility. We hear Paule Marshall's mother and her friends teaching a little girl the power of language within the setting of a powerless woman's world, a Brooklyn kitchen. Several mothers (Welty's, Marshall's, Howard's, Abbott's) trained their daughters' ear, gave a sharp sense of the voice of the spoken and written word. Others, by example and with words, taught values and the courage to live by them. We applaud Faye Moskowitz's mother, who encourages her anxious adolescent daughter to be proud of her Judaism in small-town Jackson, Michigan. We witness the senility and the dying of the mothers of Madeleine L'Engle and Simone de Beauvoir; we experience their daughters' profound compassion. In excerpts that together form a two-generational portrait, Margaret Mead sketches her mother's character and Margaret Mead's daughter, Mary Catherine Bateson, remembers Margaret Mead, in particular the attitudes behind her mother's child-rearing practices and the sexual morality she encouraged in her daughter. What runs through all these selections is an intense emotional current that joins the engaging mothers and their sensitive, alert daughters across the generations. How the daughters, who grew up to become writers, perceived the features of their mothers' gifts (which are sometimes unconventional—we marvel at Dervla Murphy's mother in County Waterford, Ireland, and at Kim Chernin's in the Bronx) has been transformed in the following selections into a luminous body of literature. (That body would be larger, were it possible financially. It would feature Dorothy Canfield Fisher's "What My Mother Taught Me," her fine introduction to her collected *Harvest of Stories*; an excerpt from Maxine Hong Kingston's *A Woman Warrior*; and Alice Walker's "In Search of Our Mothers' Garden." The two latter pieces can be found in that superb and ample collection, *The Norton Anthology of Literature by Women*.)

"We are our memory," the Argentine writer Jorge Luis Borges once wrote. That insight reverberates throughout this collection. Reading, we sift the writers' memories and through the power of the language their mothers taught them we are moved by their effort to make sense of the lives they remember when they were children, their mothers' clay. What is common to all the various incarnations here (and these writers represent a broad cultural span, from Elizabeth Bowen in late-Victorian Dublin to Audre Lorde in Depression-era Harlem) is the strength and resilience of the bond itself, as eternal and as radical as memory itself.

These collected glimpses of the mother-daughter bond take us finally to the heart of reality itself, to the essential truth of the human condition. What we find at the core of our experience is not a heart of darkness, an experience of separateness and loneliness. Rather, what we come upon is an experience of attachment: relationship and communion are the most significant clues surrounding the mystery of our human nature. They tell us the most about who we are.

Stories of inhumanity often begin when the mother, for one sad reason or another, is no longer in the child's picture. Something has gone wrong and the mother-child bond is broken. The child feels abandoned and life becomes a process of trying to recover what was lost. A recent study of Virginia Woolf, *The Invisible Presence: Virginia Woolf and the Mother-Daughter Relationship* by Ellen Bayuk Rosenman, locates the loss of the writer's mother when she was thirteen years old as the turning point in Virginia Woolf's life. The author makes a strong case for reading Woolf's fiction as an unceasing attempt to resurrect the lost mother, to recover the essential female presence, and to console her inconsolable self.

Such an interpretation of one writer's biography and art can be read as a variation on the mythological theme of Demeter and Persephone. In that story the goddess-mother presides over the cessation of the earth's fertility until her lost daughter is returned from Hades, the underground of death. Nothing can live or grow on earth while the mother-daughter bond is broken. The implication is that this bond is essential to the progress of life itself. Nothing can grow while this relational circle of love and caring remains violated.

Does this ancient myth exaggerate or hit squarely a profound human truth?

In the passion and the seriousness of their attention to their maternal presences, the writers in this collection convince me that the ancient myth bears the seed of truth. This book contains its extraordinary germinations and a few enchanting flowerings.

MOTHERS

MEMORIES, DREAMS AND REFLECTIONS
BY LITERARY DAUGHTERS

SHIRLEY ABBOTT *grew up in Hot Springs, Arkansas, and moved north after college. She has been a Fulbright scholar, an editor at* Horizon *magazine, a contributor to* Harper's, American Heritage, *and* Esquire, *and the author of several books about food and antiques. The selection that follows is taken from her book* Womenfolks: Growing Up Down South *(1983), a rich blend of personal memoir and meditation on family myth and tradition. It is both an illuminating examination of mothers and daughters and a vivid tribute to the gritty, independent women who were the South's true heroines. Shirley Abbott writes about Southern women, especially her maternal Scotch-Irish ancestors, with such insight and compassion that we feel until* Womenfolks *we've scarcely read anything true about the American South. It is as if we are seeing the territory and its people whole for the first time.*

1

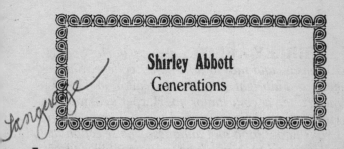

language

Shirley Abbott
Generations

In a piece about Black English for the *New York Times*, James Baldwin observed that language is "the most vivid and crucial key to identity: it reveals the private identity and connects one with, or divorces one from the larger, public, or communal identity." My mother had such a language of identity—hillbilly English, which once was just such a key to identity as James Baldwin describes. The Southern migrant in the twentieth century has been forced to carry it around like a cardboard valise, evidence that he is a transient arriving in vain at the door of Grand Hotel. Hillbilly English was the language of the dying frontier, of the farm and the backwoods in an ancient social order. Not much is left of it now except in show business. It makes the Grand Ole Opry grand, and it was what made L'il Abner funny. In the movies it marks out the rubes and the demagogues, as it has in many novels, Faulkner's or James Dickey's *Deliverance*, for example. Its wiry, leathery locutions come with a mythic

---

From *Womenfolks: Growing Up Down South.*

overlay thrown in for free—poor white trash, mean and lowdown. Ignorant. Dumb. Like Black English, it causes doors to be slammed shut. This was my mother's speech, and it separated us. Women have carved identities distinct from their mothers' by having lovers or going to law school or getting married at dawn in their bare feet, but my ticket to independence was standard English.

Folklorists, out in the high hollows with tape recorders, have been telling us for decades that the ancient speech habits of the Southern mountains date back to Renaissance English and have miraculously survived unscathed, just like the dulcimers that presumably hang on the wall of every cabin. They cite old forms like "holp" for "helped," "ary a one" for "none," and other archaisms dear to the hearts of grammarians. Dear to my heart, too, for I can remember hearing this language used in earnest. Even as late as the 1950s, hillbilly English was still a fairly pristine state in backwoods Arkansas, and I'm as eager as anybody to give it an Elizabethan pedigree.

It was as rough as a fresh-sawed board, with none of the cadences of the Tidewater accent or the soft resonances of black speech. It twanged like an out-of-tune banjo, and if Shakespeare was its great-grandsire, its more immediate ancestry was ignorance, abetted by isolation. After she moved to town, my mother struggled daily not to say "I taken" and "he don't." She learned, after several years, that what you did to a shirt collar was not "arning" and what an automobile had four of was not "tars," and that "them" was not the same as "those." She left off

3

saying she was "aimin' " to do a thing, but never got rid of "hisself" and "theirself." Alas, there were no linguists hanging around Hot Springs to reassure her that she sounded like a seventeenth-century English peasant.

How I shrank from it, as I had shrunk from my grandmother's coffin. But what a wonderful language it was. People didn't leave, they "taken off," and they takened off their clothes and takened a dose of salts. (I never figured out when to add the *ed* to it.) They never searched for a thing: they "hunted it up," and they did as they "ort." They "warshed" things out, and then they "rinched" them. My Aunt Vera, of legendary tidiness, spent a lifetime rinching her hair, her underpants and her dishrags, rinching off her porch, her feet, or her nieces who had been making mudpies. She and my mother were forever "fixin' " to do this or that, and if you asked when, they always said, "dreckly," which is "directly," but meant "when I get around to it."

If they wanted a hug from a child they commanded, "Give me some sugar," and sassy kids were threatened with "little keen switches across them bare laigs." The *a* at the end of a given name was usually transformed into *y*. (Four sisters I knew whose names were Edna, Elva, Nola, and Lola, have gone through life as Edny, Elvy, Noly, and Loly. There was a fifth, but her name had been Roxy to start with.) In hillbilly, people never scolded anybody, they "quarreled at" a person, and anyone in a bad temper was "a-quarrelin' "—"Yonder comes my papa just a-quarrelin'," or "mad as an old sore-tailed cat."

People were seldom in love; they were "foolish about" somebody. "He's just foolish about Maria." Cheese and cabbage and molasses were spoken of in the plural. "Pass me those cheese," or " . . . them cheese." "Bed" was never just bed, but "the bed." Nobody went to bed, he "got in the bed," and lazy people "laid in the bed" until whatever late morning hours they got out of the bed.

It was a language generous with pronouns. Never "let's," but "let's us." "Let's us go on over to your allses house and eat us some dinner." "Hunt you up a rockin' chair, and set down awhile." This double-barreled, nailed-down dative was used whenever it possibly could be. People were always urging me to "put you a spoonful of them good preserves" on my biscuit, or "drink you a glass of that cold buttermilk." There was something tender and owlish in this odd locution, as if one ought to perform these homely acts with thankfulness that the benefit of them was strictly personal, something that did not need to be divided up and shared.

Hard workers were the "workingest," fast runners the "runningest," sagging barns the "torndownest," smart dogs the "beatin'-est." Adjectives were generally frowned on, but you could always take the small plain ones and lay them on in threes—"a great big ole," "a tiny little bitty," "a hateful mean ole." It was as lavish and unstudied as country hospitality. The days of log rolling and corn husking were past by the time I was born, but the spirit was the same. People hardly ever issued specific invitations. The courtesy was not to invite but to go. People just showed up and were always made

5

welcome: it was an excuse to stop work. To stay less than an hour was an insult, and there was always a meal. Nobody ever was let out of a house without the goodbye ritual, which could take up to three hours. "No, now you don't have no business going off so soon, you just got here." "Now, come on, stay all night with us, don't say no." And in working out the details of a refusal or acceptance, the talk would begin again. I have wasted away on many a doorstep while my mother spent the afternoon saying goodbye at some second cousin's home.

All this was topsy-turvy from uptown manners, just as the grammar was crazy. It drove me mad. By the age of ten I had become a snob, as fearful of dangling my participles as of laying hold of the wrong fork at some well-set dinner table. Nobody north of the Mason-Dixon line would have been able to see much difference between my mother's manners and those of our city friends, but she was definitely an outsider. Furthermore, she knew she embarrassed me. I knew I was being an ass, even then, and I tried not to be embarrassed. But it was not the surface of her speech that mattered—it was its connotations, the closemouthedness, the toughness, the weight of familial devotion it carried.

"A language," Baldwin said, "comes into existence by means of brutal necessity, and the rules of the language are dictated by what the language must convey." Hillbilly was all hardship and conspicuous self-denial and rough wit. No fancy words. Nothing abstract. It was a tool for hellfire sermons, bawdy jokes, gospel songs, and insults. In its very vocabulary was contempt for all things intellectual.

But it was clean and sweet. It is as old as Black English and as great a liability. Mother spoke a pretty version of it, but I took care not to talk like "thet."

Between her and me there was much anguish. As any second-generation immigrant knows, to refuse to speak the language of one's ancestors is the ultimate breach. Yet she was able to forgive me one way or another for such tricks as going into the country with her and calling all the women "ahnt" instead of "aint."

As I have said, my mother was not an ideologue, nor given to analyzing things, and what she might have thought of the modern feminist movement I cannot say. Out on the farm the subject of women's rights was irrelevant, but she did come to believe in women's rights once she began working for wages. (In much the same way, she believed in Saint Peter waiting at the Pearly Gates. There had to be such a thing, even though she had never personally seen it.) Her job at the tourist cabins for three dollars a week was a fair enough beginning. She had many other kinds of work after that. Running a mangle in a laundry was one of the things she did before I was born. About the time my father decided to become a farmer, when I was thirteen, his health and fortunes began to fail. Mother went right back into the job market, selling clothing and shoes in various department stores, clerking and cashiering in a drugstore, taking in sewing on weekends. She both worked and kept house, and she nursed my father

7

through diabetes and other ailments that finally carried him off.

The best job mother ever had was as assistant physical therapist in a local hospital that treated arthritis. She had had to train for the post, and it had a semblance of professional status even though it was hard labor, often in a steamy therapeutic pool. She liked it, though. It was the only job she had that didn't seem pointless. She began there in 1959 and by 1967 had worked up to sixty-five dollars a week. Men on the hospital staff doing exactly the same work made more, but there was no point protesting. The threat of layoff was all too vivid. She could have been replaced the next day. Of all the Southern states only Texas ratified the Equal Rights Amendment (Tennessee and Kentucky ratified but rescinded), and one state, Mississippi, never even gave suffrage a *pro forma* Yea. Not surprisingly, Southern working women fare worse than any in the nation. "Blacks and women," according to a report of the Southern Regional Council, continued through the 1970s to hold low-status, low-paying jobs. In 1975, not one black woman was making as much as $13,000 per year, and in the sixteen Southern cities surveyed, only one per cent of all skilled workers were women. The Southern female, who is supposed to hold so special a niche in the fond masculine heart, has had rough treatment in the marketplace.

Not too surprisingly, therefore, Mother never perceived work as anything exciting or glamorous. It was something you did because you needed the money. You had no union, no seniority, and no guarantee that your responsibilities would not be increased by 50 per cent without any commensurate rise in salary. Benefits, of course, were something accruing to the employer. So whatever job she had, she took care to get to work early and stay late. When her supervisor, always a man, spoke harshly to her, she took her rebukes mildly and spoke her mind only at home. Her preference—and in this she was at one with most of the women she knew—would have been not ever to work for wages at all. Housework struck her as easy and satisfying by comparison. At least in the house she was in charge of something.

But in one way, Mother was a kind of radical, or at least events turned in such a way that she began to look like a radical. Some time in the late 1960s feminists brought forth the notion of sisterhood—of women bonded to women. Sisterhood was going to be "powerful," our Hanseatic League, our lobbying arm in the corridors of heightened awareness. But sisterhood was nothing new to me. It has been a zealously guarded secret among Southern women for years. Next to motherhood, sisterhood is what they value most, taking an endless pleasure in the daily, commonplace society of one another that they never experience in male company.

The most vivid memories of my childhood are long afternoons when my aunt Vera would come to our house with her daughter, June, and the four of us would form a kind of subversive cell. June and I would usually play, indoors and out, while our mothers sewed or quilted or canned. Sometimes the four of us would dress and get in the car and drive around Hot Springs, buying thread and snaps at the dry-goods store, visiting some spring or other and drinking from tin cups, or "ratting up and down," as my aunt called it, on Central Avenue. Hearing what they said on these afternoons, I gradually realized that my mother and her sister were not awed by men in the least, that they preferred each other's company to that of their respective husbands.

I also realized that these two women had certain unmatronly desires, usually involving beautiful dresses and travel, that otherwise went unmentioned: merely the circumspect fantasies of a pair of young housewives caught in the coils of the commonplace. And yet, sharing these fantasies made them laugh, gave them a secret life as they bent their dark heads over the sewing machine or a "pinker" that never would pink. I could not have voiced the idea, but I knew that the part of their lives they liked most was here, with each other. Not at the supper table or at work or in bed with their husbands. My father used to be jealous of these tête-à-têtes, and he had cause.

Often I spent summer afternoons in larger groups of women, not my kin. The neighborhood beauty shop is one of the foundations of society in small Southern towns. You go there to get your hair "fixed," but that isn't the real reason, any more than men congregate at the county courthouse to transact legal business. The beauty operator is invariably a middle-aged woman who found herself in need of a trade and solved the problem by getting her license and having some shampoo sinks and hair dryers installed on the glassed-in porch. All the neighborhood women would have standing appointments, as my mother did, and they'd bring their children along. It was an all-female society—no man would dare enter the place—and here, if nowhere else, women said what they thought about men. And what they thought was often fairly murderous.

Those sweet-faced wives and mothers would sit there wafting their wet, red fingernails in the air, hoping to get them dry before the comb-out was finished, saying, "Now, Maidie, spray me good, I want it to last through tomorrow. I'll sleep with my head in a bonnet." They would gossip, of course. Every teen-age romance or impending marriage, separation, illness, operation, or death got its going-over. But the leitmotif of the song they sang was their loyalty and fortitude in the face of male foolishness, and as a keen obligato, "Don't ever let them know what you really think of them. Humor them. Pretend you love them. Even love them, if you must. But play a strong card to their weak one." That was not what they said, but it was what they meant, and it is an attitude that often runs through the conversations and the writing of Southern women.

It was always the same, wherever I went. As they drank their cokes, folded their stacks of fresh towels, played bridge, or sewed, they assured one another, "Men are children. Men are little boys. They can't stand pain. They never grow up. They can't face the truth." All this information was deeply buried in metaphor. "Albert got up at three o'clock to go fishing this morning. Was just going to tiptoe out, he said. Well, he couldn't find his hipboots, and I thought he would tear the house down. I finally had to get up and find them for him. It was five by the time he left." Or, "I told him if he wanted to smoke that nasty pipe, he could smoke it outside. I wasn't going to have that smell in my living room." Or, "He's just like a little child. If you don't have supper on the table the minute he gets home, he gets mad. 'Course, after you feed him, you can get him to do anything."

This was their means to survival, a minority strategy worked out and handed along from mother to daughter. But it was a very hard bargain, hardest in some ways for the men. Southern men, and in particular the writers, are as a rule so fixated in their points of view that they seldom realize what the women are thinking about them—or doing to them. Occasionally, one of them suspects what is happening. James Dickey was quoted in the *New York Times* on the subject of Southern women. "They're very loving and affectionate, but they really think their men are dependent upon them. If their man is brilliant, they think he's brilliant because they've helped him to be brilliant. Basically they think their men are weak . . ."

Southern women are supposedly taught to bat their eyelids and be weak, but I know very few of them who are truly dependent, no matter what they may pretend. In the end, how can they have perfect respect for people they regard as small boys to be tolerated, put up with, cajoled? "If I ever finish my education, I'm going to live in the North," a young black woman said to me recently in Atlanta. "I told my daddy I was, and he didn't get mad! So then my mother scolded me, and she said, 'Don't you know that's no way to handle your daddy? If you want him to give you the money to go North, at least wait to ask him until after he's had a good meal, and then talk sweet to him. Don't just up and tell him what you are going to do.' That's always what Mother says. I went to visit my cousins in Brooklyn last summer, and they say what they think, whether anybody has had a good dinner or not."

My mother and I were double-sided people, often at cross-purposes. She felt her responsibilities toward me keenly and tried to make a woman of me (she must have despaired of the task, since I was indolent by nature and spent most of my time listening to radio serials and reading. What she taught was not necessarily what I learned. Her spoken lessons were just what any good mother of the 1940s was teaching her daughter. But what she really wanted me to know I learned by going to the movies and the beauty parlor with her and through what I overheard her saying to my aunt as they sewed. I listened well. I was a better student than she thought. But one of the things she most wanted me to learn was something I never quite absorbed: dissimulate. Hide. Never let anybody know what your true feelings are. Unlike that of the belle, however, her purpose was defensive rather than predatory.

Psychiatrists, understandably enough since most of them are men, have always focused on the passion that little girls feel for their fathers. Girls are all supposed to be in training from babyhood, sensing out the contours of love and loss as we fall in love with Daddy and are forced to postpone our pleasure. But I was in love with my mother, too. I hated her doing housework, could not bear the sight of her in an old dress and a pair of unlaced oxfords, feeding soapy bed sheets into the wringer, scraping carrots and parsnips at the sink. But one thing she had acquired in town was the ability to be glamorous, to divorce herself, by means of paints and polishes, from that other world. I loved her glamorous aspect.

She had a wonderful drawer full of cosmetics. I think the women in her family must have yearned for such things since the dawn of time. In any case, my mother thought that make up was one of the fine arts. She had an enormous dressing table, a yellow satin-veneer piece with a knee-hole and a mirrored top, and a vast standing mirror that reflected the whole bedroom. There was a little low-backed bench and four drawers; in them she kept all her wonderful implements of beauty. Not every day, but once a week, or any time she was going out shopping, she would bathe, put on her stockings and a lacy slip and high-heeled shoes, and sit down to paint. I would abandon dog, swing, book, or any other pursuit in order to watch her. I'd come indoors and post myself beside the bench.

The open drawers gave off the most ravishing smells. Down in their depths sat little white jars with pink lids, black cylinders trimmed in silver, pink glass things with tiny roses on top, high-domed boxes with face powder inside (if you opened these on your own, they'd blow dust all over the table top), fresh powder puffs, miniature caskets with

14

trick openings, compacts with pearl lids that shut with a glamorous click, vials of astringent and witch hazel, red boxes with logs of mascara inside, and pencils for what Mother always called her "eye-browls." Most seductive of all were the perfume bottles, some with glass stoppers and ribbons around the neck, one with a figurine on top. (No doubt there was enough coal-tar dye and other harrowing poisons in this array to have murdered any number of Renaissance popes. This was long before we learned to fear our own chemical magic. Maybe, in fact, the paint pots were what killed her.)

She would take her tweezers and hand mirror, search her freckled face for any wayward sprouts and swiftly uproot them. Anxious about a black hair or two on her upper lip, she would apply a thick paste, that looked like a pale green caterpillar beneath her nose. It had to set five minutes, and it had a loathsome vinegary stench. I smell it still. When she removed the goo, she looked exactly as she had before, but she would survey the defoliated terrain with the solemnity of a military tactician.

Meanwhile, I would be taking the tops off all the lipsticks and unscrewing jar lids, hoping to have a say-so in what she applied next. I liked the smoky eye shadow, the blue rouge (it *was* blue), the dark maroon lipstick, and whatever came in exotic packaging. But she seldom followed my leads, except on the evenings she went out alone. My parents never went out together, but once every few weeks or so, after doing the supper dishes, Mother would dress and disappear and neither she nor Daddy would tell me where she was going. I imagined her meeting handsome men, sipping coffee with them in the grill room of some hotel. It turned out, years later, that what she did was go to the movies by herself, while I agonized at home, pleased by the notion that she was having a romance and ravaged with jealousy at the same time—jealous of what, I still can't say.

On those rare afternoons when she did abandon her housework and go out, she would leave the blue rouge and maroon lipstick in their cases, and having brought her face to its state of daytime perfection, she would take up her car keys and shut the door on her immaculate house. She and I would set off for town together, and she seemed so beautiful to me in those moments that I loved her with all my heart—indeed I was in love with her. Unless we were going to the movies, town was a complete bust. We'd go find a parking place and go into Woolworth's for a spool of thread and a nickel's worth of candy. Maybe we'd look at a pattern book, and sometimes, to my despair, she'd bump into one of her thousands of cousins on the street and talk for half an hour. The exoticism of the afternoon would vanish sooner than the bag of candy.

Many years later I stopped to wonder why a woman of her thoroughly practical inclinations would spend upwards of an hour prettying up to go to the dime store. She certainly was not trying to attract a man. In the middle of the afternoon in Hot Springs, Arkansas, the only visible men were pumping gas in filling stations. She was not doing it for Daddy, for by the time he got home from work, she'd be in a housedress again, perspiring over the kitchen range. Nor was she competing with other women. She was doing it for fun, and for a mark of her separateness, and for a way of showing herself—and me—that even so responsible a person as herself could do something that had no purpose to it. It was her one real break with her past. Maybe she wanted to let me know, in the most subtle way, that femininity was not merely the massive, serious, strenuous thing she usually made it seem to be, but occasionally a matter of pleasing yourself. And thus she delved into that dresser drawer, which is one of the most ancient sources of womanly corruption, without being corrupted by it.

One August morning, when I was thirty-three and a long-gone Northerner, I stood beside Mother at the very same dresser drawer and once again watched her make up her face. Her right hand was faltering that day; for a reason that she claimed not to understand her fingers could not quite handle the stoppers and lids and paraphernalia. Once again, I helped a bit, undid the caps, snapped the little containers shut. I knew, although she did not quite yet realize it, that she was dying. The mastectomy four years earlier had not cured the cancer, which had instead metastasized into a clump of wild cells now thriving in the left lobe of her brain, and in her spine, her ribs, her femurs, her tibias. Nevertheless, on this morning she had awakened optimistic, feeling better, she said. She wanted to get dressed and go out. Worn out by the effort, she lay down, and in the afternoon she had the first of several seizures —an intimation of mortality, a fast and vicious dress rehearsal for her death throes six months later. Then I think she realized what was wrong, though she did not say so, even after the terror had let up. After that day, there was no more frivolity. She never opened the dresser drawer again.

The South may be the last place where dying is still sometimes a community project. My father died two years before my mother, but his stay in the hospital, as the obituaries say, was brief. Mother's illness, which went on for six months, reached out and transformed the daily routine of a dozen people. Sometimes, sitting at her bedside and knowing exactly who would arrive and at what time, I used to wonder what we all had done before she got sick. I had left my husband and my job in New York and had come to stay with her full time. I could have hired a nurse, I suppose, to stay with her at home, during the few weeks she was well enough to be at home. But the indecent passion she had felt for her mother at last laid hold of me. I couldn't bear the idea of anyone but me waiting on her, cutting up her food in tiny pieces, washing her nightgowns, cleaning her house, taking her a bedpan at 3 A.M. Exhausted at one point, I considered hiring a nurse or a housekeeper but the whole family recoiled. It had to be my hands and their hands. It was the only way we could confront our rage at what had overtaken her.

As her spine dissolved, and her speech worsened, and she lost the ability to read and write, and she became almost immobile, I took a certain grim pleasure in making her as comfortable as I could. She was doing what she could for me, too. She seldom cried out, and she never complained, even though a change of sheets or merely having the bed cranked up was almost unbearable agony. She used to pretend to be asleep every afternoon so I could read, and I read the way a chainsmoker smokes—getting through two or three paperbacks a day, piling the used-up novels on the dresser, by the chair, in the corner of the room, like unemptied ashtrays.

She finally went to the hospital so that she could have injections of morphine. (Ironically, she almost always refused them. She said they didn't kill the pain but locked her up inside it.) This was a homey, almost countrified place where the needs of the dying were understood and always had been. The nurses brought me a cot so I could spend the nights, and for almost six months I lived there with her. In order to keep ourselves intact, she and I set up an unvarying routine: we awakened at seven as the morning prayer was broadcast over the loudspeaker. I gave her water and brushed her teeth. I brought the bedpan. Her breakfast came. I helped her deal with it. Then I changed her linen and got dressed myself and went outside in search of coffee. By then it would be eight o'clock, and I would go and telephone her sister and her brothers and her best friends, all of whom wanted a morning report regardless of the fact that they came to visit every afternoon.

That got us through to half past eight. I was always stunned by the hundreds of actions one could perform in a hospital room and still use up only ninety minutes of one day. The rest of the day proceeded just the same deliberate way, each hour measured out carefully, marked by arrivals and departures. She never wanted to talk about what was happening to her; the word "cancer" was not in her vocabulary. I felt, uneasily, that we ought to be talking about it. It was well enough, I guessed, to have hidden all the facts of love in this impenetrable caul of reticence all one's life, but we were grown women now, and she was dying. Could we not even talk of that? Yet neither of us ever spoke. And once again, as I think back on it, it scarcely matters. What could we have said?

At first her self-control was hard-won: her face often had a desperate look about it, and she would weep and then stop weeping without offering any explanation. But then she got control again, and the control eventually turned into serenity. Only once, in the final months, did I see it break. She awoke one morning in November and asked what date it was. It happened to be my birthday, and for reasons that I did not immediately understand, she began to cry. "Don't worry, Mother," I kept saying. "I don't care if it's my birthday. You don't have to give me a present." I dared not tell her she didn't have to bake a cake. "Tell you what, I'll go get some cupcakes, and we'll celebrate this afternoon."

That only made things worse, and then it dawned on me. Long ago she had made the revolutionary decision to have only one child, or at least not to have twelve children and then turn them into farmhands. So as she lay on her deathbed, the event mattered to her. She was not crying because it was my birthday. She was crying because years before, on that same morning, she had been twenty-one and had had a baby. Now, in so short a time, a bewildered young woman stood beside her hoping to distract her from thoughts of death. I had assumed, as always, that her concern was for me. But she was grieving for another young woman.

In the last month of her life, she lost the power of speech almost completely: that hillside in the brain's left hemisphere where words are manufactured had apparently been eaten up, strip mined. Sometimes, with enormous effort, she could repeat a word or two if she watched my mouth very carefully. Sometimes, bending over her, I would call her Mama, and she would say the word. I could tell by the vexation in her eyes that she knew it was the wrong name for me, but it was all she could do. I'd always laugh, and she liked that. One evening her brothers and I were sitting around the hospital room, too tired to talk or think, just watching her sleep, all of us worn down with knowing that she was locked up in pain that might last for months more. She woke and saw us and moved her left hand, clearly in need of something. Her younger brother bounded up to do the guesswork—water? an injection? ice cream? No, she smiled, but we could see her growing impatient. Finally, when we had all tried everything, she made an enormous effort. Like a kid who knows the answer to a riddle, she opened her mouth and said one clear syllable: "Brush." And so her brother brushed her hair, and she fell asleep again, and next day died.

I don't know how many women like her are still left. I don't know whether her doctrine is the right one—if that is the word to apply to her beliefs. She would have understood the things that many women

21

are now determined to gain—titles, power, high salaries, the right to define themselves by male standards of success. She certainly knew firsthand why women need an education and good salaries, and it never occurred to her that they need to apologize for working outside the home, or in it either.

But the idea that happiness is likely to result from having a succession of lovers she would have thought silly. To exchange the certainties of the kitchen and the laundry room for the risky pleasures of the boudoir would have struck her as a dubious bargain. She didn't believe that feminine liberation had anything to do with sex but rather with paychecks.

Nor could she ever have agreed that housework is degrading drudgery that ought to be sloughed off on the maid, or that children drag a woman down. In fact, the whole notion that an assiduous fussing over one's own self, an endless vigil over one's own feelings and moods, an elaborate absorption in one's own body could be a source of satisfaction or a way of life would have astounded her. I think she would have gotten a good laugh over the recent discovery of certain avant-garde women that the experience of having a baby and raising it is, after all, worthwhile. But she wouldn't have laughed too hard. She never was the sort to downgrade other people's accomplishments.

She was one of the mass of women who work as housewives or as underpaid help in the outside world. Urban, educated feminists tend to dislike them for being regressive and reactionary and a passel of ingrates. I myself have become some sort of urban, educated feminist, and my mother and I are still at

22

crosspurposes. Particularly since my daughters were born, she has whispered in my ear each night as I slept, trying to remake me in her image. I battle her off as well as I can, but she touches me still, and I love her. I would not want my children to grow up without knowing what their grandmother thought.

SIMONE de BEAUVOIR'S A Very Easy Death, *the source of the following excerpt, was published in France in 1964 under the title* Une Mort Très Douce *and was greeted with stunning critical acclaim. A profoundly moving, day-by-day account of the death of the author's mother, it is a deeply personal story that reveals a face of Simone de Beauvoir hitherto unknown. Though the tone is detached (as in* Memoirs of a Dutiful Daughter*) and the eye critical (as in* The Second Sex*), the daughter's feelings are strong and loyal. Somehow they translate into a preserving and humble voice. In these pages the writer's dying mother, as well as all of suffering and grieving humanity, are honored.*

Simone de Beauvior
from
A VERY EASY DEATH

As soon as I woke up, I telephoned my sister.
Maman had come to in the middle of the night; she
knew that she had been operated upon and she
hardly seemed at all surprised. I took a cab. The
same journey, the same warm blue autumn, the
same nursing-home. But I was stepping into another story: instead of a convalescence, a deathbed.
Before, I came here to spend comparatively unemo-
tional hours; I went through the hall without paying
attention. It was behind those closed doors that the
tragedies were taking place: nothing showed through.
From now on one of these dramas belonged to me.
I went up the stairs as quickly as I could, as slowly
as I could. Now there was a sign hanging on the
door: No Visitors. The scene had changed. The bed
was in the position it had been the day before, with
both sides free. The sweets had been put away in
cupboards; so had the books. There were no flowers any more on the big table in the corner, but
bottles, balloon-flasks, test-tubes. Maman was asleep;
she no longer had the tube in her nose and it was
less painful to look at her, but, under the bed, one

26

could see jars and pipes that communicated with her stomach and her intestines. Her left arm was attached to an intravenous drip. She was no longer wearing any clothes whatever: the bed-jacket was spread over her chest and her naked shoulders. A new character had made her appearance—a private nurse, Mademoiselle Leblon, as gracious as an Ingres portrait. She had a blue headdress to cover her hair and white padded slippers on her feet: she supervised the drip and shook the flask to dilute its plasma. My sister told me that according to the doctors a respite of some weeks or even of some months was not impossible. She had said to Professor B 'But what shall we say to Maman when the disease starts again, in another place?' 'Don't worry about that. We shall find something to say. We always do. And the patient always believes it.'

In the afternoon Maman had her eyes open: she spoke so that one could hardly make out what she said, but sensibly. 'Well,' I said to her, 'so you break your leg and they go and operate on you for appendicitis!'

She raised one finger and, with a certain pride, whispered, 'Not appendicitis. Pe-ri-ton-it-is.' She added. 'What luck . . . be here.'

'You are glad that I am here?'

'No. Me.' Peritonitis: and her being in this clinic had saved her! The betrayal was beginning. 'Glad not to have that tube. So glad!' . . .

I showed Maman the book of crosswords Chantal had brought. Speaking to the nurse she faltered, 'I have a big dictionary, the new Larousse; I treated myself to it, for crosswords.' That dictionary: one of her last delights. She had talked to me about it for a long time before she bought it, and her face lit up every time I consulted it. 'We'll bring it for you,' I said.

'Yes. And *Le Nouvel Œdipe* too; I have not got all the . . .'

One had to listen very intently to catch the words that she laboured to breathe out; words whose mystery made them as disturbing as those of an oracle. Her memories, her desires, her anxieties were floating somewhere outside time, turned into unreal and poignant dreams by her childlike voice and the imminence of her death.

She slept a great deal; from time to time she took up a few drops of water through the tube; she spat in paper handkerchiefs that the nurse held to her mouth. In the evening she began to cough: Mademoiselle Laurent, who had come to ask after her, straightened her up, massaged her and helped her to spit. Afterwards Maman looked at her with a real smile—the first for four days.

Poupette decided to spend her nights at the nursing-home. 'You were with Papa and Grandmama when they died; I was far away,' she said to me. 'I am going to look after Maman. Besides, I want to stay with her.'

I agreed. Maman was astonished. 'What do you want to sleep here for?'

'I slept in Lionel's room when he was operated on. It's always done.'

'Oh, I see.'

I went home, feverish with 'flu. Leaving the overheated clinic I had caught cold in the autumnal

dampness: I went to bed, stupefied with pills. I did
not switch off the telephone: Maman might die at
any moment, 'blown out like a candle,' said the
doctors, and my sister was to call me at the least
alarm. The bell woke me with a start: four in the
morning. 'It is the end.' I picked up the receiver
and heard an unknown voice: a wrong number. I
could not get to sleep again until dawn. At half-past
eight the telephone bell again: I ran for it—an utterly unimportant message. I loathed the hearse-
black apparatus: 'Your mother has cancer. Your
mother will not get through the night.' One of these
days it would crackle into my ear, 'It is the end.'

I go through the garden. I go into the hall. You
might think you were in an airport—low tables,
modern armchairs, people kissing one another as
they say hallo or good-bye, others waiting, suitcases, hold-alls, flowers in the vases, bouquets
wrapped in shiny paper as if they were meant for
welcoming travellers about to land . . . But there is
a feeling of something not quite right in the whis-
perings, the expressions. And sometimes a man entirely clothed in white appears in the opening of the
door at the far end, and there is blood on his shoes.
I go up one floor. On my left a long corridor with
the bedrooms, the nurses' rooms and the duty-room.
On the right a square lobby furnished with an up-
holstered bench and a desk with a white telephone
standing upon it. The one side gives on to a waiting-
room; the other on to room 114. No Visitors. Beyond
the door I come to a short passage: on the left the
lavatory with the wash-stand, the bed-pan, cotton-
wool, jars; on the right a cupboard which holds

Maman's things; on a coat-hanger there is the red dressing-gown, all dusty. 'I never want to see that dressing-gown again.' I open the second door. Before, I went through all this without seeing it. Now I know that it will form part of my life for ever.

'I am very well,' said Maman. With a knowing air she added, 'When the doctors were talking to one another yesterday, I heard them. They said, "It's amazing!" ' This word delighted her: she often pronounced it, gravely, as though it were a spell that guaranteed her recovery. Yet she still felt very weak and her overriding desire was to avoid the slightest effort. Her dream was to be fed by drip all her life long. 'I shall never eat again.'

'What, you who so loved your food?'

'No. I shall not eat any more.'

Mademoiselle Leblon took a brush and comb to do her hair for her: 'Cut it all off,' Maman ordered firmly. We protested. 'You will tire me: cut if off, do.' She insisted with a strange obstinacy: it was as though she wanted to bring lasting rest by making this sacrifice. Gently Mademoiselle Leblon undid her plait and untangled her hair; she plaited it again and pinned the silvery coil round Maman's head. Maman's relaxed face had recovered a surprising purity and I thought of a Leonardo drawing of a very beautiful old woman. 'You are as beautiful as a Leonardo,' I said.

She smiled. 'I was not so bad, once upon a time.' In a rather mysterious voice she told the nurse, 'I had lovely hair, and I did it up in bandeaux round my head.' And she went on talking about herself, how she had taken her librarian's diploma, her love for books. As Mademoiselle Leblon answered, she was preparing a flask of serum: she explained to me that the clear fluid also contained glucose and various salts. 'A positive cocktail,' I observed. . . .

While she was dozing I looked at a paper: opening her eyes she asked me, 'What is happening at Saigon?' I told her the news. Once, in a tone of bantering reproof, she observed, 'I was operated on behind my back!' and when Dr P came in she said, 'Here is the guilty man,' but in a laughing voice. He stayed with her for a little while, and when he remarked, 'It is never too late to learn', she replied in a rather solemn tone, 'Yes. I have learnt that I had peritonitis.'

I said jokingly, 'You really are extraordinary! You come in to have your femur patched up, and they operate on you for peritonitis!'

'It's quite true. I am not an ordinary woman at all!'

This circumstance, this mistake, amused her for days. 'I tricked Professor B thoroughly. He thought he was going to operate on my leg, but in fact Dr P operated on me for peritonitis.'

What touched our hearts that day was the way she noticed the slightest agreeable sensation: it was as though, at the age of seventy-eight, she were waking afresh to the miracle of living. While the nurse was settling her pillows the metal of a tube touched her thigh—'It's cool! How pleasant!' She breathed in the smell of eau de Cologne and talcum powder—'How good it smells.' She had the bunches of flowers and the plants arranged on her wheeled table. 'The little red roses come from Meyrignac.

At Meyrignac there are roses still.' She asked us to raise the curtain that was covering the window and she looked at the golden leaves of the trees. 'How lovely. I shouldn't see that from my flat!' She smiled. And both of us, my sister and I, had the same thought: it was that same smile that had dazzled us when we were little children, the radiant smile of a young woman. Where had it been between then and now?

'If she has a few days of happiness like this, keeping her alive will have been worth while,' said Poupette to me. . . .

Maman had dreaded cancer all her life, and perhaps she was still afraid of it in the nursing-home, when they X-rayed her. After the operation she never thought of it for a single moment. There were some days when she was afraid that at her age, the shock might have been too great for her to survive it. But doubt never even touched her mind: she had been operated on for peritonitis—a grave condition, but curable.

What surprised us even more was that she never asked for a priest, not even on the day when she was so reduced and she said, 'I shall never see Simone again!' Marthe had brought her a missal, a crucifix and a rosary: she did not take them out of her drawer. One morning Jeanne said, 'It's Sunday today, Aunt Françoise: wouldn't you like to take Communion?' 'Oh, my dear, I am too tired to pray: God is kind!' Madame Tardieu asked her more pressingly, when Poupette was there, whether she would not like to see her confessor: Maman's expression hardened—'Too tired,' and she closed her eyes to put an end to the conversation. After the visit of another old friend she said to Jeanne, 'Poor dear Louise, she asks me such foolish questions: she wanted to know whether there was a chaplain in the nursing-home. Much I care whether there is or not!'

Madame de Saint-Ange harried us. 'Since she is in such a state of anxiety, she must surely want the comforts of religion.'

'But she doesn't.'

'She made me and some other friends promise to help her make a good end.'

'What she wants just now is to be helped to make a good recovery.'

We were blamed. To be sure we did not prevent Maman from receiving the last sacraments; but we did not oblige her to take them. We ought to have told her, 'You have cancer. You are going to die.' Some devout women would have done so, I am sure, if we had left them alone with her. (In their place I should have been afraid of provoking the sin of rebellion in Maman, which would have earned her centuries of purgatory.) Maman did not want these intimate conversations. What she wanted to see round her bed was young smiling faces. 'I shall have plenty of time to see other old women like me when I am in a rest-home,' she said to her grand-nieces. She felt herself safe with Jeanne, Marthe and two or three religious but understanding friends who approved of our deception. She mistrusted the others and she spoke of some of them with a certain amount of ill-feeling—it was as though a surprising instinct enabled her to detect those people whose presence might disturb her peace of mind. 'As for those women at the club, I shall not go to see them again. I shall not go back there.'

People may think, 'Her faith was only on the surface, a matter of words, since it did not hold out in the face of suffering and death.' I do not know what faith is. But her whole life turned upon religion; religion was its very substance: papers that we found in her desk confirm this. If she had looked upon prayer as nothing but a mechanical droning, telling her beads would not have tired her any more than doing the crossword. The fact that she did not pray convinces me that on the contrary she found it an exercise that called for concentration, thought and a certain condition of the soul. She knew what she ought to have said to God—'Heal me. But Thy will be done: I acquiesce in death.' She did not acquiesce. In this moment of truth she did not choose to utter insincere words. But at the same time she did not grant herself the right to rebel. She remained silent: 'God is kind.' . . .

Why did my mother's death shake me so deeply? Since the time I left home I had felt little in the way of emotional impulse towards her. When she lost my father the intensity and the simplicity of her sorrow moved me, and so did her care for others— 'Think of yourself,' she said to me, supposing that I was holding back my tears so as not to make her suffering worse. A year later her mother's dying was a painful reminder of her husband's: on the day of the funeral a nervous breakdown compelled her to stay in bed. I spent the night beside her: forget-

ting my disgust for this marriage-bed in which I had
been born and in which my father had died, I watched
her sleeping; at fifty-five, with her eyes closed and
her face calm, she was still beautiful; I wondered
that the strength of her feelings should have overcome her will. Generally speaking I thought of her
with no particular feeling. Yet in my sleep (although my father only made very rare and then
insignificant appearances) she often played a most
important part: she blended with Sartre, and we
were happy together. And then the dream would
turn into a nightmare: why was I living with her
once more? How had I come to be in her power
again? So our former relationship lived on in me in
its double aspect—a subjection that I loved and
hated. It revived with all its strength when Maman's
accident, her illness and her death shattered the
routine that then governed our contacts. Time vanishes behind those who leave this world, and the
older I get the more my past years draw together.
The 'Maman darling' of the days when I was ten
can no longer be told from the inimical woman who
oppressed my adolescence; I wept for them both
when I wept for my old mother. I thought I had
made up my mind about our failure and accepted it;
but its sadness comes back to my heart. There are
photographs of both of us, taken at about the same
time: I am eighteen, she is nearly forty. Today I
could almost be her mother and the grandmother of
that sad-eyed girl. I am so sorry for them—for me
because I am so young and I understand nothing;
for her because her future is closed and she has
never understood anything. But I would not know

how to advise them. It was not in my power to wipe out the unhappiness in her childhood that condemned Maman to make me unhappy and to suffer in her turn from having done so. For if she embittered several years of my life, I certainly paid her back though I did not set out to do so. She was intensely anxious about my soul. As far as this world was concerned, she was pleased at my successes, but she was hurt by the scandal that I aroused among the people she knew. It was not pleasant for her to hear a cousin state, 'Simone is the family's disgrace.'

The changes in Maman during her illness made my sorrow all the greater. As I have already said, she was a woman of a strong and eager temperament, and because of her renunciations she had grown confused and difficult. Confined to her bed, she decided to live for herself; and yet at the same time she retained an unvarying care for others—from her conflicts there arose a harmony. My father and his social character coincided exactly: his class and he spoke through his mouth with one identical voice. His last words, 'You began to earn your living very young, Simone: your sister cost me a great deal of money,' were not of a kind to encourage tears. My mother was awkwardly laced into a spiritualistic ideology; but she had an animal passion for life which was the source of her courage and which, once she was conscious of the weight of her body, brought her towards truth. She got rid of the ready-made notions that hid her sincere and lovable side. It was then that I felt the warmth of an affection that had often been distorted by jealousy and that she expressed so badly. In her papers I have found

touching evidence of it. She had put aside two letters, the one written by a Jesuit and the other by a
friend; they both assured her that one day I should
come back to God. She had copied out a passage
from Chamson in which he says in effect, 'If, when
I was twenty, I had met an older, highly-regarded
man who had talked to me about Nietszche and
Gide and freedom, I should have broken with home.'
The file was completed by an article cut out of a
paper—*Jean Paul Sartre has saved a soul.* In this
Rémy Roure said—quite untruthfully, by the way—
that after *Bariona* had been acted at Stalag XII D an
atheistical doctor was converted. I know very well
what she wanted from these pieces—it was to be
reassured about me; but she would never have felt
the need if she had not been intensely anxious as to
my salvation. 'Of course I should like to go to
Heaven: but not all alone, not without my daughters,' she wrote to a young nun.

Sometimes, though very rarely, it happens that
love, friendship or comradely feeling overcomes the
loneliness of death: in spite of appearances, even
when I was holding Maman's hand, I was not with
her—I was lying to her. Because she had always
been deceived, gulled, I found this ultimate deception revolting. I was making myself an accomplice
of that fate which was so misusing her. Yet at the
same time in every cell of my body I joined in her
refusal, in her rebellion: and it was also because of
that that her defeat overwhelmed me. Although I
was not with Maman when she died, and although I
had been with three people when they were actually
dying, it was when I was at her bedside that I saw

Death, the Death of the dance of death, with its
bantering grin, the Death of fireside tales that knocks
on the door, a scythe in its hand, the Death that
comes from elsewhere, strange and inhuman: it had
the very face of Maman when she showed her gums
in a wide smile of unknowingness.

'He is certainly of an age to die.' The sadness of
the old; their banishment: most of them do not
think that this age has yet come for them. I too
made use of this cliché, and that when I was referring to my mother. I did not understand that one
might sincerely weep for a relative, a grandfather
aged seventy and more. If I met a woman of fifty
overcome with sadness because she had just lost her
mother, I thought her neurotic: we are all mortal;
at eighty you are quite old enough to be one of the
dead . . .

But it is not true. You do not die from being
born, nor from having lived, nor from old age. You
die from *something*. The knowledge that because of
her age my mother's life must soon come to an end
did not lessen the horrible surprise: she had sar-
coma. Cancer, thrombosis, pneumonia: it is as violent and unforeseen as an engine stopping in the
middle of the sky. My mother encouraged one to be
optimistic when, crippled with arthritis and dying,
she asserted the infinite value of each instant; but
her vain tenaciousness also ripped and tore the re-
assuring curtain of everyday triviality. There is no
such thing as a natural death: nothing that happens
to a man is ever natural, since his presence calls the
world into question. All men must die: but for
every man his death is an accident and, even if he
knows it and consents to it, an unjustifiable violation.

ELIZABETH BOWEN *was born in Dublin in 1899 and spent her childhood there and at Bowen's Court in Kildorrery, County Cork. As the following selection from* Memories of a Dublin Childhood *reveals, her native city is the setting for her earliest memories, and her parents, especially her mother, are their leading characters. With the publication of her major trilogy of novels* (The House in Paris, The Death of the Heart, *and* The Heat of the Day) *Elizabeth Bowen moved into the ranks of the major modern novelists. Critics regard her fiction on the same level as that of Virginia Woolf, Katherine Mansfield, and Henry James.*

Elizabeth Bowen
from
MEMORIES OF A DUBLIN CHILDHOOD

My mother was not a County Cork woman, nor, like most of the earlier Bowen brides, did she come from the counties of Tipperary or Limerick. Her family, the Colleys, were originally of Castle Carbery, County Kildare; they had been in Ireland since Queen Elizabeth's reign. The Castle itself was now since some time in ruins, and most of the land round it had been sold. The Colleys lived at the time of my mother's marriage (and continued to live until I was four years old) at Mount Temple, Clontarf—a Victorian house that, from the top of its lawns, looked with its many windows out across Dublin Bay. My father, as a young Cork man alone in Dublin, had been introduced to the Colleys by mutual friends. In the course of a series of Sunday calls he had soon singled out my mother from the Mount Temple group of handsome, vivacious sisters. She was the unusual one—capricious, elusive, gently intent on her own thoughts. She and my father had in common a vagueness as to immediate things—so much so that her brothers and sisters wondered how she and he ever did arrive at anything so practical as an agreement to marry. They wondered, also, how Florence would keep house— and indeed she found this difficult at the start.

My father's and mother's families had in common the landowning Protestant outlook and Unionist politics. He and she, however, were individual people, departures from any family type. Tradition was, it is true, to be felt behind them, and in indifferent matters conditioned their point of view. But in matters in which they felt deeply they arrived at conclusions that were their own. True to their natures as man and woman, he was the more thoughtful, she the more feeling one. His mind had been formed by learning unknown to her: he lived by philosophy, she lived by temperament. His forehead, his talk, his preoccupations, were unmistakably those of an intellectual man, though a streak of young spontaneity in his nature redeemed him from stiffness or pedantry. As for her, because of her grace and vagueness, as well as her evident pleasure in the pretty and gay, she would not have been called an intellectual woman—for the blue-stocking reigned as the type then. But she read and she talked, and her thoughts were no less active for being half-submerged in her continuous dream. . . .

"Nursery"

My Herbert Place nursery, the first-floor drawing-room below it, and the dining-room under that, all had a watery quality in their lightness from the upcast reflections of the canal. The house was filled, at most daytime hours, by the singing hum of the sawmill across the water, and the smell of new-planed wood travelled across. Stacks of logs awaiting the saw over-topped the low tarred fence that ran along the bank on the opposite side. The wood-yard was fed from some of the barges that moved slowly up or down the canal, sinking into then rising again from locks. Not much wheeled traffic went past our door, but from each end of Herbert Place, intermittently, came the ring and rumble of trams going over bridges.

Herbert Place faced east: by midday the winter sun had passed from the front rooms, leaving them to grey-green reflections and their firelight, that brightened as dusk drew in.

My nursery reached across the breadth of the house; being high up, it had low windows, and bars had been fixed across these to keep me from falling out. On the blue-grey walls hung pictures, and two of these pictures I do remember sharply—they were openings into a second, more threatening reality. The first must, I think, have been chosen for its heroic subject when my mother still expected me to be Robert: it was Casabianca standing against the flames. The boy stood in ecstasy on the burning deck. In the other, a baby in a wooden cradle floated smilingly on an immense flood, stretching out its two hands to a guardian cat that sat upright on the quilt at the cradle's foot. All round, from the lonely expanse of water rose only the tips of gables, chimneys, and trees. The composure of the cat and the baby had been meant, I suppose, to rule all disaster out of the scene. But for me there was constant anxiety—what would become of the cradle

42

in a world in which everyone else was drowned? In fact, these two pictures induced in me a secret suspended fear of disasters—fires and floods. I feared to be cut off in high buildings, and the beautiful sound of rain was ruined for me by a certainty that the waters must rise soon. Watching my moment, I used to creep to a window to make sure that nothing was happening yet. (When, later, I lived by the sea in England, I was in equal dread of a tidal wave.) In no other way was I a nervous child—and had my mother guessed that the pictures would give me fancies she would have certainly had them taken down.

Apart from the Casabianca, there to stimulate courage—for my father and mother, like all Anglo-Irish people, saw courage apart from context, as an end in itself—my nursery was planned to induce peace. Peace streamed, it is true, from "The Herald Angels" in their black-and-gold frame—a flight of angels swept over a snowy landscape, casting light on the shepherds' upturned brows. And all around the nursery, under the pictures, ran a dado of nursery-rhyme scenes. I spied on its figures through the bars of my cot, and my mother taught me to know their names. She was free with the jingle of nursery rhymes, but reserved in the telling of fairy tales. She did not wish me, she said, to believe in fairies, for fear that I might confuse them with angels. So, when I heard of fairies from other sources I thought of them as being trivial and flashy and (for some reason) always of German birth. Of Irish fairies I heard nothing at all. My mother's fears of confusion were baseless, for having seen pictures of both fairies and angels, I distinguished one from the other by the shape of their wings—fairies' wings were always of the butterfly type, while angels' had the shape and plumage of birds'. The smiling, sweeping, plumy presence of angels was suggested constantly to me—if I were to turn around quickly enough I might surprise my own Guardian behind me. My mother wished me to care for angels: I did. . . .

"Stephen's Green"

For quiet walking we crossed the canal. But Dublin, the city behind Herbert Place, was magnetic. Miss Baird* liked centres of life; she liked Grafton Street; she liked Stephen's Green with its patterns of lawns and lake, its peopled footbridge, its mounds and its boskage that was romantic even in wintertime. Though English, she was born Continental; the most nearly foreign governess that I had. She could divine (in the water-divining sense) any possible scene of fashion. Often, and not really I think from kindness, we went out to feed the ducks in Stephen's Green. I carried the bag of crusts; she carried a muff. Towards the point where we took up our station, on a kerb of the lake, the water-fowl converged with a darting smoothness, their ripples making spokes of a fan.

Among the floating and bloating crusts the reflections were broken up. The birds jabbed brutally with their beaks. I tried to insist on justice: there

---

* Bowen's governess

was always a slow duck or a wistful duck that did not get anything. Round me and the lake the rock-stuck mounds and the arbour-work against the evergreens sometimes glittered or glistened in sunshine that was frosty or damp, but were sometimes haunted or derelict under a brown veil. The lake's polish varied with our days. Under my nostrils the smell of sopping bread filled the air. The trams running round us, outside the trees and railings, according to weather sounded distant or near. The throbbing tune of a barrel organ underran the hum and rumble of traffic: for minutes together a tune took command of the city. Everyone seemed to listen; it seemed to suspend the world.

At one of these minutes I remember my mother standing on the bridge over the lake, looking for us. She sometimes came here on an impulse to join Miss Baird and me. Her hat was perched on the hair piled over her pointed face; I could have known her only by the turn of her head as she looked along the lake for my scarlet coat. I was as easy to see as a pillar-box. She started toward us through the strolling and standing people as though through a garden that was her own.

My mother's feeling for Stephen's Green was native, subtle, nostalgic, unlike Miss Baird's. As a young girl between classes at Alexandra College, she had walked and sat here—sometimes in love with a person, always in love with an idea. The most intense moments of her existence all through her life had been solitary. She often moved some way away from things and people she loved, as though to convince herself that they did exist. Perhaps she never did quite convince herself, for about her caresses and ways with me I remember a sort of rapture of incredulity. Her only child had been born after nine years of waiting—and even I was able to understand that she did not take me or her motherhood for granted. She was so much desolated that she unnerved me when anything went wrong between her and me. If my mother was a perfectionist, she had the kind of wisdom that goes with that make-up. She explained to me candidly that she kept a governess because she did not want to scold me herself. To have had to keep saying "Do this," "Don't do that," and "No," to me would have been, as she saw it, a peril to everything. So, to interpose between my mother and me, to prevent our spending the best part of our days together, was the curious function of every governess. It was not that there were more pressing claims on my mother's time: she was not a worldly woman (though she did like pleasure) and my father was out the greater part of the day. When she was not with me she thought of me constantly, and planned ways in which we could meet and could be alone.

I know now the feeling with which she stood on the bridge, looked along the lake till she came to my scarlet coat, then thought: "That is my child!"

When I had been born my mother was thirty-four—so that in these winters I write about she was approaching the end of her thirties. I do not remember her clothes distinctly; I only see the fluid outline of her. I believe that she had a sealskin jacket and that her skirts swept barely clear of the ground. One of my father's brothers sent back from

South Africa grey ostrich feathers for her and white for me. She possessed an ermine wrap and a string of pearls, and diamond and other rings that she wore on her blue-veined hands. Her style of dressing was personal; a touch of haughtiness set her against fashion. Susceptible to her charm, the glow of her face and being, I could feel its action on people round us—of this she was never conscious herself. She could withdraw into such a complete abstraction that she appeared to enter another world. Her beauty—for I know now it was beauty—was too elusive and fine for a child to appreciate: I thought I only thought she was lovely because I loved her.

She wore her bronze-coloured hair (which was threaded with silver early) in a pompadour over her forehead; at the back the hair was brushed up from the nape of her neck, then coiled on the top of her head. She shored up the weight of it with curved tortoise-shell combs. Her eyes, alternately pensive and quizzical, were triangular, with arched upper lids; they were of a grey-blue that deepened, and she had large pupils. Her dark eyebrows were expressive. When she smiled her nose turned down at the tip, and the smile sent her cheeks up in subtle curves. In her cheeks showed the blue-pink of a sweet-pea. She flushed easily, when she was startled or angry, drank red wine, or sat too near a fire—for this last reason there were hand-screens, of stretched silk painted with flowers, all over the drawing-room at Herbert Place. Her complexion had the downy bloom of a peach, and she dusted this over with fuller's earth. She used *Peau d'Espagne* scent. Her name, Florence, suited her.

KIM CHERNIN *is the author of several books including* The Obsession: Reflections on the Tyranny of Slenderness, Eve's Dilemma, *and* The Hungry Self. *She now lives in Berkeley, California, where she has a writing consultation practice. When* In My Mother's House: A Daughter's Story, *the source of the following selection, was published in 1983, Grace Paley wrote: "We have this book because Kim Chernin longed to know her mother, 'save' an important life, and communicate her to the next generation (as well as the rest of us). There are stories in this book that I will never forget." Tillie Olsen called it "a profound portrayal of the ever-changing, deepening relationship between mother, daughter, and eventually, granddaughter. A book that will be an American resource." In* My Mother's House *is the brave and ultimately triumphant story of Rose Chernin, Russian immigrant and passionate Old Left activist, and her daughter Kim, the narrator of this riveting memoir of conflict, confrontation, and reconciliation among four generations of Chernin women. It is an unforgettable history of family love, twentieth-century politics, and human forgiveness.*

Kim Chernin
from
IN MY MOTHER'S HOUSE

The Proposal

July 1974

She calls me on the telephone three times the day before I am due to arrive in Los Angeles. The first time she says, "Tell me, you still like cottage cheese?" "Sure," I say, "I love it. Cottage cheese, yogurt, ricotta . . ." "Good," she says, "we'll have plenty."

The second conversation is much like the first. "What about chicken? You remember how I used to bake it?"

The third time she calls the issue is schav—Russian sorrel soup, served cold, with sour cream, chopped egg, and onion, large chunks of dry black bread. "Mama," I say. "Don't worry. It's you I'm coming to visit. It doesn't matter what we eat."

She worries. She is afraid she has not been a good mother. An activist when I was growing up, Communist Party organizer, she would put up our dinner in a huge iron pot before she left for work each morning, in this way making sure she neglected no essential duty of a mother and wife. For this, however, she had to get up early. I would watch her, chopping onions and tomatoes, cutting a chicken up small, dicing meat, while I ate breakfast, sitting on a small stepladder at our chopping board.

Now, thirty years later, she's afraid she won't be able to give whatever it is I come looking for when I come for a visit. I'm laughing, and telling my daughter about her three calls, and I am weeping.

"What's schav?" my daughter asks me as we get off the plane in Los Angeles. "There's Grandma," I say, "ask her," as I wave to my mother, trying to suggest some topic of conversation for this eleven-year-old American girl and the woman in her seventies who was born in a small Jewish village in Russia.

My mother catches sight of us and immediately begins talking in an excited voice over the heads of people in line before us as we come through the disembarcation lane. I love this about her, this extravagance of feeling, the moodiness that goes along with it.

"Mama," I call out, waving excitedly, while my daughter looks at her feet and falls back with embarrassment as I push forward into my mother's arms.

She takes me by the elbow as we make our way toward the baggage, giving me sideways her most cunning look. What does she see? I look at myself with her eyes. Suddenly, I'm a giant. Five feet, four and a half inches tall the last time I measured myself, now I'm strolling along here as if I'm on stilts. She has to tip back her head to look into my eyes. This woman, whose hands were once large enough to hold my entire body, does not now reach as high as my daughter's shoulder.

We are all trying to think of something to say. We hurry past murals on the terminal walls. Finally, it is my mother who speaks. "Who are you running from?" she says, tugging me by the arm. "Let me get a look at you."

She stops and looks into my eyes. Then she looks at Larissa. Deeply perceptive, this look of hers. Assessing. Eyes narrowing. "A beauty," she whispers to me as Larissa goes off to stand near the baggage chute. But then she straightens her back and tilts her head up. "It's good you came now," she whispers. "It's important."

She comes up close to me, her shoulder resting against mine. "There's something I didn't tell you."

"You don't have to tell me," I say as quietly as possible. "I already know."

"You know?" She looks doubtful, but only for a moment. "Hoie," she sighs, "you were always like this. Who can keep anything from you?"

"Is she in pain?"

"Pain, sorrow, who can distinguish? There is, let me tell you, a story here. If you would write it down in a book, nobody would believe you."

I know better than to ask about the story. In my family they hint and retreat and tell you later in their own good time.

"But this is not for now," she says, turning her head sharply. "She won't last long, that much I know."

"What do the doctors say?"

"I should wait for doctors to tell me about my

own sister?" Her voice has an edge to it, an impatience. But I know her by now. With this tone she attempts to master her own pain.

I want to put my arms around her, to comfort her for the loss of Aunt Gertrude. But I'm afraid she'll push me away, needing her own strength more than she needs my comfort.

"You know doctors," she continues, softening. "For every one thing they tell you, there are two things hidden under the tongue."

"And you?" I ask, because it seems to me she'll let the question come now. "How are you?"

She gestures dismissively with her hand and I know what will follow. "*Gezunt vi gezunt,*" she snorts, with her grim, shtetl humor: "Never mind my health, just tell me where to get potatoes."

Larissa waves. She has been making faces at me, as if the luggage is much too heavy for her to carry; she drags it along, wiping her forehead with an imaginary rag.

"What's this?" my mother calls out. "We leave the child to carry the luggage?"

But I am wringing my hands. I have put my fists against my temples, rocking myself with exaggerated woe. My mother looks at me, frowning, puzzled. There is a playfulness between Larissa and me, a comradeship she does not understand. When I was pregnant with Larissa I used to dream about running with her through the park, a small child at play with a larger one called mother.

But now my mother cries out, "Wait, wait, we'll help you, don't strain like this."

She is confused by our sudden bursts of wildness;

she frowns and seems to be struggling to understand the meaning of playfulness.

"It's a joke, Mama," I have to tell her, "a game we play."

Then, with hesitation, she smiles. But it is here I see most clearly the difference in our generations. Hers, with its eye fixed steadily on survival. Mine freer, more frivolous, less scarred and, in my own eyes, far less noble.

Now she has understood what Larissa is doing.

"Another one, look at her," she calls out, shaking her hands next to her head, leaning forward. "Both crazy."

We take up the suitcases and walk out toward the car. Larissa is carrying the two small duffel bags that make it clear we have come for only a few days.

But my mother has not overlooked this symbolism. And now, refusing my hand when I reach out for her, she says, "Three and a half years you haven't been to visit. You think you're living in the North Pole?"

"Berkeley, the North Pole, what's the difference?" I say, irresistibly drawn into her idiom. "It would take a team of huskies to drag me away from my work."

"Your work," she says, with all the mixed pride and ambivalence she feels about the fact that I live alone with my daughter, supporting both of us as a private teacher, involved in a work of solitary scholarship and poetry she does not understand.

"Still the same thing?" she asks, a tone of uncertainty creeping into her voice. "Mat-ri-archy?"

Reluctantly, I nod my head. But it is not like us to avoid a confrontation. "Tell me," she says, in a hushed, conspiratorial tone, as if she were making an alliance with my better nature. "Tell me, this is serious work you are doing?"

Once, years ago, coming down to visit I grew so angry that when we reached home I called a taxi and returned to the airport again.

"Mama," I say, my voice already too vehement, "listen to me." Larissa falls back and walks beside me. "In doing this work I am breaking taboos as great as those you broke when you became a Communist."

I know that my daughter wants me to lower my voice. Her face is puckered and worried. I put my hand on her shoulder, changing my tone.

"Believe me, where women are concerned, there are still ideas it is as difficult to think as it was once difficult for Marx to understand the fact that bourgeois society was built upon the exploitation of the workers."

Since I was a small girl I have been fighting with my mother. When the family was eating dinner some petty disagreement would arise and I'd jump up from the table, pick up a plate and smash it against the wall. I'd go running from the room, slamming doors behind me.

By the age of thirteen I insisted that Hegel was right and not Marx. "The Idea came first," I cried out from the bathroom, which had the only door in the house that locked. "The Spirit came before material existence."

In the afternoons I read books. I started on the

left side of the bookcase, at the top shelf, and thumbed my way through every book in the library. *The Classics of Marxism, Scottsboro Boy, State and Revolution* by Lenin, a story about the Huck Bella Hop in the Philippines, stories about the Spanish civil war.

I understood little of what I read, but I built a vocabulary, a mighty arsenal of weapons to use against my mother.

Then, when she came into the house, I was ready for her. Any opinion she uttered, I took the opposite point of view. If she liked realism, I preferred abstract art. If she believed in internationalism, I spoke about the necessity to concentrate on local conditions.

Twenty years later nothing has changed. We still refuse to understand one another, both of us still protesting the fact we are so little alike.

Her voice rises; she has clenched her jaw. "You're going to tell me about the exploitation of the workers?"

I answer belligerently, shaking with passion. "There is the same defiance of authority in the scholarship I do, the same passion for truth in the poetry I write as there has been in your life."

"Truth? We're going to discuss truth now?"

"And it changes, doesn't it? From generation to generation?"

The silence that follows this outburst is filled up through every cubic inch of itself by my shame. We are not even out of the airport and already I've lost my temper. And this time especially I had wanted so much to draw close to her. Surely, it must be possible after all these years.

"Mama," I say, throwing my arm around her shoulders with the same conspiratorial appeal she has used in approaching me. "You know what I found out? Marx and Engels, both of them, believed there was once a matriarchal stage of social organization. Yes, I'm serious. I'll tell you where you can read it."

"Marx and Engels?" she says. "You don't say. Marx and Engels?"

But now she sighs, shaking her head. "So all right, I am what I am, we can't be the same person. But I don't like to see you spending your life like this, that much I know."

She pauses, looking over at me, and I can see in her eyes the same resolution I have made.

"Let it go, I don't want to quarrel with you. But when I think . . . a woman like you. So brilliant, so well-educated. You could contribute to the world. With your gifts, what couldn't you accomplish?" Then, in her most endearing voice she says, "You're a poet. I accept this. But now I've got something to say to you. And I don't want you to say no before you give it some thought."

I look down at her face, so deeply marked with determination. "Tell me," I say, in spite of myself, for I know she won't tell me now, no matter what I do.

She looks around her. She has always liked a little suspense. She looks over at Larissa, she looks down at our bags. She reaches in her purse and feels around for her keys.

And then finally, taking my arm, she says, confidingly, almost with humor, "So, what's the hurry? We've got time."

At dinner Larissa toys with her food. Who can blame her? From the moment we entered the house my mother has been feeding her. In the first ten minutes she brought out a plate of cookies baked for us by Aunt Sara, my father's brother's wife. Since then, I've seen my mother standing at the kitchen door, her hands at her waist, watching my daughter. "A good eater," she says to no one in particular as Larissa accepts a slice of Jell-O mold. "This is what you used to be like," she adds, turning to me, "before you took it in your head to get so thin."

In the kitchen, lined up on the counter, there are several large platters wrapped in tin foil. They are the gifts brought by my various aunts when they heard I was coming down for a visit. Raisin strudel from Aunt Anne, rolled cinnamon twists from Sara Sol's, a bowl of chopped liver, kugel in an oval pan.

I have always been held in high esteem by my family. "A *chochma*, a wise one," they'd say about me even as a child. "Born with a clear star over her head," his oldest sister would say to my father. "A golden tongue," they'd murmur when I burst out in some extravagant childhood story.

Even to this day, in spite of the fact that I have brought home to them so few tangible signs of worldly fame, they admire me.

They manage to forgive me for my two divorces. They struggle to understand the way I live.

"We never had a poet in the family before," my father's oldest brother said to me before he died. "We're proud of you. If you were born a son, you maybe would have become even a rabbi."

Their family traces itself back to the Vilna Goan, a famous rabbinical scholar of the eighteenth century. But my mother, whenever she heard this, would always snort. "Hach, little people, trying to make themselves feel important."

Her own family was more radical, more violent in its passion, more extreme in its life choices. Each side has always expected me to carry on its tradition. As it is, I have inherited my mother's fierce, revolutionary fervor, my father's quiet inclination for scholarship, and someone else's wild, untutored mystical leanings. They all worry about me because I have become too thin. But the food they have brought me, in love and in tribute, today has been eaten by my daughter.

Larissa moves her food over to the side of her plate, shovels it back toward the center, and makes fork marks in the baked squash.

My mother casts a disapproving glance at her. "Chopped liver she doesn't like. Schav she doesn't like. So eat a mouthful of chicken. Chicken they are eating also among the fifth generation born Americans."

At this, my mother's sister, Aunt Gertrude, who is sitting next to me, throws back her head and emits a dry, conciliatory laugh. It is impossible to recognize in this frail, withdrawn woman, the aunt of my childhood, the woman who joined the Peace Corps at the age of fifty-three, and went off to serve as a nurse in Ethiopia. I have heard that one day she rode a donkey over the mountains, taking supplies to villages of the interior. The image of her has lived on with me, an aging woman with gaunt face and brilliant eyes, her white hair beginning to yellow, the habitual smoker's cough, the clop of the animal's hooves and she rides, talking, smoking, gesturing, over the bad roads of the mountains of Ethiopia.

When I lean close to her I can smell the acrid sweetness I have known since childhood, when my sister was dying. It makes me want to run toward her, to grab her so tight death cannot get hold of her, and it makes me want to run away. I glance toward her from the corner of my eye, knowing she would not like to be stared at. And she, growing conscious of my tact, pressed my foot beneath the table.

Her touch is so light I can scarcely feel it, but it has the power to jog my memory. Profoundly moved, I recall the games we used to play together when I was a child visiting at her house, little pokings and pattings, accompanied by puffs from her cigarettes, perfect rings of smoke, the smell of caffeine and the good odor of soap.

She had some secret sorrow, never spoken of, never completely hidden from me. But I knew, even as a small girl, that if you loved this woman you should pretend to believe that she was happy.

"There you be, cookie," she'd say in her husky voice when she came looking for me. I would jump up and throw my arms around her neck, charmed by her gruff tenderness.

She worked hard; she grew old early. "Something's eating her," my mother would say to my father. And I watched the wrinkles gnawing at her face, deepening perceptibly every time I saw her.

Silence comes to our table. Gertrude sipping her black tea, my mother tapping her fork against her plate, my own chair shifting restlessly as it attempts in all futility to establish itself in some permanent niche in the world.

And suddenly I know precisely what my mother has been hinting at since I arrived in Los Angeles. It comes to me from the silence as if it had been clearly and distinctly uttered. Now, in front of my aunt and my daughter, she is going to ask me something impossible to refuse.

She takes a deep breath, looks around the room as if she has misplaced something, and then delivers herself of one of those weighty utterances which had been troubling the atmosphere all day. "Do you know why I'm alive today?" she says, as if it were a question of her own will that she has lived to be an old woman. "Do you want to know why I'm still living?" And then, when Larissa looks toward her expectantly: "Because," she says, "there's still injustice in the world. And I am a fighter."

My mother's conversation frequently assumes this rhetorical tone. It comes, I suppose, from the many years she has been a public speaker. Even her English changes at such moments. It loses its Yiddish inflection and her voice rings out as if she were speaking through a megaphone. But today I know that all these statements are intended for me.

"Never mind how old I am," she says. "Never mind when I was born. Or where, or to what mother. There's only one important fact about a life. And that one is always a beginning. A woman who lives for a cause, a woman with dedication and unbreakable devotion—that's a woman who deserves the name of woman."

Has she been rehearsing this little speech? I ask myself. Has she been going over it again and again in her mind, as she waited for me at the airport?

As we leave the table she looks out the window, bends her knees slightly, and tips back her head, trying to catch sight of the moon. "Not yet," she mutters and walks toward the room where Larissa has been building a fire.

Here, everything has a story. The charcoal sketch of Harriet Tubman, given to her by Langston Hughes. The book of Tina Modotti's photographs, a gift from a young radical woman. And now I realize there is something new in this room, which she has been wanting me to notice. It is visible in the light from the small lamp attached to an oil painting of my sister in her red Komsomol scarf. It says:

TO ROSE CHERNIN FOR 25 YEARS OF MILITANT LEADERSHIP TO THE COMMITTEE FOR THE DEFENSE OF THE BILL OF RIGHTS. IN APPRECIATION OF YOUR LIFELONG DEVOTION AND STRUGGLE ON BEHALF OF THE FOREIGN-BORN AND ALL VICTIMS OF POLITICAL AND RADICAL OPPRESSION. PRESENTED AT THE 25TH ANNUAL BANQUET, JANUARY 18, 1974.

She watches me as I study the plaque, unconsciously reciting the words aloud to Larissa. Then she waves at it with a disparaging shake of her hand. "So what else could they say? You think someone would write: 'To Rose Chernin: A Mean Person'?"

She is standing next to the fire, her foot on the rocker of Gertrude's chair. They are twisting newspaper into tight coils. Larissa pokes at the glowing coals with a wire hanger. But my mother has been waiting to speak with me. And now she says, "My mother knew how to read and to write. Isn't it so, Gertrude? Mama was a literate woman."

This fact makes no impression upon my daughter. She has no context for wondering at this achievement, so rare, so remarkable in a Jewish woman of the shtetl. On me, however, these words make a tremendous impression. The tone in which my mother speaks them moves me even to tears. "Mama was a literate woman," she repeats with a strangely wistful pride. Now she looks significantly at me and I know that we have come finally to the end of all this hinting.

"You are a writer," she says. "So, do you want to take down the story of my life?"

I am torn by contradiction. I love this woman. She was my first great aching love. All my life I have wanted to do whatever she asked of me, in spite of our quarreling.

She's old, I say to myself. What will it take from you? Give this to her. She's never asked anything from you as a writer before. Give this. You can always go back to your own work later.

But it is not so easy to turn from the path I have imagined for myself. This enterprise will take years. It will draw me back into the family, waking its ghosts. It will bring the two of us together to face all the secrets and silences we have kept. The very idea of it changes me. I'm afraid. I fear, as any daughter would, losing myself back into the mother.

I sit down on the edge of the gray chair that used to be my father's favorite reading place. It occurs to me that I should reason with her, tell her how much it means to me now to go my own way. "Mama," I say, intending to bring everything out into the open. And then she turns toward me expectantly, a raw look of hope and longing in her eyes.

I learned to understand my mother's life when I was a small girl, waiting for her to come home in the afternoons. Each night I would set the table carefully, filling three small glasses with tomato juice while my father tossed a salad. Then we would hear my mother's car pull up in front of the house and I could go into the living room and kneel on the gray couch in front of the window to watch her come across the lawn, weighed down with newspapers and pamphlets and large blue boxes of envelopes for the mailing I would help to get out that night.

She was a woman who woke early, no matter how late she went to bed the night before. Every morning she would exercise, bending and lifting and touching and stretching, while I sat on the bed watching her with my legs curled up. Then, a cold shower and she would come from it shivering, smelling of rosewater, slapping her arms. She ate toast with cottage cheese, standing up, reading the morning paper. But she would always have too little time to finish her coffee. I would watch her taking quick sips as she stood at the door. "Put a napkin into your lunch," she'd call out to me, "I forgot the napkin." And there was always a cup with a lipstick stain standing half full of coffee on the table near the door.

Later, the Party gave her a car and finally she learned how to drive it. But in the early years she went to work by bus. Sometimes when I was on vacation I went downtown with her.

In her office she took off her shoes and sat down in a wooden chair that swiveled. Always, the telephone was ringing. A young black man. Framed on a false murder charge. And so she was on her feet again, her fist clenched. By twelve o'clock she would have made friends with the young man's mother. And for years after that time some member of his family would drive across town on his birthday to pick up my mother and take her home to celebrate.

It was the invariable pattern of her life, as I learned to know it when I was a little girl, still hoping to become a woman like my mother. To this day I rise early, eat a frugal meal, take a cold shower and laugh as I slap my arms, bending and stretching, touching and reaching.

But I cannot describe my day with these bold, clear strokes that sketch in her life. This strange matter of becoming a poet, its struggle so inward and silent. How can I tell her about this life that has so little to show for itself in the outer world?

But I should never underestimate my mother. Since I was a child she has been able to read my thoughts. And now she turns from the bookshelf where she has been showing my daughter the old books she brought back during the thirties from the Soviet Union. She looks at me with that serious, disapproving gaze which taught me, even as a small child, always to lie about myself. And now she comes toward me, in all the extraordinary power of her presence, to touch me with her index finger on my shoulder.

"I went to Cuba last year," she says. "I took with me . . . what was it? Twenty-five people. All of them younger than myself. And you know what they did at night? Did I tell you? They went to sleep. Now could I sleep in a place like that? I ask you. So I took this one and that one, we went out into the streets, we walked, we went into restaurants. I don't care what the doctors tell me. I'm not going to rest. Do I have to live to be a hundred? What matters to me, so long as I'm living, I'm alive."

For me, these words have all the old seductive charm I experienced as a small girl, learning to know this woman. I loved her exclamation of surprise when someone came to our door, her arms flying out, her pleasure at whoever it was, dropping in on the way to a meeting. It was open house at our house on Wednesday nights. We never knew who might drop in. We'd pull up an extra chair, my father would go off to add lettuce to the salad, I'd pour another glass of tomato juice, and my mother would climb up on a stepladder to bring down a tin of anchovies. Every Wednesday morning she prepared a big pot of beef stroganoff or a spaghetti sauce with grated carrots and green pepper, which I would heat up, to simmer slowly, when I came home from school.

But how could I become my mother? She arrived in this country as a girl of twelve. An immigrant, struggling for survival, she supported her family when her father ran off and deserted them. To me she gave everything she must have wanted for herself, a girl of thirteen or fourteen, walking home from the factory, exhausted after a day of work.

What she is grows up out of her past in a becoming, natural way. She was born in a village where most women did not know how to read. She did not see a gaslight until she was twelve years old. And I? Am I perhaps what she herself might have become if she had been born in my generation in America?

This thought, although it remains unspoken, startles my mother. She looks over at me as if I have called her. And now she reaches out and pats my face, her hand falling roughly on my cheek.

She clears her throat. There comes into her voice a strangely confessional tone. "I'd come into your room at night," she says, "there you'd be. Looking out the window." She breathes deeply, shaking her head at some unpleasant impression life has left upon her. "I thought, this one maybe will grow up to be a *Luftmensch*. You know what it means? A dreamer. One who never has her feet on the ground."

She stops now, looking at me for understanding.

She is vulnerable, uncertain whether she can continue. "We were poor people. Immigrants. For everything we had to struggle." I do not take my eyes from her face. And then the words rush from her, their intensity unexpected, shattering both of us. "The older I get the more I think about Mama. Always I struggled. Never to be like Mama. Never like that poor, broken woman . . ."

Larissa has been taking books out of the shelves, stacking them up on the floor, overturning the stacks. She seems surprised at the crash as her face turns toward her grandmother, who nods conciliation, as she never did to me, the child of her anxious years.

My grandmother could not adjust to the New World. I have heard this all my life. She was sent to a mental hospital. She attempted suicide. My mother would talk about the beautiful letters she wrote. "A Sholom Aleichem," my mother would say. "The most heartbreaking stories," my aunt echoed. Then she added, "She must have wanted to become a writer."

She, too, was a dreamer and she lived through most of her days in that sorrow of mute protest which in her generation was known as melancholia. My mother, her daughter, was obsessed by the fate of her mother and this obsession has descended to me. But who could have imagined these old stories would awaken my child to an interest in the family? She is growing up, I say to myself, she is becoming conscious, my heart already stirred by the magnitude of this, she is entering the mythology of this family.

The twilight comes into the room. It spreads itself

out on the stacks of magazines, the lacquered Chinese dish, the little carved man with a blue patch in his wooden trousers. Everyone begins to look as if they have been brushed with understanding. For here finally is the clear shape of the story my mother wants me to write down—this tale of four generations, immigrants who have come to take possession of a new world. It is a tale of transformation and development—the female reversal of that patriarchal story in which the power of the family's founder is lost and dissipated as the inheriting generations decline and fall to ruin. A story of power.

My mother has stopped talking. She raises her eyebrows, asking me to respond to her. Soon I know if I hold silence she will take a deep breath and straighten her shoulders. "Daughter," she will say, in a voice that is stern and admonishing, "always a woman must be stronger than the most terrible circumstance. You know what my mother used to say? Through us, the women of the world, only through us can everything survive."

An image comes to me. I see generations of women bearing a flame. It is hidden, buried deep within, yet they are handing it down from one to another, burning. It is a gift of fire, transported from a world far off and far away, but never extinguished. And now, in this very moment, my mother imparts the care of it to me. I must keep it alive, I must manage not to be consumed by it, I must hand it on when the time comes to my daughter.

Larissa tugs at my sleeve. She is pointing to the window. I wonder why I feel such shame that I am crying, why I want to hide my face in my hands. I see my mother standing by the window, the dark folds of the drape gathered on either side of her. And there, above her head, where my daughter is now pointing, we see the slender cutting of a sickle moon, and my mother stands in silence, her arms folded upon her breast.

My mother sighs. But even in this expression of weariness or sorrow, I feel the power of the woman, as she straightens her shoulders, strides back into the room, sits down on the coffee table in front of me, and takes my hands.

"You never knew how to protect yourself," she says, "You never knew. I would stand there and watch you weep. You wept for everything. The whole world seemed to cause you pain. And I would say to myself, This one I will strengthen. This one I will make a fighter. And you, why can't you forgive me I wanted to teach you how to struggle with life? Why can't you forgive?"

My head moves down. I cannot restrain myself any longer. I know what I am going to do and I must take the risk. I feel my own lips, cold, unsure of themselves, pressed against my mother's hand. Very softly, whispering, I say to her, "Mama, tell me a story."

She lifts her head, her breast rises. "Good," she says. "From the mother to the daughter."

And so, eagerly now, I surrender. Deeply moved, I shall do what she has asked. I sit down on the floor, leaning against the knees of a white-haired old woman. And yes, with all the skill available to me as a writer, I will take down her tales and tell her story.

She was born in the first years of this century, in that shtetl culture which cannot any longer be found in this world. Her language is that haunting mixture of English, Yiddish, and Russian, in which an old world preserves itself. It is a story that will die with her generation. My own child will know nothing of it if it is not told now.

How could I have imagined that I, who am one of the few who could translate her memory of the world into the language of the printed page, had some more important work to do? . . .

Epilogue

August 1981

She calls us on the telephone two times the day before we are due to arrive in Los Angeles. The first time she says: "You know that spinach loaf I make? You think Larissa would like it?" "The spinach loaf? With carrots and wheat germ? She'd love it." "Good," says my mother, "I already baked it."

Our second conversation is like the first. "I found a recipe," she says. "I made kugel. Just like Mama used to make. But now the question is, should we go out instead for dinner maybe?"

Her third call comes the next day, a few hours before we are leaving. "Maybe we should go out after all," she says. "How many times in a life does a person get accepted to Harvard?"

"Mama," I say, "are you kidding? I told Larissa about that spinach loaf. We didn't eat since yesterday morning. Just to have a big appetite when we arrive."

"You don't say," she sighs, "since yesterday." And then she realizes I'm kidding. "You," she says, "you can't fool me. Didn't you just tell me you were cooking breakfast?" . . .

During dinner the phone keeps ringing. "I can't talk now," my mother says, standing next to the table. "My daughter and my granddaughter are here."

Then, setting the phone down, she says, "If you would dream a life could you dream something better?"

Larissa goes into the kitchen and turns off the tea kettle. My mother leans over and whispers in my ear. "I'm almost eighty years old," she says. "Look at my life. My mother, the one literate woman in our shtetl. And today, my own granddaughter going to Harvard."

While we are drinking tea she stands up suddenly and goes off into her bedroom. She has moved since Gertrude's death and has bought herself a little house in a beautiful project at the foot of the Baldwin Hills. My high school is three or four blocks away. Now black people are living in those hills we can see so clearly from her patio. All the others have moved away.

She comes back into the room wearing a little pair of knit slippers. The doctor has told her to rest and she is trying. "I have some money for you two," she says. "What do I need it for? At my age, the needs are little. If I get sick I know you won't let me die because of a few dollars."

"I'm glad you know that about me," I say, strangely relieved that she does.

"I know you. A mother knows her child," she says.

After dinner Larissa goes out for a jog. We can see her, in her red running shorts, looping around the lawns, past the roses and camelias, beneath the olive trees. But then we turn back into the room and my mother sits down in her large chair, near the bookcase. I look at her, balancing her checkbook. She has developed a child's very deep concentration. To open her purse, to look through it searching for her glasses, takes time, a deliberate focusing of attention. It removes her from me, sets her apart in her own world, with that serious frown which makes a kingdom out of a sandbox.

She crosses her legs and takes off one shoe. She is the size of a ten-year-old child, but her head is large and her expression very grave; it gives to this woman, born in a shtetl, who has lived her whole life among the people, a curious air of nobility.

Since I saw her last she has entered into old age. The masks have been thrust off and she has regained the ability to pass rapidly from one pure state of feeling to another. Above all, she loves with such intensity that she cannot keep still. And so she cries out, "What shall I do with all this joy? Do you know how happy you have made me? How will I keep it inside?" And then she presses her hand to her heart and squeezes down, her eyes spilling.

At ten o'clock we make up a bed in the living room. Larissa falls asleep quickly but I hear my mother moving about in her room. Drawers open and close, there is a patter of little feet and then I see her, peeping in at me, trying to determine if I am sleeping. I wave to her, and she crooks her finger at me, beckoning.

Her room is large and perfectly ordered. There is a bright afghan on the bed, crocheted for her by a deportee from her committee. On the wall near the window a large oil painting of two Chinese women soldiers, sitting with their guns and reading together from a book. On the dresser there are photographs. And then I see something new. She comes over to stand beside me. "That's what I wanted to show you," she says. "I found it. In the drawer with the letters. My friend Anna Gloria is a printer. She made this for you and put a frame on it." She reaches up to take it down from the wall. "So read," she says, pushing it into my hands. Her love for me has taken possession of her face. She shakes me lightly by the shoulder. I remember a large hall; hundreds of people there, at long tables covered in white cloths. I came all dressed up, and I went up to the stage when my name was announced. I talked into a microphone. And even before I opened my mouth I saw the old women, sitting together, nudging and whispering, the handkerchiefs coming out.

"Shall I recite it for you?"

"Oy," she says, pressing her hand to her heart, "would you do that?"

I glance down at the page, but I realize at once that I don't need it. For more than twenty years I have remembered every word of this speech I gave at her birthday celebration after she was released from jail.

> I would like to greet you on my mother's fiftieth birthday, and tell you what her great fight for freedom and equal rights for all peoples has meant to me. All my life she has taught me to fight for my rights and for the rights of other minority groups. . . . My mother has been a guiding light and a strong influence. . . . I also know now that more than anything in the world I would like to follow in her footsteps and earn from you people the love that she has earned.

I stop, remembering how true these words once were for me. And now, as I go on reciting, I can for the first time in my life acknowledge the longing which even then I saw in her face.

She has been sitting on her bed, her legs drawn up and her bathrobe tucked carefully around her. When I finish, she holds out her hand. "There it is," she says, "there it is. Always the people."

I notice that she has taken a small drawer out of her dresser. She pats the bed next to her and I sit. Then, she reaches into the drawer and takes out a little velvet box. "This is my wedding ring," she says, handing me the thin silver band. "And here's the ring your father gave me when we were married twenty-five years." She reaches over and opens my hand. "It's time for me to divest," she says.

My hands shake as I receive the rings. "Look inside," she whispers. "You'll see the dates." I turn it and hold it up to the light. Inside, in a delicate script, it says: *P.K.R.C. June 21, '26.* She is rummaging in the drawer again. She takes out a beautiful silver necklace and hands it to me. "Heirlooms we don't have in our family. But stories we've got." As I put it around my neck she begins to rock herself, her hands gripping her knees. Softly, she hums a tune I remember from many, many years ago. "It's the story of Stenka Razin," she says. "You remember? The great peasant leader. This necklace your father got for me when we were traveling down the Volga."

She goes back to looking in the drawer. "Good, here it is, I thought I lost it maybe." The drawer yields up a pin with a hammer and sickle. This, too, is passed on to me. She brings out a gold pendant in the shape of a triangle. It holds a red stone set in gold and I can see at once that it is valuable. "This one, a lady gave me after a speech. She came up, she took it from her neck and put it on mine. 'Because of the work you've done, Rose Chernin,' she said. You see this inscription? G12732. That was her number from the concentration camp." She reaches over and puts the pendant around my neck. "You'll take good care," she says. "This is my life here."

I realize that Larissa is standing in the doorway, watching. She has been asleep and she looks very young, her hair tossed about, her cheeks flushed. Is it really true that she is going away from home in a few months? My mother opens her arms and to my immense surprise my daughter comes over, lies down on the bed and puts her head on my mother's lap. I take her feet and hold them, squeezing tightly. My mother says to her, "When you were a little girl you'd come to visit. I'd give you a bath, dinner of course, and then I'd pick you up and put you to bed. And you'd say, 'When I grow up I'm going to carry *you* around. Because *you* are a little Grandma.'"

As she says this I remember a dream. I was walking about all over the world carrying a burden in my arms. In the beginning I was afraid that the burden would be too much for me. But then, as I kept walking, I found that the burden was growing lighter and lighter and I could not tell, looking down, whether it was my mother or my child.

Larissa stretches herself and turns over onto her back. "I remember Grandpa Kusnitz," she says, in a sleepy voice. "He used to spin me around in the air. And I remember Bill Taylor," she says. "He was huge. A black man, and he took me with him one time on the plane to Los Angeles. You remember, Grandma?"

My mother strokes her hair, humming the Russian lullaby she used to sing to me. *"Spe moi angel, moi precrasni, bayoushki bayou. Ticha smotret mesyats yasni, callibel twayou."*

Larissa goes on talking. "I remember walking in a carriage, with Mama and Peter in Dublin. We saw trees and Mama gave me a green leaf with prickly edges."

My mother gestures to me and takes my elbow and pulls me down so that she can whisper in my ear. "Think of it," she says, "a mother and daughter together like this."

Larissa says, "And a granddaughter."

She curls up against me and puts my hand on her head. It's the last time, I think. The last time. It'll never happen again. And my daughter says, "I remember when we came to America. I was one year old. We stopped in New York. In the Bronx. We stayed with Sonia Auerbach and she made me a bed in a drawer."

My mother reaches up for a pillow and puts it under Larissa's head. *"Ticha smotret mesyats yasni,"* she sings. And Larissa says, "I know what it means. The bright moon looks on quietly."

My mother goes on humming, Larissa's eyes open and close. And my mother says, "Did I ever tell you about Zayde?"

We have both heard this story before. She told it seven years ago, when I first began to write down her life.

"Well," she says, taking a breath, "when we lived in the shtetl, Friday was always the longest day of the week. And why? Because, of course, we were waiting for Zayde . . ."

But this time she talks with a voice so gentle it will run, I know, right into Larissa's dreaming.

And then it is Sunday, the last day of our visit. Larissa has gone over to see some of my mother's friends who live in the project. A few houses down there is a woman I've known since childhood, a professor of Marxism at the university. Dorothy Healey, who was in jail with my mother, will be moving in next year. Yesterday, when we went out for a walk, an older man came over to meet me. "A comrade," my mother whispered, taking my hand and placing it in his.

These people have lived their whole lives caring about the world. Little by little the dogma has dropped away, and now only the sense of human possibility remains. It makes them tender, in spite of their militancy. And for me they make this housing project strangely like a shtetl.

We are sitting on the little patio behind her house. It is spring, but leaves are falling. A breeze rises suddenly and my mother says, "Do you know the poem by Lermontov? I remember it from when I was a girl."

I look at her, unable to talk.

"Wichaju adin na da rogu," she recites, very grandly. *"Skvoz tuman kremnesti poot blestet/Noch ticha pustenya vnemlet bogu/E zvezda zvezdoyu gavareet."*

She puts her two hands on her cheeks and rocks herself. "Do you know what it means?" I nod, but she translates anyway. "I walk out on the road alone. The path shines through the fog. The night is still. The desert is aware of God. And the stars speak to one another. Why do I feel so lonely?"

There are tears in her eyes. I wonder what she is thinking when she falls silent. I do not dare to say a word and finally she says, "It is as beautiful today as it was seventy years ago."

There are words but I do not speak them. I wonder whether in this struggle to become myself I have become what she was as a girl. I say, "Do you remember when you used to recite that poem to me?"

"Do I remember?" Her eyebrows fly up, her eyes sparkle. "You used to climb into my lap. You'd say, 'Mama, tell me.' 'What,' I'd say, 'what shall I tell you child?' And you, very serious, used to answer, '*Wichaju*, Mama, *wichaju* . . .'"

We do not move. We do not look at one another. But I feel the way something is imparted to me, palpably, passing between us. And then, grabbing my hand, pressing it against her heart, she says, "You remind me of Lermontov. Did I ever tell you that?"

I look around me in this garden behind my mother's house. It has become a wave of light, an affirmation that rises not only beyond sorrow, but from a sense of wondering joy. I glance quickly at my mother, who has fallen silent, and I watch with disbelief the way the distance between us, and all separation, heals over. We are touched by a single motion of forgiveness. Her hand touches my cheek, she calls me by my childhood name, she says, "The birds sing louder when you grow old."

It has grown dark; the breeze is growing cold and yet we sit on here, where the shadows gather, my mother and I together. Above us, on the hills, lights are shimmering in a dusk that seems to be falling earlier for them.

My mother says, "There is a saying I learned in Russia, when I was a child. '*Da nashevo berega, dabro nie daplievot.*' Do you want to translate?"

"Nothing good ever swims to our shores."

"*Da, da,*" she says, "a peasant saying. And do you believe it?"

"Not anymore."

"And yet the people are wise."

"Sometimes a life can grow beyond wisdom."

"So it seems. So it seems."

It is late. My mother is tired. She reaches over to hold my hand. Suddenly, she speaks familiar words in a voice I have never heard before. It is pure feeling. It says, "I love you more than life, my daughter. I love you more than life."

In her own lifetime (1873–1954), and especially outside of France, **SIDONIE-GABRIELLE COLETTE** *was best known as a novelist, as the creator of Chéri, Gigi, Claudine. But over the same half century, she published an even larger body of autobiography—memoirs, portraits, notebooks, letters. Her achievement as a novelist, critic, and journalist was acknowledged during her last years by the awarding of the medal of the Legion of Honor and her election to the Academie Goncourt. When she died in Paris, she was the author of more than eighty books. Robert Phelps has selected and translated* Letters from Colette *(1981) and has edited her magnificent autobiography,* Earthly Paradise, *from which the following excerpt is taken.*

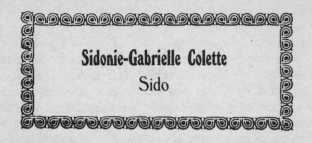

Sidonie-Gabrielle Colette
Sido

Always up at dawn ...

Always up at dawn and sometimes before day, my
mother attached particular importance to the cardinal points of the compass, as much for the good as
for the harm they might bring. It is because of her
and my deep-rooted love for her that first thing
every morning, and while I am still snug in bed, I
always ask: "Where is the wind coming from?" only
to be told in reply: "It's a lovely day," or "The
Palais-Royal's full of sparrows," or "The weather's
vile" or "seasonable." So nowadays I have to rely
on myself for the answer, by watching which way a
cloud is moving, listening for ocean rumblings in
the chimney, and letting my skin enjoy the breath
of the West wind, a breath as moist and vital and
laden with portents as the twofold divergent snort-
ings of some friendly monster. Or it may be that I
shrink into myself with hatred before that fine cold
dry enemy the East wind, and his cousin of the

From *Earthly Paradise*.

North. That was what my mother used to do, as she covered with paper cornets all the little plant creatures threatened by the russet moon "It's going to freeze," she would say, "the cat's dancing."

Her hearing, which remained keen, kept her informed too, and she would intercept Aeolian warnings.

"Listen over Moûtiers!" she used to say, lifting her forefinger where she stood near the pump, between the hydrangeas and the group of rose bushes. That was her reception point for the information coming from the west over the lowest of the garden walls. "Do you hear? Take the garden chairs indoors, and your book and hat. It's raining over Moûtiers; in two or three minutes more it'll be raining here."

I strained my ears "over Moûtiers"; from the horizon came a steady sound of beads plopping into water and the flat smell of the rain-pitted pond as it sluiced up against its slimy green banks. And I would wait for a second or two, so that the gentle drops of a summer shower, falling on my cheeks and lips, might bear witness to the infallibility of her whom only one person in the world—my father— called "Sido."

It was the reflected glow ...

It was the reflected glow of your blazing line along the terrace, O geraniums, and yours, O foxgloves, springing up amid the coppice, that gave my childish cheeks their rosy warmth. For Sido loved red

and pink in the garden, the burning shades of roses,
lychnis, hydrangeas, and red-hot pokers. She even
loved the winter cherry, although she declared that
its pulpy pink flowers, veined with red, reminded
her of the lights of a freshly killed calf. She made a
reluctant pact with the East wind. "I know how to
get on with him," she would say. But she remained
suspicious and, out of all the cardinal and collateral
points of the compass, it was on that icy treacherous
point, with its murderous pranks, that she kept her
eye. But she trusted him with lily-of-the-valley bulbs,
some begonias, and mauve autumn crocuses, those
dim lanterns of cold twilights.

Except for one mound with a clump of cherry
laurels over-shadowed by a maidenhair tree—whose
skate-shaped leaves I used to give to my school
friends to press between the pages of their atlases—
the whole warm garden basked in a yellow light that
shimmered into red and violet; but whether this red
and violet sprang then, and still spring, from feelings of happiness or from dazzled sight, I could not
tell. Those were summers when the heat quivered
up from the hot yellow gravel and pierced the plaited
rushes of my wide-brimmed hats, summers almost
without nights. For even then I so loved the dawn
that my mother granted it to me as a reward. She
used to agree to wake me at half past three and off
I would go, an empty basket on each arm, toward
the kitchen gardens that sheltered in the narrow
bend of the river, in search of strawberries, black
currants, and hairy gooseberries.

At half past three, everything slumbered still in a
primal blue, blurred and dewy, and as I went down

the sandy road the mist, grounded by its own weight, bathed first my legs, then my well-built little body, reaching at last to my mouth and ears, and finally to that most sensitive part of all, my nostrils. I went alone, for there were no dangers in that freethinking countryside. It was on that road and at that hour that I first became aware of my own self, experienced an inexpressible state of grace, and felt one with the first breath of air that stirred, the first bird, and the sun so newly born that it still looked not quite round.

"Beauty," my mother would call me, and "Jewel of pure gold"; then she would let me go, watching her creation—her masterpiece, as she said—grow smaller as I ran down the slope. I may have been pretty; my mother and the pictures of me at that period do not always agree. But what made me pretty at that moment was my youth and the dawn, my blue eyes deepened by the greenery all around me, my fair locks that would only be brushed smooth on my return, and my pride at being awake when other children were asleep. . . .

In her garden my mother . . .

In her garden my mother had a habit of addressing to the four cardinal points not only direct remarks and replies that sounded, when heard from our sitting room, like brief inspired soliloquies, but the actual manifestations of her courtesy, which generally took the form of plants and flowers. But in addition to these points—to Cèbe and the rue des Vignes, to Mother Adolphe, and Maître de Fourolles—there was also a zone of collateral points, more distant and less defined, whose contact with us was by means of stifled sounds and signals. My childish pride and imagination saw our house as the central point of a mariner's chart of gardens, winds, and rays of light, no section of which lay quite beyond my mother's influence.

I could gain my liberty at any moment by means of an easy climb over a gate, a wall, or a little sloping roof, but as soon as I landed back on the gravel of our own garden, illusion and faith returned to me. For as soon as she had asked me: "Where have you come from?" and frowned the ritual frown, my mother would resume her placid, radiant garden face, so much more beautiful than her anxious indoor face. And merely because she held sway there and watched over it all, the walls grew higher, the enclosures which I had so easily traversed by jumping from wall to wall and branch to branch, became unknown lands, and I found myself once more among the familiar wonders.

"Is that you I hear, Cèbe?" my mother would call. "Have you seen my cat?"

She pushed back her wide-brimmed hat of burnt straw until it slid down her shoulders, held by a brown taffeta ribbon around her neck, and threw her head back to confront the sky with her fearless gray glance and her face the color of an autumn apple. Did her voice strike the bird on the weathercock, the hovering honey buzzard, the last leaf on the walnut tree or the dormer window which, at the first light, swallowed up the barn owls? Then—though it was certain to happen, the surprise was never failing—from a cloud on the left the voice of a prophet with a bad cold would let fall a "No, Madame Colê—ê—tte!" which seemed to be making its way with great difficulty through a curly beard and blankets of fog, and slithering over ponds vaporous with cold. Or perhaps: "Ye—es, Madame Colê—ê—tte!," the voice of a shrill angel would sing on the right, probably perched on the spindle-shaped cirrus cloud which was sailing along to meet the young moon. "She's he—e—ard you. She's go—oing through the li—i—lacs."

"Thank you!" called my mother at random. "If that's you, Cèbe, just give me back my stake and my planting-out line, will you! I need them to get my lettuces straight. But be careful. I'm close to the hydrangeas!" As if it were the offering of a dream, the prank of a witches' Sabbath, or an act of magical levitation, the stake, wound around with ten yards of small cord, sailed through the air and came to rest at my mother's feet.

On other occasions she would offer to lesser, invisible spirits a tribute of flowers. Faithful to her ritual, she threw back her head and scanned the sky: "Who wants some of my double red violets?" she cried.

"I do, Madame Colê—ê—tte!" answered the mysterious one to the East, in her plaintive, feminine voice.

"Here you are, then!" and the little bunch, tied together with a juicy jonquil leaf, flew through the air, to be gratefully received by the plaintive Orient. "How lovely they smell! To think I can't grow any as good!"

"Of course you can't," I would think, and felt inclined to add: "It's all a question of the air they breathe."

"I could live in Paris ..."

"I could live in Paris only if I had a beautiful garden," she would confess to me. "And even then! I can't imagine a Parisian garden where I could pick those big bearded oats I sew on a bit of cardboard for you because they make such sensitive barometers." I chide myself for having lost the very last of those rustic barometers made of oat grains whose two awns, as long as a shrimp's feelers, crucified on a card, would turn to the left or the right according to whether it was going to be fine or wet.

No one could equal Sido, either, at separating and counting the talc-like skins of onions. "One—two—three coats; three coats on the onions!" And letting her spectacles or her lorgnette fall on her lap, she would add pensively: "That means a hard winter. I must have the pump wrapped in straw. Besides, the tortoise has dug itself in already, and the squirrels round about Guillemette have stolen quantities of walnuts and cobnuts for their stores. Squirrels always know everything."

If the newspapers foretold a thaw, my mother would shrug her shoulders and laugh scornfully. "A thaw? Those Paris meteorologists can't teach me anything about that! Look at the cat's paws!" Feeling chilly, the cat had indeed folded her paws out of sight beneath her, and shut her eyes tight. "When there's only going to be a short spell of cold," went on Sido, "the cat rolls herself into a turban with her nose against the root of her tail. But when it's going to be really bitter, she tucks in the pads of her front paws and rolls them up like a muff."

All the year round she kept racks full of plants in pots standing on green-painted wooden steps. There were rare geraniums, dwarf rose bushes, spiraeas with misty white and pink plumes, a few "succulents," hairy and squat as crabs, and murderous cacti. Two warm walls formed an angle which kept the harsh winds from her trial ground, which consisted of some red earthenware bowls in which I could see nothing but loose, dormant earth.

"Don't touch!"

"But nothing's coming up!"

"And what do you know about it? Is it for you to decide? Read what's written on the labels stuck in the pots! These are seeds of blue lupin; that's a narcissus bulb from Holland; those are seeds of winter cherry; that's a cutting of hibiscus—no, of course it isn't a dead twig!—and those are some seeds of sweet peas whose flowers have ears like little hares. And that . . . and that . . ."

"Yes, and that?"

My mother pushed her hat back, nibbled the chain of her lorgnette, and put the problem frankly to me:

"I'm really very worried. I can't remember whether it was a family of crocus bulbs I planted there, or the chrysalis of an emperor moth."

"We've only got to scratch to find out."

A swift hand stopped mine. Why did no one ever

model or paint or carve that hand of Sido's, tanned and wrinkled early by household tasks, gardening, cold water, and the sun, with its long, finely tapering fingers and its beautiful, convex, oval nails?

"Not on your life! If it's the chrysalis, it'll die as soon as the air touches it, and if it's the crocus, the light will shrivel its little white shoot and we'll have to begin all over again. Are you taking in what I say? You won't touch it?"

"No, Mother."

As she spoke, her face, alight with faith and an all-embracing curiosity, was hidden by another, older face, resigned and gentle. She knew that I should not be able to resist, any more than she could, the desire to know, and that like herself I should ferret in the earth of that flowerpot until it had given up its secret. I never thought of our resemblance, but she knew I was her own daughter and that, child though I was, I was already seeking for that sense of shock, the quickened heartbeat, and the sudden stoppage of the breath—symptoms of the private ecstasy of the treasure seeker. A treasure is not merely something hidden under the earth or the rocks or the sea. The vision of gold and gems is but a blurred mirage. To me the important thing is to lay bare and bring to light something that no human eye before mine has gazed upon.

She knew then that I was going to scratch on the sly in her trial ground until I came upon the upward-climbing claw of the cotyledon, the sturdy sprout urged out of its sheath by the spring. I thwarted the blind purpose of the bilious-looking, black-brown chrysalis, and hurled it from its temporary death into a final nothingness.

"You don't understand . . . you can't understand. You're nothing but a little eight-year-old murderess —or is it ten? You just can't understand something that wants to live." That was the only punishment I got for my misdeeds; but that was hard enough for me to bear.

Sido loathed flowers to be sacrificed. Although her one idea was to give, I have seen her refuse a request for flowers to adorn a hearse or a grave. She would harden her heart, frown, and answer "No" with a vindictive look.

"But it's for poor Monsieur Enfert, who died last night! Poor Madame Enfert's so pathetic, she says if she could see her husband depart covered with flowers, it would console her! And you've got such lovely moss roses, Madame Colette."

"My moss roses on a corpse! What an outrage!"

It was an involuntary cry, but even after she had pulled herself together she still said: "No. My roses have not been condemned to die at the same time as Monsieur Enfert."

But she gladly sacrificed a very beautiful flower to a very small child, a child not yet able to speak, like the little boy whom a neighbor to the east proudly brought into the garden one day, to show him off to her. My mother found fault with the infant's swaddling clothes, for being too tight, untied his three-piece bonnet and his unnecessary woolen shawl, and then gazed to her heart's content on his bronze ringlets, his cheeks, and the enormous, stern black eyes of a ten months' old baby boy, really so much more beautiful than any other boy of ten months! She gave him a *cuisse-de-nymphe-émue* rose, and he accepted it with delight, put it in his mouth, and sucked it; then he kneaded it with his powerful little hands and tore off the petals, as curved and carmine as his own lips.

"Stop it, you naughty boy!" cried his young mother.

But mine, with looks and words, applauded his massacre of the rose, and in my jealousy I said nothing.

She also regularly refused to lend double geraniums, pelargoniums, lobelias, dwarf rose bushes and spiraea for the wayside altars on Corpus Christi day, for although she was baptized and married in church, she always held aloof from Catholic trivialities and pageantries. But she gave me permission, when I was between eleven and twelve, to attend catechism classes and to join in the hymns at the evening service.

On the first of May, with my comrades of the catechism class, I laid lilac, camomile, and roses before the alter of the Virgin, and returned full of pride to show my "blessed posy." My mother laughed her irreverent laugh and, looking at my bunch of flowers, which was bringing the May bugs into the sitting room right under the lamp, she said: "Do you suppose it wasn't already blessed before?"

I do not know where she got her aloofness from any form of worship. I ought to have tried to find out. My biographers, who get little information from me, sometimes depict her as a simple farmer's wife and sometimes make her out to be a "whimsical bohemian." One of them, to my astonishment, goes so far as to accuse her of having written short literary works for young persons!

In reality, this Frenchwoman spent her childhood in the Yonne, her adolescence among painters, journalists, and musicians in Belgium, where her two elder brothers had settled, and then returned to the Yonne, where she married twice. But whence, or from whom, she got her sensitive understanding of country matters and her discriminating appreciation of the provinces, I am unable to say. I sing her praises as best I may, and celebrate the native lucidity which, in her, dimmed and often extinguished the lesser lights painfully lit through the contact of what she called "the common run of mankind."

I once saw her hang up a scarecrow in a cherry tree to frighten the blackbirds, because our kindly neighbor of the west, who always had a cold and was shaken with bouts of sneezing, never failed to disguise his cherry trees as old tramps and crown his currant bushes with battered opera hats. A few days later I found my mother beneath the tree, motionless with excitement, her head turned toward the heavens in which she would allow human religions no place.

"Sssh! Look!"

A blackbird, with a green and violet sheen on his dark plumage, was pecking at the cherries, drinking their juice and lacerating their rosy pulp.

"How beautiful he is!" whispered my mother. "Do you see how he uses his claw? And the movements of his head and that arrogance of his? See how he twists his beak to dig out the stone! And you notice that he only goes for the ripest ones."

"But, mother, the scarecrow!"

"Sssh! The scarecrow doesn't worry him!"

"But, mother, the cherries!"

My mother brought the glance of her rain-colored eyes back to earth: "The cherries? Yes, of course, the cherries."

In those eyes there flickered a sort of wild gaiety, a contempt for the whole world, a lighthearted disdain which cheerfully spurned me along with everything else. It was only momentary, and it was not the first time I had seen it. Now that I know her better, I can interpret those sudden gleams in her face. They were, I feel, kindled by an urge to escape from everyone and everything, to soar to some high place where her own writ ran. If I am mistaken, leave me to my delusion.

But there, under the cherry tree, she returned to earth once more among us, weighed down with anxieties, and love, and a husband and children who clung to her. Faced with the common round of life, she became good and comforting and humble again.

"Yes, of course, the cherries . . . you must have cherries too."

The blackbird, gorged, had flown off, and the scarecrow waggled his empty opera hat in the breeze.

In those days there were bitter winters ...

In those days there were bitter winters and burning summers. Since then I have known summers which, when I close my eyes, are the color of ocher-yellow earth, cracking between stalks of corn; and beneath the giant umbels of wild parsnip, the blue or gray of the sea. But no summer, save those of my childhood, enshrines the memory of scarlet geraniums and the glowing spikes of foxgloves. No winter now is ever pure white beneath a sky charged with slate-colored clouds foretelling a storm of thicker snow-flakes yet to come, and thereafter a thaw glittering with a thousand waterdrops and bright with spear-shaped buds. How that sky used to lower over the snow-laden roof of the haylofts, the weathercock, and the bare boughs of the walnut tree, making the she-cats flatten their ears! The quiet vertical fall of the snow became oblique and, as I wandered about the garden catching its flying flakes in my mouth, a faint booming as of a distant sea arose above my hooded head. Warned by her antennae, my mother would come out on the terrace, sample the weather, and call out to me:

"A gale from the west! Run and shut the sky-lights in the barn! And the door of the coachhouse! And the window of the back room!"

Eager cabin boy of the family vessel, I would rush off, my sabots clattering, thrilled if, from the depths of that hissing turmoil of white and blue-black, a flash of lightning and a brief mutter of thunder, children of February and the West wind,

together filled one of the abysses of the sky. I
would try then to shudder and believe that the end
of the world had come.

But when the din was at its height, there would
be my mother, peering through a big brass-rimmed
magnifying glass, lost in wonder as she counted the
branched crystals of a handful of snow she had just
snatched from the very jaws of the West wind as it
flung itself upon our garden.

"There is about a very beautiful child ..."

"There is about a very beautiful child something I
can't define which makes me sad. How can I
make myself clear? Your little niece C. is at this
moment ravishingly beautiful. Full-face she's still
nothing much, but when she turns her profile in a
certain way and you see the proud outline of her
pure little nose below her lovely lashes, I am
seized with an admiration that somehow disturbs
me. They say that great lovers feel like that before the object of their passion. Can it be then
that, in my way, I am a great lover? That's a
discovery that would much have astonished my
two husbands!"

So she was able, was she, to bend over a human
flower with no harm to herself, no harm save for
that "sadness"; was sadness her word for that melancholy ecstasy, that sense of exaltation which up-
lifts us when we see the waxen purity of faces
dissolving into an arabesque never resembling its

original, never twice the same: the dual fires of the eyes, the nostrils like twin calyxes, the little sea cave of the mouth quivering as it waits for its prey? When she bent over a glorious childish creature she would tremble and sigh, seized with an anguish she could not explain, whose name is temptation. For it would never have occurred to her that from a youthful face there could emanate a perturbation, a mist like that which floats above grapes in their vat, or that one could succumb to it. My first communings with myself taught me the lesson, though I failed to observe it sometimes: "Never touch a butterfly's wing with your finger."

"I certainly won't . . . or only just lightly . . . just at the tawny-black place where you see that violet glow, that moon lick, without being able to say exactly where it starts or where it dies away."

"No, don't touch it. The whole thing will vanish if you merely brush it."

"But only just lightly! Perhaps this will be the time when I shall feel under this particular finger, my fourth, the most sensitive, the cold blue flame and the way it vanishes into the skin of the wing— the feathers of the wing—the dew of the wing . . ." A trace of lifeless ash on the tip of my finger, the wing dishonored, the tiny creature weakened.

There is no doubt that my mother, who only learned, as she said, "by getting burnt," knew that one possesses through abstaining, and only through abstaining. For a "great lover" of her sort—of our sort—there is not much difference between the sin of abstention and that of consummation. Serene and gay in presence of her husband, she became disturbed, and distracted with an unexplained passion, when she came in contact with someone who was passing through a sublime experience. Confined to her village by her two successive husbands and four children, she had the power of conjuring up everywhere unexpected crises, burgeonings, metamorphoses, and dramatic miracles, which she herself provoked and whose value she savored to the full. She who nursed animals, cared for children, and looked after plants was spared the discovery that some creatures want to die, that certain children long to be defiled, that one of the buds is determined to be forced open and then trampled underfoot. Her form of inconstancy was to fly from the bee to the mouse, from a newborn child to a tree, from a poor person to a poorer, from laughter to torment! How pure are those who lavish themselves in this way! In her life there was never the memory of a dishonored wing, and if she trembled with longing in the presence of a closed calyx, a chrysalis still rolled in its vanished cocoon, at least she respectfully awaited the moment. How pure are those who have never forced anything open! To bring my mother close to me again I have to think back to those dramatic dreams she dreamed throughout the adolescence of her elder son, who was so beautiful and so seductive. At that time I was aware that she was wild, full of false gaiety, given to maledictions, ordinary, plain-looking, and on the alert. Oh, if only I could see her again thus diminished, her cheeks flushed red with jealousy and rage! If only I could see her thus, and could she but understand me well enough to recognize herself in what she would most strongly have reproved! If only I, grown wise in my turn, could show her how much her own image, though coarsened and impure, survives in me, her faithful servant, whose job is the menial tasks! She gave me life and the mission to pursue those things which she, a poet, seized and cast aside as one snatches a fragment of a floating melody drifting through space. What does the melody matter to one whose concern is the bow and the hand that holds the bow?

She pursued her innocent ends with increasing anxiety. She rose early, then earlier, then earlier still. She wanted to have the world to herself, deserted, in the form of a little enclosure with a trellis and a sloping roof. She wanted the jungle to be virgin but, even so, inhabited only by swallows, cats, and bees, and the huge spider balancing atop his wheel of lace silvered by the night. The neighbor's shutter, banging against the wall, spoiled her dream of being an unchallengeable explorer, a dream repeated every day at the hour when the cold dew seems to be falling, with little irregular plops, from the beaks of the blackbirds. She got up at six, then at five, and at the end of her life a little red lamp wakened her, in winter, long before the Angelus smote the black air. In those moments while it was still night my mother used to sing, falling silent as soon as anyone was able to hear. The lark also sings while it is mounting toward the palest, least inhabited part of the sky. My mother climbed, too, mounting ceaselessly up the ladder of the hours, trying to possess the beginning of the beginning. I know what that particular intoxication is like. But what she sought was a red, horizontal ray, and the pale sulphur that comes before the red ray; she wanted the damp wing that the first bee stretches out like an arm. The summer wind, which springs up at the approach of the sun, gave her its first fruits in scents of acacia and woodsmoke; when a horse pawed the ground and whinnied softly in the neighboring stable, she was the first to hear it. On an autumn morning she was the only one to see herself reflected in the first disk of ephemeral ice in the well bucket, before her nail cracked it.

The time came ...

The time came when all her strength left her. She was amazed beyond measure and would not believe it. Whenever I arrived from Paris to see her, as soon as we were alone in the afternoon in her little house, she had always some sin to confess to me. On one occasion she turned up the hem of her dress, rolled her stocking down over her shin, and displayed a purple bruise, the skin nearly broken.

"Just look at that!"

"What on earth have you done to yourself this time, Mother?"

She opened wide eyes, full of innocence and embarrassment.

"You wouldn't believe it, but I fell downstairs!"

"How do you mean—'fell'?"

"Just what I said. I fell, for no reason. I was going downstairs and I fell. I can't understand it."

"Were you going down too quickly?"

"Too quickly? What do you call too quickly? I was going down quickly. Have I time to go downstairs majestically like the Sun King? And if that were all . . . But look at this!"

On her pretty arm, still so young above the faded hand, was a scald forming a large blister.

"Oh goodness! Whatever's that!"

"My footwarmer."

"The old copper footwarmer? The one that holds five quarts?"

"That's the one. Can I trust anything, when that footwarmer has known me for forty years? I can't imagine what possessed it, it was boiling fast, I went to take if off the fire, and crack, something gave in my wrist. I was lucky to get nothing worse than the blister. But what a thing to happen! After that I let the cupboard alone. . . ."

She broke off, blushing furiously.

"What cupboard?" I demanded severely.

My mother fenced, tossing her head as though I were trying to put her on a lead.

"Oh, nothing! No cupboard at all!"

"Mother! I shall get cross!"

"Since I've said, 'I let the cupboard alone,' can't you do the same for my sake? The cupboard hasn't moved from its place, has it? So, shut up about it!"

The cupboard was a massive object of old walnut, almost as broad as it was high, with no carving save the circular hole made by a Prussian bullet that had entered by the right-hand door and passed out through the back panel.

"Do you want it moved from the landing, Mother?"

An expression like that of a young she-cat, false and glittery, appeared on her wrinkled face.

"I? No, it seems to me all right there—let it stay where it is!"

All the same, my doctor brother and I agreed that we must be on the watch. He saw my mother every day, since she had followed him and lived in the same village, and he looked after her with a passionate devotion which he hid. She fought against all her ills with amazing elasticity, forgot them, baffled them, inflicted on them signal if temporary defeats, recovered, during entire days, her vanished strength; and the sound of her battles, whenever I spent a few days with her, could be heard all over the house till I was irresistibly reminded of a terrier tackling a rat.

At five o'clock in the morning I would be awakened by the clank of a full bucket being set down in the kitchen sink immediately opposite my room.

"What are you doing with that bucket, Mother? Couldn't you wait until Josephine arrives?"

And out I hurried. But the fire was already blazing, fed with dry wood. The milk was boiling on the blue-tiled charcoal stove. Nearby, a bar of chocolate was melting in a little water for my breakfast, and, seated squarely in her cane armchair, my mother was grinding the fragrant coffee which she roasted herself. The morning hours were always kind to her. She wore their rosy colors in her cheeks. Flushed with a brief return to health, she would gaze at the rising sun, while the church bell rang for early Mass, and rejoice at having tasted, while we still slept, so many forbidden fruits.

The forbidden fruits were the overheavy bucket drawn up from the well, the firewood split with a billhook on an oaken block, the spade, the mattock, and above all the double steps propped against the gable window of the woodhouse. There were the climbing vine whose shoots she trained up to the gable windows of the attic, the flowery spikes of the too-tall lilacs, the dizzy cat that had to be rescued from the ridge of the roof. All the accomplices of her old existence as a plump and sturdy little woman, all the minor rustic divinities who once obeyed her and made her so proud of doing without servants, now assumed the appearance and position of adversaries. But they reckoned without that love of combat which my mother was to keep till the end of her life. At seventy-one, dawn still found her undaunted, if not always undamaged. Burnt by the fire, cut with the pruning knife, soaked by melting snow or spilled water, she had always managed to enjoy her best moments of independence before the earliest risers had opened their shutters. She was able to tell us of the cats' awakening, of what was going on in the nests, of news gleaned, together with the morning's milk and the warm loaf, from the milkmaid and the baker's girl, the record in fact of the birth of a new day.

It was not until one morning when I found the kitchen unwarmed, and the blue enamel saucepan hanging on the wall, that I felt my mother's end to be near. Her illness knew many respites, during which the fire flared up again on the hearth, and the smell of fresh bread and melting chocolate stole under the door together with the cat's impatient paw. Those respites were periods of unexpected alarms. My mother and the big walnut cupboard were discovered together in a heap at the foot of the stairs, she having determined to transport it in secret from the upper landing to the ground floor. Whereupon my elder brother insisted that my mother should keep still and that an old servant should sleep in the little house. But how could an old servant prevail against a vital energy so youthful and mischievous that it contrived to tempt and lead astray a body already half fettered by death? My brother, returning before sunrise from attending a distant patient, one day caught my mother red-handed in the most wanton of crimes. Dressed in her nightgown, but wearing heavy gardening sabots, her little gray septuagenarian's plait of hair turning up like a scorpion's tail on the nape of her neck, one foot firmly planted on the crosspiece of the beech trestle, her back bent in the attitude of the expert jobber, my mother, rejuvenated by an indescribable expression of guilty enjoyment, in defiance of all her promises and of the freezing morning dew, was sawing logs in her own yard.

"Sir, you ask me ..."

"Sir,

"You ask me to come and spend a week with you, which means I would be near my daughter, whom I adore. You who live with her know how rarely I see her, how much her presence delights me, and I'm touched that you should ask me to come and see her. All the same I'm not going to accept your kind invitation, for the time being at any rate. The reason is that my pink cactus is probably never going to flower. It's a very rare plant I've been given, and I'm told that in our climate it flowers only once every four years. Now, I am already a very old woman, and if I went away when my pink cactus is about to flower, I am certain I shouldn't see it flower again.

"So I beg you, sir, to accept my sincere thanks and my regrets, together with my kind regards."

This note, signed *"Sidonie Colette, née Landoy,"* was written by my mother to one of my husbands, the second. A year later she died, at the age of seventy-seven.

Whenever I feel myself inferior to everything about me, threatened by my own mediocrity, frightened by the discovery that a muscle is losing its strength, a desire its power, or a pain the keen edge of its bite, I can still hold up my head and say to myself: "I am the daughter of the woman who wrote that letter—that letter and so many more that I have kept. This one tells me in ten lines that at the age of seventy-six she was planning journeys and undertaking them, but that waiting for the possible bursting into bloom of a tropical flower held everything up and silenced even her heart, made for love. I am the daughter of a woman who, in a mean, close-fisted, confined little place, opened her village home to stray cats, tramps, and pregnant servant girls. I am the daughter of a woman who many a time, when she was in despair at not having enough money for others, ran through the wind-whipped snow to cry from door to door, at the houses of the rich, that a child had just been born in a poverty-stricken home to parents whose feeble, empty hands had no swaddling clothes for it. Let me not forget that I am the daughter of a woman who bent her head, trembling, between the blades of a cactus, her wrinkled face full of ecstasy over the promise of a flower, a woman who herself never ceased to flower, untiringly, during three quarters of a century."

The American dramatist **LILLIAN HELL-MAN,** *whose plays include* The Children's Hour, The Little Foxes, *and* Another Part of the Forest, *was born in New Orleans to Max Hellman, a shoe merchant whose parents had migrated to Louisiana from Germany, and to Julia Newhouse, a "sweet eccentric" from a prosperous family whom Hellman remembers on the following pages from her memoir* An Unfinished Woman. *Hellman's parents moved to New York when she was five years old and though she continued to visit her New Orleans relatives (in both works of nonfiction,* Pentimento *and* An Unfinished Woman, *we see the young Hellman in New Orleans and New York) she grew up to become in all respects a metropolitan personality and writer. Because of her plays and her politics, she acquired a reputation as an uncompromising moralist, a strong hater, and a woman of unusual mettle, which is, obliquely, the quality she remembers in her "passive" mother.*

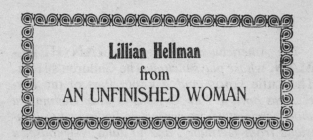

Lillian Hellman
from
AN UNFINISHED WOMAN

I was born in New Orleans to Julia Newhouse from Demopolis, Alabama, who had fallen in love and stayed in love with Max Hellman, whose parents had come to New Orleans in the German 1845–1848 immigration to give birth to him and his two sisters. My mother's family, long before I was born, had moved from Demopolis to Cincinnati and then to New Orleans, both desirable cities, I guess, for three marriageable girls.

But I first remember them in a large New York apartment: my two young and very pretty aunts; their taciturn, tight-faced brother; and the silent, powerful, severe woman, Sophie Newhouse, who was their mother, my grandmother. Her children, her servants, all of her relatives except her brother Jake were frightened of her, and so was I. Even as a small child I disliked myself for the fear and showed off against it.

The Newhouse apartment held the upper-middle-class trappings, in touch of things and in spirit of people, that never manage to be truly stylish. Heavy weather hung over the lovely oval rooms. True, there were parties for my aunts, but the parties, to a peeping child in the servants' hall, seemed so muted that I was long convinced that on fancy occasions grown people moved their lips without making sounds. In the days after the party one would hear exciting stories about the new suitors, but the suitors were never quite good enough and the parties were, obviously, not good enough for those who might have been. Then there were the Sunday dinners with great-uncles and aunts sometimes in attendance, full of open ill will about who had the most money, or who spent it too lavishly, who would inherit what, which had bought what rug that would last forever, who what jewel she would best have been without. It was a corporation meeting, with my grandmother unexpectedly in the position of vice-chairman. The chairman was her brother Jake, the only human being to whom I ever saw her defer. Early, I told myself that was because he was richer than she was, and did something called managing her money. But that was too simple: he was a man of great force, given, as she was given, to breaking the spirit of people for the pleasure of the exercise. But he was also witty and rather worldly, seeing his own financial machinations as natural not only to his but to the country's benefit, and seeing that as comic. (I had only one real contact with my Uncle Jake: when I graduated from school at fifteen, he gave me a ring that I took to a 59th Street hock shop, got twenty-five dollars, and bought books. I went immediately to tell him what I'd done, deciding, I think, that day that the break had to come. He stared at me for a long time, and then he laughed and said the words I later used in *The Little Foxes*: "So you've got spirit after all. Most of the rest of them are made of sugar water.")

But that New York apartment where we visited several times a week, the summer cottage when we went for a visit each year as the poor daughter and granddaughter, made me into an angry child and forever caused in me a wild extravagance mixed with respect for money and those who have it. The respectful periods were full of self-hatred and during them I always made my worst mistakes. But after *The Little Foxes* was written and put away, this conflict was to grow less important, as indeed, the picture of my mother's family was to grow dim and almost fade away.

It was not unnatural that my first love went to my father's family. He and his two sisters were free, generous, funny. But as I made my mother's family all one color, I made my father's family too remarkable, and then turned both extreme judgments against my mother.

In fact, she was a sweet eccentric, the only middle-class woman I have ever known who had not rejected the middle class—that would have been an act of will—but had skipped it altogether. She liked a simple life and simple people, and would have been happier, I think, if she had stayed in the backlands of Alabama riding wild on the horses she so often talked about, not so lifelong lonely for the black men and women who had taught her the only religion she ever knew. I didn't know what she was saying when she moved her lips in a Baptist church or a Catholic cathedral or, less often, in a synagogue, but it was obvious that God could be found anywhere, because several times a week we would stop in a church, any church, and she seemed to be at home in all of them.

But simple natures can also be complex, and that is difficult for a child, who wants all grown people to be sharply one thing or another. I was puzzled and irritated by the passivity of my mother as it mixed with an unmovable stubbornness. (My father had not been considered a proper husband for a rich and pretty girl, but my mother's deep fear of her mother did not override her deep love for my father, although the same fear kept my two aunts from ever marrying and my uncle from marrying until after his mother's death.)

Mama seemed to do only what my father wanted, and yet we lived the way my mother wanted us to live. She deeply wanted to keep my father and to please him, but no amount of protest from him could alter the strange quirks that Freud already knew about. Windows, doors and stoves haunted her and she would often stand before them for as long as half an hour, or leaving the house, would insist upon returning to it while we waited for her in any weather. And sad, middle-aged ladies would be brought home from a casual meeting on a park bench to fill the living room with woe: plain tales of sickness, or poverty, or loneliness in the afternoon often led to their staying on for dinner with my bored father.

I remember a time when our apartment was being painted and the week it was supposed to take stretched into three because one of the two paint-

ers, a small, sickly man with an Italian accent, soon
found that my mother was a sympathetic listener.
He would, in duty, climb the ladder at nine in the
morning, but by eleven he was sitting on the sofa
with the tale of the bride who died in childbirth, the
child still in Italy, his mother who ailed and half
starved in Tuscany, the nights in New York where
he knew nobody to eat with or talk to. After lunch,
cooked by our bad-tempered Irish lady, and served
to him by my mother to hide the bad temper, he
would climb the ladder again and paint for a few
hours while my mother urged him to stop work and
go for a nice day in the sunshine. Once, toward the
end of the long job—the other painter never returned after the first few days—I came home carrying books from the library, annoyed to find the
painter in my favorite chair. As I stood in the
doorway, frowning at my mother, the painter said,
"Your girl. How old?"

"Fifteen," said my mother.

"In Italy, not young, fifteen. She is healthy?"

"Very healthy," said my mother. "Her generation has larger feet than we did."

"I think about it," said the painter. "I let you
know."

I knew my mother didn't understand what he
meant because she smiled and nodded in the way
she always did when her mind had wandered, but I
was angry and told my father about it at dinner. He
laughed and I left the table, but later he told my
mother that the painter was not to come to the
house again. A few years later when I brought
home for dinner an aimless, handsome young man

who got roaring drunk and insisted upon climbing down the building from our eighth-floor apartment, my father, watching him from the window, said, "Perhaps we should try to find that Italian house painter." My mother was dead for five years before I knew that I had loved her very much.

When the novelist **MAUREEN HOWARD**
(Bridgeport Bus, Before My Time, Grace Abound-
ing) *published her memoir of childhood in Irish-
American Bridgeport, Connecticut, and beyond,
the critic Frank Kermode wrote that in* Facts of
Life *(from which the following excerpt is taken),
"Maureen Howard has solved the peculiar problems of autobiography with her usual skill, and
her prose has an authentic note of self-irony and
candor. She keeps her eye for the ridiculous and
knows how to write the prose appropriate to a
slightly painful hilarity. She also knows how to
preserve her own and others' dignity while expos-
ing affectation and vanity. Of course she can do
these things because she really is an exceptionally
good writer." She begins her award-winning autobiography with a portrait of her mother, Loretta
Burns, a lady refined but fey. The mother is a
wonderful character and her daughter, as unsenti-
mental and critical a witness as you could find,
makes us feel it. On the pages that follow, we hear
and see Loretta Burns and marvel at such nonfiction that reads so much like a first-rate novel.*

117

Maureen Howard
from
FACTS OF LIFE

"Ah, did you once see Shelley plain," one of my mother's beloved lines, delivered on this occasion with some irony as we watched Jasper McLevy, the famed Socialist mayor of Bridgeport, climb down from his Model A Ford. "Laugh where we must, be candid where we can," was another of her lines, a truncated couplet, one of the scraps of poems, stories, jingles that she pronounced throughout the day. Like station breaks on WICC, her quotations punctuated the hours. Vacuum off: "One thing done and that done well / is a very good thing as many can tell." Out on the back stoop to take in the thick chipped bottles of unhomogenized milk, she would study the sky over Parrott Avenue— "Trust me Clara Vere de Vere from yon blue heavens above us bent . . ." George and mother and me, pressed against the sun-parlor doors watching a September hurricane play itself out. Ash cans rattling down the drive, gutters clotted with leaves, shingles flying, the rambler rose torn from its trellis whipping the cellar door. Her gentle, inappropriate

118

crooning: "Who has seen the wind?/ Neither you nor I: / But when the trees bow down their heads, . . ."

My mother was a lady, soft-spoken, refined; alas, she was fey, fragmented. I do not know if it was always so, but when we were growing up, broken off bits of art is what we got, a touch here and there. A Lehmbruck nude clipped out of *Art News* tacked in the pantry, a green pop-eyed Sienese Madonna folded in the Fannie Farmer cookbook. She was sturdy when we were children, with high cheekbones and red hair, like a chunky Katharine Hepburn, so the fragility, the impression of fragility was all in her manner, her voice. Her attitude toward anything as specific as a pile of laundry was detached, amused. It might not be our dirty socks and underwear that she dealt with at all, but one of our picture books or a plate of cinnamon toast. As she grew older her fine red hair faded to yellow, then to white, but it was still drawn back from her face and pinned at the neck as she wore it in college. Her clothes were old but very good. And my mother—the least independent of women—always used her maiden name, her married name tacked on as though she were listing herself in her *Smith Alumnae Quarterly*. Loretta Burns Kearns. Somewhat wistful. You do remember me? Loretta Burns?

I sensed that my mother was a misfit from the first days when, dressed in a linen hat and pearls, she walked me out around the block. She was too fine for the working-class neighborhood that surrounded us. "Flower in the crannied wall/ I pluck you out of the crannies." Down Parrott Avenue around to French Street we marched, taking the air— "As I was going up the stair/ I met a man who wasn't there./ He wasn't there again today. . . ." I never knew when I was growing up whether my mother didn't have time to finish the poems what with the constant cooking, cleaning, washing, or whether this was all there was, these remnants left in her head.

To the crowded A & P we charged on a Saturday morning—ours not to make reply, ours not to reason why, ours but to do and die. If she gave us a ride back to school after lunch and the scent of spring was heavy over the schoolyard fence as the nuns filed in from the convent, my mother would sing out to us, triumphant behind the wheel of the old brown Auburn: "Come down to Kew in lilac-time. . . . And there they say, when dawn is high and all the world's a blaze of sky . . . Come down to Kew in lilac-time (it isn't far from London!)"

"There once was a molicepan who met a bumble-stum. . . ." A witless ditty—it must have been hilarious in her public-speaking class at college and never failed to please at lunch or dinner. But it wasn't mere nonsense or chestnuts from the laureates she quoted. My mother had studied German and I believe been quite a serious student before life caught up with her. *"So long man strebt, er ist erlost,"* she said. As long as man strives he is saved. *"Wer reitet so spät durch Nacht und Wind?"* We were treated to disjointed lines, lots of *Faust*, some Schiller and Heine, the final watery gurglings of the Rhine maidens and, of course, *"Freude, schöner Götterfunken . . ."*

It sounded beautiful gibberish to me as did the Latin verbs she conjugated to the remote pluperfect tense, but for my mother it was to prove that she could still do it, could reel it off with ease—as naturally as an athlete doing push-ups before the flab sets in. *"Amāveram, amāveras, amāverat."* That was the trick my mother could do and other mothers couldn't, as well as smock my dresses by hand and overcook the meat to please my father and not speak to George when he was rotten, but be elegantly wounded, disappointed in her son, like a grieving queen.

She kept a plain brown copybook to mark down all our childhood diseases and achievements. This chronicle is of no general interest: while it is gratifying for me to know that I went to the World's Fair in 1939 with the last scabs of my chicken pox and still had a wonderful time, it is terrifying to read my first poem (age seven) about the Baby Jesus and George's loathsome moral verse (age six)—both efforts already corrupted by the worst literary traditions. "Thus should a little child be merry/ In snowy, blowy January."

We were dressed in our Sunday best and taken to the concert series at Klein Memorial Hall. My father wouldn't go near the stuff. Helen Traubel stomped onto the stage in a black tent and something like gym shoes. The Budapest Quartet, all young and buoyant, stunned us with the knowledge of their own brilliance. The Connecticut Symphony ground out their Debussy and Ravel, their sloppy Beethoven, their inevitable Gershwin jolly-up. Me and my mother and George, proud and rather excited by the grandeur we could pull off in Bridgeport. The audience—a sprinkling of local music teachers, a solid core of middle-class Jewish shopkeepers and professionals who were more sophisticated than the Irish in town, and that set of rich old ladies who stumble into concert halls all over the world, canes and diamonds, hearing aids, rumpled velvet evening capes from long ago.

We never made it to Kew where all the world's a blaze of sky, but to the first little temple of civic culture, the Klein Memorial out near Bassick High School beyond the Cadillac showroom. On those special nights we were there. The price of the tickets was something awful, but my mother wanted this for us. I ran off pictures in my head, beautiful scenery, lakes and rills, mountains and fens. I called upon the great myth that one *must* be moved. I strained, while the violins soared, for deeper finer thoughts, but it was beyond my childish endurance. I tap, tap, tapped my patent-leather pump into my brother's ankle until it drove him mad, found that I had to cough, begged to go to the water fountain and was kept in my seat by a Smith Brothers' cough drop from my mother's purse.

What did it mean to her? Was my mother full of a passionate yearning like those starved women of taste who carted their pianos across the prairie? God knows, Bridgeport was raw land in the thirties. Before my father died, she sat in perfect harmony with him in front of the Lawrence Welk show. She was lost in the old sappy songs, lost. Walled in by her vagueness, all the fragments of herself floating like the million orange, green and purple dots that formed the absurd image, the bobbing head of the lisping bandmaster. My parents took my anger as a joke. Disgust swelled from me: I was not ready for compassion.

Or did Loretta Burns know that her chance was gone and only want those ineffable finer things for me and George? Well, we sure got them. We got the whole culture kit beyond her wildest dreams. There came a day when George knew who was dancing what role in which ballet that very evening up at City Center. For the pure clean line of a particular Apollo he would leave his gray basement on St. Mark's Place—burnt-out pots, ravioli eaten cold from the can, grit in the typewriter keys. His coffee-stained translations from the Spanish and Greek littered the floor. No closets. No bathtub. Now, as an adult, my brother takes with him wherever he lives an intentional chaos that is impressive, a mock poverty. Orange crates and real Picassos. Thousands of records and books but no dishes, no curtains. Money handled like trash. Twenty-dollar bills crumpled in ashtrays, checks left to age, income tax ignored. He is quite successful really. Her boy has become a strange man, but not to himself and he is not unhappy. My brother, a middle-aged man, can come to visit (filthy jeans and Brooks Brothers blazer), take William Carlos Williams off the shelf and read a passage, rediscovered: "At our age the imagination across the sorry facts"—then tell me why it is so fine, and it *is* fine. We are grown: now I can see the poem perfectly. As we talk beneath my Greenwich Village skylight he threads his speech with lines—like our mother, of course.

While I'm split, split right down the middle, all sensibility one day, raging at the vulgarities that are packaged as art, the self-promotion everywhere, the inflated reputations. In such a mood I am unable to sit in a theater or pick up a recently written book. I am quite crazy as I begin to read in stupefying rotation—*Anna Karenina, Bleak House, Persuasion, Dubliners, St. Mawr, Tender Is the Night, The Wings of the Dove*. I play the Chopin Mazurkas until the needle wears out. Drawings are the only works I can bear to look at. The atmosphere I demand is so rarefied it is stale and I know it.

Then again, everything is acceptable to me. In an orgy I view the slickest movie or love story on TV, suck in the transistor music and thrill to the glossy photographs of sumptuous salads and stews, the magnificent bedrooms and marble baths in *House and Garden*. Our great living junk art. The Golden Arches of McDonald's rise, glorious across the landscape, contempo-monolithic, simple in concept as Stonehenge if we could but see it. Then the nausea overtakes me in Bloomingdale's "art gallery" or as I listen to all that Limey Drah-ma on Public Television. Sick. I am often sick of art.

It would never have occurred to my mother that the finer things might be complicated for us, less than sheer delight. She simply stopped after her children left home. There were no more disembodied lines, not even the favorite "Little Orphant Annie's come to our house to stay," or "Where are you going young fellow my lad/ On this glittering morning in May?/ I'm going to join the colors, Dad . . ." No. She settled into Lawrence Welk, "Double Jeopardy," Dean Martin no less, and she had all her life been such a lady. She read the *Bridgeport Post* and clipped the columns of some quack who had many an uplift remedy for arthritis and heart disease. She followed the news of the Kennedys in *McCall's* magazine, until the last terrible years when she was widowed, when the blood circulated fitfully to her cold fingers and her brain. Then, from a corner of her dwindling world, she resurrected Ibsen's *Rosmersholm* in a German translation and underlined in a new ballpoint pen the proclamations of Rebecca West, all that heroic bunkum about the future, the strength of women, and her festering spiritual love.

Mother sat on the brown velvet couch day after day, rejecting tapioca and Jell-O, smiling at the pictures in her art books like a child . . . such pretty flowers . . . all the colors . . . by some Dutchman . . . in a bouquet. The fat ladies she laughed at were Renoir's, bare bottoms by a hazy stream. Her mind skipped the shallow waters of her past like a stone. George and her own father were one man. My father—her great love whom she had married against all opposition—now, my father was merely "that fellow" and there was a photo she found of Loretta Burns with a whole band of robust Smith girls, each one warmly recalled, who'd gone hiking up Mount Tom on a fine autumn day in her sophomore year. Sometimes she could not place me and so she entertained me graciously, gave me pieces of crust and cake. She was tiny now, nestled in the couch. Her thoughts fluttered away from her: "By the shores of Gitche Gumee,/ By the shining Big-Sea-Water," she said. Gaily she'd recite her most cherished line of Heine:

Ich weiss nicht was soll es bedeuten
Dass ich so traurig bin . . .

What does it mean that I am so sad? She seemed happy to remember the words at all.

My Life in Art

"Oh, the Irish"—my mother patronized her own. Too much love and exasperation was learned at her knee: the Irish—the whole insufferable lot of them—crass, low in their tastes but what could you really say against them—crooked politicians and venal priests, alcoholic virgins tottering to Mass. They were charming. We were taught to take the Irish lightly. In our house high seriousness was never the order of the day.

As kids in grammar school we said— "Well, that's the Irish"—when the nuns sent us home with books of chances on the Buick sedan, when the new Stations of the Cross were more lurid than the old. Later, when I came as a visitor to town I presumed at once that it was some thick mick mayor, true to form, who had destroyed the Victorian Gothic mansion, a dream of grandeur set in a vast garden on Golden Hill Street. I've come across that house, the Wheeler Mansion, in books on American architecture. The Metropolitan Museum took slides of every room before it was leveled. Bridgeport, a vaudeville joke of a town, had little and it opted for less. None of this seemed funny anymore: the arrogance of the mayor's sleazy taste, the hatred it implied of our meager heritage, his disdain for the duped Yankee millionaire who'd left his prized home to the citizens of Bridgeport. True, many of the fine houses in Ireland were burned to the ground after 1916—the wrath of those people, getting back their own—but the vengeance here was petty, trashed down by the Republican City Council. It was 1958. Joe McCarthy was still a great favorite of the *Bridgeport Post*. Who needed professors from out of town taking notes on an old house? Who needed gargoyles and turrets, pictures, rugs, copper beeches with a hundred years' growth? The Wheeler land was to stand empty for years, a useless punishment to the town. After my diatribe against the Irish my father said: "The new mayor is Italian."

This only increased my fury. "Well then," I cried, "it's Bridgeport, pure Bridgeport."

Our family was alone in the parish, mocking the world we came from—the tap routines and accordion music on Saint Patrick's night, the *Catholic Messenger* with its simpering parables of sacrifice, its weekly photos of saintly missionaries and their flock of mocha children with souls like ours, rescued for eternity. My parents were good Catholics and never meant us to find our religion a farce. It was as perfect to them as to any knee-bobbing, bead-telling spinster. The Catholic Church with its foreshortened American history and tangled puritanical roots was as inviolate to my mother and father as it was to the last-ditch aristocrats of Evelyn Waugh.

Mass, Communion, fish on Fridays, the Legion of Decency, were all part of our life. The Holy Days were honored. Belief without question: observation without piety. Once during Lent—it must have been after a scalding sermon condemning our wanton modern pleasures, so few in the thirties (radio programs, a Saturday matinee, an evening of cards)—we knelt together in the living room and attempted the family rosary. My father, playing up his role, intoning the Aves as he'd learned them in the seminary, mother backing him in a whisper, George and me mumbling after. By the time we got up from the floor, stiff with embarrassment, we all knew that charade would never be repeated. But we set out the crèche with solemnity at Christmas and the week before Easter the palms were dutifully carried home from church and wound round the finial of the dresser mirror to gather dust. Religion was a serious business, but the Irish were fair game. In laughing at them we laughed at ourselves, didn't we, Catholics in good standing, pure potato-famine Irish, gone fine with our cut glass and linens from McCutcheon's.

Our piano lessons, taught by Sister Mary Patronella, a large woman who dosed with Listerine so that she might breathe freely over her pupils, cost fifty cents an hour and were not worth the price. Then ballet for me, elocution, clarinet for George—

none of my mother's efforts to spring us from our cultural poverty or the dim children in our neighborhood came to much. She found extraordinary people to widen our horizons. A distraught mother (with a house full of waifs in undershirts gnawing at pieces of Bond Bread) instructed us in drawing and watercolors. Shading, outline, perspective: the point of each academic exercise was lost in the woman's confusion: our studio her kitchen table, old jelly jars to dip our brushes, chipped saucers to mix our colors and her kids whining in the doorway. For a while our Saturday mornings were a penance.

There followed, for me, a vivid year of modern dance. Only imagine the heroics of it: a tiny Jewish girl in her twenties, tense as a young bird, dedicated to Art, operating out of a storefront behind venetian blinds. A few potted plants, photos of Isadora, Ted Shawn and Ruth St. Denis piously tacked on the walls. Through her gauze drapery Miss Weinstein was all bone and dancer's muscle. Her body was covered for Bridgeport, though sometimes when the mothers had gone off—they were not allowed to attend class with their clumpy purses and absurdly disguised shapes—sometimes, our teacher would fling off her kimono and reveal herself to us, free and naked under the Grecian dress, leaping, swaying around the shop for her small audience. We felt the walls thrust out beyond the dry cleaners next door. The stamped tin ceiling arched heavenward into the insurance office above. Here was perfect space; and the phonograph playing away. Her breasts were like small muscles, too. Her buttocks and stomach flat. We were to believe the human body was beautiful:

Miss Weinstein made it so, her neck tendons stretched to the sublime. The idea was alien to me. My arms and legs and all the mysteries between were called a temple of the Holy Ghost. All the nuns' warnings—never to see, never to touch. One sad warped Sister of Saint Joseph took the girls aside each spring and near to hysteria instructed us in ingenious arrangements of lace handkerchiefs into rosettes that, pinned with a miraculous medal on our more revealing cotton dresses, would distract the eye from our childish bosoms—our very bodies being instruments of the devil. For the school play we had undressed with large white towels held in our teeth, covering our shame. Then came the modern dance. Ruby Weinstein was ridiculous in her abandon, but the ten preadolescent girls in her class never snickered. Nipples and navels were reasonable in the atmosphere she created. I'd never seen pubic hair, but it was quite the right thing on Miss Weinstein as she danced for us.

In our home-sewn togas we expressed ourselves, leaping (as though against the wind), swaying (branches in spring), falling (in death to the cold floor). There was no technique at all, save the perfect imitation of our teacher. There was no critique, no one student singled out for grace or elevation of style. The only choreographed piece, which we danced finally and disastrously for our mothers, was performed to the "Narcissus Song." We rushed from the corners of the store to a round 1930's mirror set on the floor, fell in love with our respective images, tossed our heads, sighed, leapt, swayed, fell to the contemplation of our beauty again and expired, all ten of us, by the side of the reflecting pool.

At home I played my own record of "Narcissus" when "they" were out. I dashed from the sun parlor to the center of the living room carpet timing each move, the coy little testing of the water with my toe, the flirtatious smile. There was no mirror needed. The true narcissism of adolescence lay a few years ahead: the self-enchantment of my dancing was enough. Imagined away the plumpness and pigtails. Turned to dust my colorless school clothes. Fantasies in an empty house. It was the beginning of my long career as an escape artist. Secrecy was important. No one on the block, no one at Saint Patrick's School should know that I studied the modern dance. I was the only Christian in Miss Weinstein's class, and though the girls were friendly I was content to go off alone in the car with my mother. I did not want art confused with real life. The dread ballet classes of former years had been an ordeal—all the little daughters of doctors and dentists, *socialites* from Fairfield in squirrel coats and Tyrolean skirts, the heiress of a girdle empire escorted by a black maid.

No, what Ruby Weinstein offered was pure. Art. Freedom. I had come to know in my childish way these grand abstractions. Grace and Beauty. All written on the blossoming soul with an indiscriminate use of capital letters. Such inflation seems horrifying to me now. I have no clear idea what freedom is and grace belongs to children, to one perfect stroke, or to the talented who put in a lifetime of hard work. So I leapt out of Ruby's corner with my

illusions on the afternoon of our spring recital to
adore myself, pink toga and pigtails, but I was
Narcissus no more. They laughed. The mothers,
squeezed back against the shop window in a line of
folding chairs, swapped smiles and laughed, not
cruelly but with a sweet indulgence. We were little
girls again, consigned to another clumsy step in our
advance toward the womanly state. Someday we
would have purses and hats, hateful permanent waves
and face powder soiling the collars of our print
dresses. We would sit in a row like vegetable women,
amused by art, wondering if there was enough in
the house for supper. End of the record. I died by
the side of the pool.

Polite applause, the scraping of chairs and then
Miss Weinstein sprang forth wearing underclothes
beneath her gauze, decent this day. To urgent unknown music she danced for them, danced against
them. Her strong small body became a force: the
sequence of leaps, back falls, contractions, spun
from her endlessly, like magic scarves. The little
studio was charged with her conviction. She was not
afraid to expose herself: this was her Art. She danced
till the end of the old seventy-eight and danced
beyond to silence. Yes, her performance had a manic
energy, was routine artsy, but Ruby's dedication
was the real thing. Stunned by such beauty I went
straight to my dreams again, while the mothers,
bewildered but with full respect, clapped and clapped.
There was a sudden intimacy in the storefront
studio— "It's meant so much." "Next year, Miss
Weinstein," they said, "in the fall." We stood by
the jars of lilacs she had placed on the window shelf

for our final meeting. There was no next year. Ruby Weinstein was passing through Bridgeport.

In the car my mother called me by a pet name. "You were very good, Mimi." That was untrue. She had laughed with the rest. There was no comfort in the old name. I remember this moment and others like it when she would draw away as though the years to come were accomplished and she had lost control of me. "How will it turn out for you?" she seemed to say. Then in a soothing voice she went back, back further to the nursery rhyme that was always mine—"Reeny-Pen-Pone/ Lived all alone." I was her strange, fat child, wounded, clutching my toga in a brown paper bag. She had done her best.

JEAN KERR is the author of several plays—including Mary, Mary *(one of the longest running plays in Broadway history) and* Finishing Touches *—and the best-selling books* Penny Candy, The Snake Has All The Lines, *and* How I Got To Be Perfect, *from which the following portrait of the author's resourceful Irish mother is taken. Kerr, the wife of New York drama critic Walter Kerr, is the mother of a daughter and the five sons whom she immortalized in the best-seller* Please Don't Eat the Daisies.

Jean Kerr
My Wild Irish Mother

I'm never going to write my autobiography and it's all my mother's fault. I didn't hate her, so I have practically no material. In fact, the situation is worse than I'm pretending. We were crazy about her—and you know I'll never get a book out of that, much less a musical.

Mother was born Kitty O'Neill, in Kinsale, Ireland, with bright red hair, bright blue eyes, and the firm conviction that it was wrong to wait for an elevator if you were only going up to the fifth floor. It's not just that she won't wait for elevators, which she really feels are provided only for the convenience of the aged and infirm. I have known her to reproach herself on missing one section of a revolving door. And I well remember a time when we missed a train from New York to Washington. I fully expected her to pick up our suitcases and announce, "Well, darling, the exercise will be good for us."

When I have occasion to mutter about the finan-

From *How I Got to Be Perfect*.

cial problems involved in maintaining six children in a large house, Mother is quick to get to the root of the problem. "Remember," she says, "you take cabs a lot." In Mother's opinion, an able-bodied woman is perfectly justified in taking a taxi to the hospital if her labor pains are closer than ten minutes apart.

The youngest daughter of wealthy and indulgent parents, Mother went to finishing schools in France and to the Royal Conservatory of Music in London. Thus, when she came to America to marry my father, her only qualifications for the role of housewife and mother were the ability to speak four languages, play three musical instruments, and make *blancmange*. I, naturally, wasn't around during those first troubled months when Mother learned to cook. But my father can still recall the day she boiled corn on the cob, a delicacy unknown in Ireland at that time, for five hours until the cobs were tender. And, with a typical beginner's zeal, Mother "put up" twenty bushels of tomatoes for that first winter before it struck her that neither she nor Dad really liked canned tomatoes.

By the time I was old enough to notice things, Mother was not only an excellent cook. She could make beer, an accomplishment that set her apart and endeared her to many in those Prohibition days. Of course, Mother didn't drink beer, so it was hard for her to judge whether she was on the right track or not. And it was always an anxious moment when my father took his first sip of each new batch and declared, "Yes, Kit, I think you're getting warmer."

But beer brewing is a very involved process, as

the Budweiser people will tell you, and the crock used to stand for weeks in the pantry before it was time for the bottling. I don't know how big the crock was, but I know that it stood taller than I did. One of my earliest memories—I must have been four—is of sitting on the floor handing the bottle caps to Mother. On this particular occasion the crock was nearly empty when Mother gave a little shriek. Something, something—perhaps a mouse—was at the bottom of the crock.

She took a long fork and gingerly fished out a small, sodden object. I knew in a flash what it was, but I was too terrified to speak. Then I heard Mother say, in a very strained voice, "Jean you must *always* tell Mommy where you put your shoes."

Together we sat in silence and stared at the rows and rows of shiny bottles all ready to go into the cases down in the cellar. Then Mother jumped up. A thought had struck her. She tossed the shoe into the garbage and announced briskly, "You know what? I think it will help the aging process." And it must have, too, because everyone said it was the best batch she ever made.

Just as she made beer she never drank, Mother would cook things she had no intention of eating. Where food is concerned, she is totally conservative. She will study the menu at an expensive restaurant with evident interest and then say, "Darling, where do you see lamb chops?" Or she will glance with real admiration at a man at a nearby table who seems actually to be consuming an order of cherrystone clams. "Aren't Americans marvelous?" she'll remark. "They will eat anything."

On the other hand she was always willing to prepare all manner of exotic dishes for Dad and the rest of us. In the old days the men who worked for my father frequently gave him gifts of game—venison, rabbit, and the like. Occasionally we children would protest. I recall becoming quite tearful over the prospect of eating deer, on the theory that it might be Bambi. But Mother was always firm. "Nonsense," she would say, "eat up, it's just like chicken."

But one night she went too far. I don't know where she got this enormous slab of meat; I don't think my father brought it home. It stood overnight in the icebox in some complicated solution of brine and herbs. The next day the four of us were told that we could each invite a friend to dinner. Mother spent most of the day lovingly preparing her roast. That night there were ten of us around the dining-room table, and if Mother seemed too busy serving all the rest of us to eat anything herself, that was not at all unusual. At this late date I have no impression of what the meat tasted like. But I know that we were all munching away when Mother beamed happily at us and asked, "Well, children, how are you enjoying the bear?"

Forks dropped and certain of the invited guests made emergency trips to the bathroom. For once, all of Mother's protestations that it was just like chicken were unavailing. Nobody would touch another bite. She was really dismayed. I heard her tell Dad, "It's really strange, Tom—I thought all Americans liked bear."

Mother's education, as I have indicated, was rather one-sided. While she knew a great deal about such "useless" things as music and art and literature, she knew nothing whatever, we were quick to discover, about isosceles triangles or watts and volts or the Smoot-Hawley Tariff. As we were growing up, we made haste to repair these gaps.

One of the most charming things about Mother was the extraordinary patience with which she would allow us youngsters to "instruct" her. I remember my brother Hugh, when he was about eight, sitting on the foot of Mother's bed and giving her a half-hour lecture which began with the portentous question, "Mom, how much do you know about the habits of the common housefly?"

At that, it's remarkable how much of this unrelated information stayed with her. Just recently I was driving her to a train and she noticed, high up in the air, a squirrel that was poised on a wire that ran between two five-story buildings. "Look at that little squirrel 'way up on that wire," she said. "You know, if he gets one foot on the ground, he'll be electrocuted."

But if her knowledge of positive and negative electricity is a little sketchy, there is nothing sketchy about her knowledge of any subject in which she develops an interest. Mother always adored the theater and was a passionate playgoer from the time she was five years old. However, during the years when she was sobbing gently over *The Lily of Killarney* in Cork City, she was blissfully unaware of the menacing existence of American drama critics or the fact that their printed opinions had a certain measurable effect on the box office. Even when she came to America, she still had the feeling that five nights was probably an impressive run for a Broadway show.

Time passed, and my husband and I became involved in the theater. Mother began to get the facts. When, quite a few years ago, we were living in Washington and came up to New York for the opening of a revue we had written, I promised Mother that I would send her all the reviews, special delivery, as soon as they appeared. In those days, before the demise of *The Sun*, there were eight metropolitan dailies. Eventually we got hold of all the papers and I was able to assess the evidence. All but one of the morning papers were fine, and while there were certain quibbles in the afternoon papers, the only seriously negative notice appeared in *The Sun*. Ward Morehouse was then the critic on *The Sun* but happened to be out of town at the moment, and the review was written by his assistant, or, as I was willing to suppose, his office boy. So, with that special brand of feminine logic that has already made my husband prematurely gray, I decided to omit this particular notice in the batch I was sending to my mother, on the theory that (a) it wasn't written by the *real* critic, and (b) nobody in Scranton, Pennsylvania, knew there was a paper called *The Sun* anyway. This was a serious miscalculation on my part, as I realized later in the day when I got Mother's two-word telegram. It read, "Where's Morehouse?"

Let me say that her interest in the more technical aspects of the theater continues unabated. Not long ago we were in Philadelphia, deep in the unrefined bedlam that surrounds any musical in its tryout

141

stage. The phone rang. It was Mother. Without any preliminary word of greeting, she asked in hushed, conspiratorial tones, "Darling, have you pointed and sharpened?"

"Good Lord, Mother," I said, "what are you talking about?"

"I'm talking about the show, dear," she said, sounding like a small investor, which she was. "*Variety* says it needs pointing and sharpening, and I think we should listen to them."

To the four low-metabolism types she inexplicably produced, Mother's energy has always seemed awesome. "What do you think," she's prone to say, "do I have time to cut the grass before I stuff the turkey?" But her whirlwind activity is potentially less dangerous than her occasional moments of repose. Then she sits, staring into space, clearly lost in languorous memories. The faint, fugitive smile that hovers above her lips suggests the gentle melancholy of one hearing Mozart played beautifully. Suddenly she leaps to her feet. "I know it will work," she says. "All we have to do is remove that wall, plug up the windows, and extend the porch."

It's undoubtedly fortunate that she has the thrust and the energy of a well-guided missile. Otherwise she wouldn't get a lick of work done, because everybody who comes to her house, whether to read the gas meter or to collect for UNICEF, always stays at least an hour. I used to think that they were one and all beguiled by her Irish accent. But I have gradually gleaned that they are telling her the story of their invariably unhappy lives. "Do you remember my lovely huckleberry man?" Mother will ask.

"Oh, *yes* you do—he had red hair and ears. Well, his brother-in-law sprained his back and hasn't worked in six months, and we're going to have to take a bundle of clothes over to those children." Or, again: "Do you remember that nice girl in the Scranton Dry Goods? Oh, yes you do, she was in lamp shades and she had gray hair and wore gray dresses. Well, she's having an operation next month and you must remember to pray for her." Mother's credo, by the way, is that if you want something, anything, don't just sit there—pray for it. And she combines a Job-like patience in the face of the mysterious ways of the Almighty with a flash of Irish rebellion which will bring her to say—and I'm sure she speaks for many of us—"Jean, what I am really looking for is a blessing that's *not* in disguise."

She does have a knack for penetrating disguises, whether it be small boys who claim that they have taken baths or middle-aged daughters who swear that they have lost five pounds. She has a way of cutting things to size, particularly books, which she gobbles up in the indiscriminate way that a slot machine gobbles up quarters. I sent her a novel recently because it had a Welsh background and because the blurb on the jacket declared, "Here is an emotional earthquake—the power and glory of a great love story combined with the magic of child-hood." Later, I asked her if she liked it. "Not really," she said. "It was nothing but fornication, all seen through the eyes of a nine-year-old boy." The first time I had a collection of short pieces brought out in book form, I sent an advance copy to Mother. She was naturally delighted. Her enthusiasm fairly bubbled off the pages of the letter. "Darling," she wrote, "isn't it marvelous the way those old pieces of yours finally came to the surface like a dead body!"

I knew when I started this that all I could do was list the things Mother says, because it's not possible, really, to describe her. All my life I have heard people break off their lyrical descriptions of Kitty and announce helplessly, "You'll just have to meet her."

However, I recognize, if I cannot describe, the lovely festive air she always brings with her, so that she can arrive any old day in July and suddenly it seems to be Christmas Eve and the children seem handsomer and better behaved and all the adults seem more charming and—

Well, you'll just have to meet her.

MADELEINE L'ENGLE, *the author of the Newberry Award-winning children's classic,* A Wrinkle in Time, *has written a trilogy of nonfiction,* The Crosswicks Journal. *The following excerpt is taken from the trilogy's second volume,* The Summer of the Great-Grandmother, *in which the daughter-writer watches her much-loved ninety-year-old mother's descent into senility. Pain and beauty and memory are themes, but a profound cosmic harmony prevails until and beyond the point of her mother's death. Madeleine L'Engle, who has combined a writing and teaching career with raising three children and managing a New York apartment and a Connecticut farmhouse (called "Crosswicks"), writes prolifically on feminism, religion, and in this memoir, growing old, with a comforting and rare common sense.*

╔══════════════════════════════╗
Madeleine L'Engle
from
THE SUMMER OF THE
GREAT-GRANDMOTHER
╚══════════════════════════════╝

This is the summer of the great-grandmother, more her summer than any other summer. This is the summer after her ninetieth birthday, the summer of the swift descent.

Once, when I was around twelve, we took a twenty-mile toboggan ride down a Swiss mountainside. The men guiding the toboggan were experienced mountaineers; the accelerating speed was wildly exciting. Mother and I both clutched the sides of the toboggan as we careened around sharply banked curves. The guides could keep it on the hard-packed snow of the path, but they could not stop it in its descent. My mother's plunge into senility reminds me of that toboggan ride.

When I look at the long green and gold days of this summer, the beautiful days are probably more beautiful, and the horrible days more horrible, than in actuality. But there's no denying that it's a summer of extremes.

It might be said with some justification that all our summers are summers of extremes, because when the larger family gathers together we are a group of opinionated, noisily articulate, varied and variable beings. It is fortunate for us all that Crosswicks is a largish, two-hundred-and-some-year-old farmhouse; even so, when four generations' worth of strong-willed people assemble under one roof, the joints of the house seem to creak in an effort to expand. If we all strive toward moderation, it is because we, like the ancient Greeks, are natively immoderate.

This is our fourth four-generation summer. Four Junes ago Mother's namesake and first great-grandchild, Madeleine, was born. We call her Léna, to avoid confusion in this household of Madeleines. Charlotte, the second great-granddaughter, was born fourteen months later. My mother is very proud of being the Great-grandmother.

But she is hardly the gentle little old lady who sits by the fireside and knits. My knowledge of her is limited by my own chronology; I was not around for nearly forty years of her life, and her pre-motherhood existence was exotic and adventurous; in the days before planes she traveled by camel and donkey; she strode casually through a world which is gone and which I will never see except through her eyes. The woman I have experienced only as a loving and gentle mother has, for the past several years, been revealing new and demanding facets. When she wants something she makes her desires known in no un-certain terms, and she's not above using her cane as a weapon. She gathers puppies and kittens into her lap; she likes her bourbon before dinner; she's a witty raconteur; and the extraordinary thing about her descent into senility is that there are occasional wild, brilliant flashes which reveal more of my mother-Madeleine than I ever knew when she was simply my mother.

But she is my mother; there is this indisputable, biological fact which blocks my attempts at objectivity. I love her, and the change in her changes me, too.

She was born in the Deep South, spent her married life wandering the globe, in New York and London, and now, in her old age, prefers the more clement weather of North Florida for the winters. But her presence in Crosswicks has always been part of the summers. A friend asked me, "Did you invite your mother to spend the summers with you or did she invite herself?"

I was a little taken aback. "There wasn't ever any question of inviting. We just said, 'When are you coming?' "

"Did you discuss it with Hugh?"

I don't think it ever needed discussion. My mother and my husband have always loved each other—after the very first when Mother wasn't happy about the idea of my marrying an actor. She and Hugh are much alike, in character, in temperament. A stranger would be apt to take Mother and Hugh for mother and son, and me for the in-law. We have always thought of her as part of Crosswicks. She helped make it grow from the dilapidated, unloved old building it was when we first saw it, a quarter of a century ago, to the home it is now. She helped plan my workroom out over the garage, a beautiful study which the children named the Tower. When we lived in Crosswicks year round, while our children were little, she usually spent one of the winter months with us; when we moved back to New York for the school year, this was even more fun for her, because we could go to the theatre, the opera.

I have been so used to having my mother be my friend as well as my mother, to having her be Hugh's friend, that I was surprised at the idea of "inviting" her to spend the summer, and at the implication that this is not the usual way of things.

Perhaps it's not, but having Mother spend the summer in Crosswicks is part of the chronology of the house.

Hugh and I drive to New York, to the airport, to meet her and bring her the hundred miles to Crosswicks. I am shocked when I see her. The plane flight has been harder on her than we had anticipated; the toboggan has continued its descent at an accelerating pace since we saw her at the ninetieth-birthday celebration on April 30. She is confused during the two and a half hours' drive. I hold her hand and try to point out familiar landmarks.

"I don't remember it," she says anxiously. Only occasionally will she see a building, a turn of the road, a special view, and say, "I know this! I've been here before . . . Haven't I?"

We stop at our usual halfway place, the Red Rooster, for lunch, but Mother is too nervous to eat, and we stay only a few minutes, while Hugh and I quickly swallow hamburgers. I continue to hold her hand, to pet her. My emotions are turned off; I do not feel, any more than one feels pain after a deep cut. The body provides its own anesthesia for the first minutes after a wound, and stitches can be put in without novocaine; my feelings are equally numbed. We complete the drive, and I am anxious only to get Mother home, and to bed, in the room which has been hers for a quarter of a century. My thoughts do not project beyond this to the rest of the summer.

I feel very tired, and somehow as though somebody had kicked me. . . .

I am tired, and numb. Mother's first two nights in Crosswicks I do not get any sleep, despite my fatigue. She needs more attention during the night than we had expected. The two girls who do night duty are young and completely inexperienced in nursing; Vicki has another year in high school; she was born during the years we lived in Crosswicks year round; it is difficult for me to realize that she is now a young woman, and a very capable young woman. Janet, too, I have known all her life; her father died when she was a baby, and her mother only a summer ago, and I wonder if she does not feel a certain irony in taking care of an old woman who has lived long past normal life expectancy. And I feel that the two girls need help, not physical help, simply my being there, awake and available if they need me.

After the first two wakeful nights it is clear to me how competent they are, and that I must get some rest.

*   *   *

It's a good thing to have all the props pulled out from under us occasionally. It gives us some sense of what is rock under our feet, and what is sand. It stops us from taking anything for granted. It has also taught me a lot about living in the immediate moment. I am somehow managing to live one day, one hour at a time. I have to. Hugh is in Crosswicks for four days, and somehow or other I am able simply to be with him, without projecting into the future. When he goes back to New York he will be going to the neurologist.

Each evening after dinner I walk the dogs down the lane for a few minutes, to catch my breath and regain perspective. The girls prepare the great-grandmother for bed, and we learned the first night that this is done more easily if I am out of the house; if I am there she calls for me, and will not do anything for any of us.

This night, when I return, she has been put to bed, and the larger family—Hugh, Bion, Josephine, the girls, assorted friends and neighbors (Maria and Peter are not back from their honeymoon)—have gathered in the living room to play poker with ancient poker chips. Alan is out in the Tower writing. I'm not a poker player either, so I go in to say good night to Mother and sit with her for a while. Our quiet times together have always been in the morning, over coffee, and at night before bedtime. For a moment, a flash, she is there, is herself, and we laugh at Tyrrell lying on her back, all four legs spread out, tail wagging in this upside-down position. Thomas, the amber cat, is also on his back, lying beside the big dog, rear legs abandoned, fore-

151

paws folded prayerfully across his chest. Titus, the yellow puffball kitten, is in Mother's lap, purring.

Then the moment is gone. "Something's wrong," my mother says. "I don't know what it is, but something's wrong."

"It's all right, Mother. Nothing is wrong."

"It is, it is. Something's wrong. I want to go home." This has been a constant refrain since her arrival. "I want to go home. I want to go home."

"You *are* home, Mother. You're with your family, with all your children."

"I want to go home."

Yesterday Alan put his arms around me to give me comfort, and said, "Yes, she wants to go home, but she doesn't mean down South."

Her fear touches off an enormous wave of protectiveness in me, and I know no way to keep her terror at bay.

"I want to go home," she repeats.

I sit on the bed beside her, and hold her hand. She fumbles with the other hand for the bell we have rigged up for her. A summer ago she used it sparingly; this summer it seems that the raucous buzz goes off every few minutes. "Mother, you don't need to ring for the girls. I'm right here."

"Where are they?"

"In the living room."

"What are they doing?"

"Playing poker."

She reaches again for the bell.

"Don't call them, Mother. I'm right here." I am obviously a poor substitute. Why am I hurt? This is not my mother who is rejecting me, my mother who was always patient, tolerant, wise.

Then she turns toward me, reaches for me. "I'm scared, I'm scared."

I put my arms around her and hold her. I hold her as I held my children when they were small and afraid in the night; as, this summer, I hold my grandchildren. I hold her as she, once upon a time and long ago, held me. And I say the same words, the classic, maternal, instinctive words of reassurance. "Don't be afraid. I'm here. It's all right."

"Something's wrong. I'm scared. I'm scared."

I cradle her and repeat, "It's all right."

What's all right? What am I promising her? I'm scared too. I don't know what will happen when Hugh goes to the neurologist. I don't know what's going to happen with my mother this summer. I don't know what the message may be the next time the phone rings. What's all right? How can I say it?

But I do. I hold her close, and I kiss her, and murmur, "It's all right, Mother. It's all right."

I mean these words. I do not understand them, but I mean them. Perhaps one day I will find out what I mean. They are implicit in everything I write. I caught a hint of them during that lecture, even as I was cautioning against false promises. They are behind everything, the cooking of meals, walking the dogs, talking with the girls. I may never find out with my intellectual self what I mean, but if I am given enough glimpses perhaps these will add up to enough so that my heart will understand. It does not; not yet. . . .

I must turn my heart fully to Mother, and not let

it be torn too much by her infinitely pathetic degeneration. I must not retreat when she is horrid with me, but let it roll off—almost impossible, but I will try. And I must not project into the future and worry about this descent being a long one.

It has not come all at once; there were strong intimations of it more than five years ago, at the time of Josephine and Alan's wedding; and it was definitely accelerated when Mother was given general anesthesia for an intestinal resection when she was eighty-seven. But until this year her mind has been like a summer sky with small white clouds occasionally moving across and blotting out the light of the sun. Each year the sky has become cloudier; there have been fewer periods of sunlight. This summer the sunlight in the sky of my mother's mind, when it shines at all, glimmers through cloud. . . .

I realize, with a pang, how privileged we are to be able to keep my mother with us. This is how it should be, but what would I do if we lived in a tiny house and did not have the girls and Clara to help? Would I be able to keep her with us, or would I have to put her in a "home" —what an obscene misuse of a word! Homes for the aged, nursing homes, are one of the horrors of our time, but for many people there is no alternative. And even though we have room, and the girls to help us, there are still those who think that my mother should be put away. Put away. Everything in me revolts at the thought. But my belief that we are supposed to share all of life with each other, dying and decay as well as feasting and fun, is being put to the test.

This summer I look at my mother sitting on the small sofa during the hour before dinner and I do not know her; I am looking at a stranger, not because she is old and shrunken and lined, but because the light behind her face is no longer there. Up until a few years ago she was an example of a woman who has experienced life fully, and who grows yearly more beautiful with age. There is little character or loveliness in the face of someone who has avoided suffering, shunned risk, rejected life. It was only when suffering, risk, and life were taken from her by atherosclerosis that Mother's face became an unfamiliar one. (I asked Pat, "What do you call it? Arteriosclerosis) Atherosclerosis?" "Most lay people say arterio, but it's athero.")

A house, like a human being, reflects its experiences. And I do not think that a house can be a happy house if no one has cried in it, if no one has died in it. If this seems contradictory, I can't help it. I rebel against death, yet I know that it is how I respond to death's inevitability that is going to make me less or more fully alive. The house helps me here, because it is a warm and welcoming house, full of life, and yet during the past two hundred years it must have contained many deaths.

Death is the most ordinary thing in the world, and so is birth. Someone is being born at this very moment. Someone is dying. Ordinary, and yet completely extraordinary. The marvel of having my babies is something I will never forget. The feeling of staggering uniqueness I had at the death of my father, the death of several close friends, was very different, but equally acute. Death may be an ordinary, everyday affair, but it is not a statistic. It is something that happens to people.

The most ordinary of deaths is the death of a parent. In this twentieth century we are likely to outlive our mothers and fathers, and more parents are dying senile than ever before. Perhaps this is why old age is respected less. So what I am experiencing this summer (though our doctor tells us that Mother is far from dying) is something I share with a great many other people. And I feel the need to reach out and say, "This is how it is for me. How is it for you?"

Who is this cross old woman for whom I can do nothing right? I don't know her. She is not my mother. I am not her daughter. She won't eat anything I cook, so we resort to games. I do the cooking as usual—and I'm quite a good cook; it's one of my few domestic virtues, and the only part of housekeeping which I enjoy—and someone will say, "Eat Alan's soup, Grandmother. You know you like Alan's soup." Or, "Have some of Hugh's delicious salad." She won't eat the salad, when Hugh is in New York, until we tell her that Hugh made the dressing before he left.

I know that it is a classic symptom of atherosclerosis, this turning against the person you love most, and this knowledge is secure above my eyebrows, but very shaky below. There is something atavistic in us which resents, rejects, this reversal of roles. I want my mother to be my mother.

And she is not. Not any more. Not ever again.

I go searching for her.

My first memories of her are early, and are memories of smell, that oft-neglected sense, which is perhaps the first sense we use fully. Mother always smelled beautiful. I remember burrowing into her neck just for the soft loveliness of scented skin.

After smell came sound, the sound of her voice, singing to me, talking. I took the beauty of her voice for granted until I was almost grown up.

Scent. Sound. Vision.

I remember going into her room just before dinner, when she was sitting at her dressing table, rubbing sweet-smelling creams and lotions into her face. She had a set of ivory rollers from Paris, which I liked to play with; and a silver-backed nail buffer. Sometimes she let me buff my own nails until they were a pearly pink. The cake of French rouge, and the buffing, makes for a much prettier nail than lacquer.

I watched her brush her hair, a dark mahogany with red glints, thick and wavy, with a deep widow's peak. On the bed her evening dress was laid out; I remember one of flowered chiffon, short in front and long in back, that short-lived style of the twenties. Her shoes were bronze kid, and as tiny as Cinderella's.

My father, too, dressed for dinner every night, even when they were not having company or going out. Mother said that Father would dress for dinner in the desert or the jungle, and that he often told her that without him she'd be on the beach in two weeks. I doubt that. Until recently, I have never seen her anything but immaculate, erect, patrician. Now she has diminished; she is tiny and slumped and we have to dress her and fix her hair, but she is aware that she still has beautiful legs and she likes to show them. She responds to men, and she likes young people, which is not unusual.

Her father, my grandfather, who died at a hundred and one, responded to women and liked young people. One of the worst things about our attitude toward old people is the assumption that they ought to be herded together with other old people. Grandfather lived past that stage; he had, as he remarked, no contemporaries. He played golf until he was ninety-five, having cut down, at ninety, from thirty-six holes to eighteen because his younger companions couldn't keep up with him. He made the great mistake of retiring at ninety-five, and from then on began the slide into senility.

My mother tended him, with considerable assistance. Nevertheless, the psychological drain was on her, and it told in other ways, too. She has never been very strong, and several times during Grandfather's last years she told me that she did not think she would live to be very old. "But I don't want to," she added. "Don't grieve for me if I die. I don't ever want to be like Papa."

"Of course I'll grieve for you. But I don't want you to be like Grandfather, either."

Grandfather was dominant, powerful, ruthless, charming, wicked, brilliant, made and spent fortunes. It was strange to see the great man becoming an ancient baby. One night when he was around a hundred, Mother was sitting with him after he'd been put to bed, sitting with her father much as I now sit with my mother. He clasped her hand tightly, looked at her like a child, and asked, "Who is going to go with me when I die?"

We bring nothing with us into the world, and certainly we can take nothing out. We die alone. But I wish that most deaths today did not come in nursing homes or in hospitals. Death is an act which should not happen in such brutal settings. Future generations may well regard our hospitals and "rest" homes and institutions for the mentally ill with as much horror as we regard Bedlam.

Meanwhile, at Crosswicks I blunder along, and will continue to blunder as long as I can, although I am well aware that at the end of the summer there will be decisions to be made. Several years ago I promised Mother that I would never put her in a nursing home, and I may have to break that promise, deny what I affirm, because I will have no choice.

Her first night in Crosswicks this summer I called Vicki and Janet aside. "Sometimes at night Grandmother rings her bell too late, and can't make it to the bathroom in time. If this happens, call me. You're only supposed to listen for her at night, and take her to the bathroom if she needs to go, not to clean up if she's—incontinent."

Incontinent. I hesitated over the word. And my motives in telling the girls to call me if Mother soils herself were certainly mixed—but then, I have never had a completely unmixed motive in my life.

Part of it was consideration for the girls. They are not being paid to take over the more unpleasant parts of nursing. Another reason is that I did not want anybody to witness the humiliation of my aristocratic mother.

The girls do not call me. Almost every morning when I come hurrying downstairs they are washing the great-grandmother, changing the sheets—the washing machine goes constantly, sheets, diapers, work clothes—I am very grateful, this summer, for all my mechanical kitchen and laundry helpers. The girls are patient and gentle with Mother. I think they, too, feel that this is an unfair ploy on the part of life; it is wrong that we should lose control of our most private functions.

Old age has been compared to being once again like a baby; it is called second childhood. It is not. It is something very different. Charlotte is not yet two, and not yet completely toilet trained. Her soiled diapers have the still-innocuous odor of a baby's. As we grow older we, as well as our environment, become polluted. The smell of both urine and feces becomes yearly stronger.

In hospitals, in nursing homes, when people become incontinent this weakness is used against them. We have all heard far too many tales of elderly patients ringing for the bedpan, waiting fifteen minutes, half an hour, and finally not being able to control themselves any longer; and then, when the overworked nurse eventually arrives, the patient is scolded for lack of control.

There are not enough nurses, or aides, or order-
lies. A hospital is no longer a good place for a
person who is ill. I have my own account. After the
birth of our first child, during the postwar boom of
babies in the late 1940's, the eminent gynecologist
who delivered Josephine did not check the pla-
centa, and a large amount remained inside me.
Three and a half weeks later, I hemorrhaged mas-
sively and was rushed to the hospital in the middle
of the night. In this enlightened twentieth century I
had childbed fever, and came very close to dying.
One night I rang for the bedpan and, after waiting
for over an hour, I wet the bed. And was roundly
berated. I was young enough to fight back.

Mother is beyond that, and the idea of having her
abused over a soiled bed is one of many reasons
why putting her in a hospital or nursing home is still
impossible to me.

One morning I dress Mother in a fresh nightgown
while Vicki and Janet finish with the bed. Most
mornings, Mother hardly seems to notice what has
happened, or to care. She will murmur, "I'm cold. I
want to go back to bed"—she who used to be so
fastidious, so sweet-smelling. But this morning as I
sit with my arms around her while the girls ready
the bed, she leans against me and, suddenly herself,
she says, "Oh, darling, I'm so ashamed about
everything."

My heart weeps. . . .

Once when Mother and I were in New York,
during a college vacation, we had lunch together in

a pleasant downtown restaurant before going to the theatre, and I remember, with the same clarity with which I remember the little embroidered dress, that I leaned across the table and said, "Oh, Mother, it's such *fun* to be with you!" And it was. We enjoyed things together, the theatre, museums, music, food, conversation.

When I was pregnant with Josephine I told Mother, "All I could possibly hope for with my children is that they love me as much as I love you."

Josephine, when she was five or six years old, lightened my heart one evening when she flung her arms around me and said, "Oh, Mama, you're so *exciting!*" What more glorious compliment could a child give a parent? My parents were exciting to me, but their lives were far more glamorous than mine. When Jo made that lovely, spontaneous remark I felt anything but exciting; I was in the midst of a difficult decade of literary rejection, of struggling with small children and a large house; and that remark of Jo's restored my faith in myself, both as a writer and as a mother. Even though I knew I might never again be published; even though I could not see any end to the physical struggle and perpetual fatigue, Josephine helped heal doubt. It is a risky business to hope, but my daughter gave me the courage to take the risk.

I wonder if I ever, unknowingly, gave my mother like courage? I am well aware of all the things I have done which have distressed her, but perhaps simply the fact that I have always loved her may sometimes have helped.

ANNE MORROW LINDBERGH, *the author of many books including* Gift from the Sea, *wife of Charles Lindbergh and mother of five children, wanted at an early age to be and in fact was a writer; to her "an experience was not finished, not truly experienced, unless written down or shared with another." Much of what she felt and thought she shared with her mother. The group of letters that follow, collected in* Bring Me a Unicorn: Diaries and Letters of Anne Morrow Lindbergh 1922–1928, *were written to her mother in the first months of Anne Morrow's undergraduate years at Smith College, where her mother had also attended. Throughout her daughter's many published volumes of letters and diaries, the mother of Anne Morrow Lindbergh is a beloved presence, a radiant center, a source of strength and comfort. But such intense maternal love and filial affection do not cancel out the inevitable pain in the drama of growing up. As Anne Morrow Lindbergh wrote in* Gift from the Sea, *"Woman must come of age by herself—she must find her true center alone."*

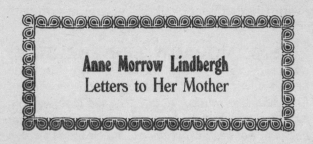

[Smith College, Northampton, September 23, 1924]
[Beginning of Freshman year]

My darling Mother!
The end of the first day! You were so lovely, dear,
to leave me the books under the pillow. I found
them the next morning when I was making my bed
and it made me so happy, especially the lovely
"sentiment" in the beginning. I read the first lesson,* right away.

The room looked so beautifully neat and tidied
and fixed when I came back. How adorable of you
to empty the trunk and put away all my things for
me. You did so much for me, Mother, when you
were up here. I hardly thanked you at all but there
were so many things you did to make it easier and
nicer and more comfortable. Everything that was
hard. I love my room. It is so nice to open the door
and find all my things. Such a wonderful feeling. I

From *Bring Me a Unicorn: Diaries and Letters of Anne Morrow
Lindbergh 1922–1928.*
*In a book of daily prayers, or "lessons."

want to *hug* the room! I went to chapel this morning with Elisabeth and walked out arm in arm with someone! It was very nice.

I love the walk past the President's, every morning. I see Paradise [Pond] and Mt. Tom and think of you.

[Northampton, September 28, 1924]
Sunday

Mother, darling—

I should like to write you pages and pages but I simply can't. I never knew anything like the rush in college. It is simply terrifying. Every moment I spend *not* rushing I feel that I'm wasting, that I should be rushing to a class or something or studying. At first the whole thing was too terrifying for words—the social as well as the work side—but especially the work side. Not in the day but at night like a perfect demon hanging over me. And I got quite panicky but it is gradually getting better and better although it still seems new and very strange and I feel very shy and young and incapable.

Elisabeth and I went to Vespers today. It was simply beautiful. President Neilson* talked wonderfully about opportunity and the responsibility of it. The text was from Kings and a wonderful one I must find, something like this: "I will give thee two thousand horses if thou, on thy part, wilt put men to ride on them."

This is so hurried you won't be able to read it. People are all *so* nice and things are getting better

---

*William Allan Neilson, President of Smith College, 1917–39.

and better. The more I think of it the more I realize what a wonderful thing you've given me. But I am just wondering whether I can ride the two thousand horses!

[Northampton, March 4, 1925]

Mother, darling,
I have been doing awfully poor work lately—I don't know why—in everything; an awful slump. I'm beginning to pick up now. Greek in particular has been hard this term but I'm talking it over with Miss Gifford* tomorrow. It isn't really serious.

I have one wonderful thing to tell you before the supper bell rings. I handed my first long, worked-over theme in to Miss Kirstein† yesterday. Today I met, going to class, a girl from the other half of our section—Miss Kirstein† had read my theme in class (that doesn't mean anything for she often reads poor ones for examples) —but *she said she liked it* and the class liked it and she said she had always felt that R. L. Stevenson was smug but she never found anyone else that did. Then she read another Freshman paper and remarked that the Freshmen were setting a rather high standard for the class! Which is, of course, a joke. Then I came to class and she was giving out papers and she handed me mine and said, "That was very nice *indeed*, Miss Morrow," and then handing me two enchanting books of rhymes said, "I thought you might enjoy

*Natalie M. Gifford, instructor of Greek.
†Mina Kirstein, teacher of creative writing; author, under her married name, Mina Curtiss.

these—they aren't as good as those others, but you may take them home and read them, if you like." I am so smothered with joy. She hardly ever says anything—a few delightful remarks on the paper and *this* on the outside: "Very nice, indeed, written with insight and taste and the rare ability to choose the right quotations." Oh, *Mother!*

[Northampton, April 22, 1925]

Mother darling—
I am terribly sorry not to have written for so long but it has been so frantically crowded and I have been very discouraged and I couldn't bear to write "from the depths"!

It is a little better now. The work seems to be piling up frightfully and the coils are tightening. Finals are pushing from the other side and it gives you a permanent hounded feeling.

And I'm *not* doing any outside things. Not a thing! Really. I don't see anyone that isn't in my classes or in my house and all the time that's not spent at classes is spent studying. Perhaps I get stale.

Writing for Miss Kirstein takes *hours*, too. And it needs consecutive hours. I haven't any consecutive hours except at night and on Sunday. Sunday is always one long stretch of work from morning until quite late, without even the break of going to classes.

I do wish I had some alibi for such inefficiency— something like having appendicitis or being in love, or brain fever—but I haven't *any* excuse—I am a healthy contented sane creature but I seem to work like molasses.

167

I think a great deal of it is because I can't seem able ever to drop it from my mind and get away from it and come back refreshed. That is awfully silly of me, but wherever I go I take it all with me—all the paraphernalia of work—mental paraphernalia. I look at a birch tree through a mist of gym shoes, course cards, alarm clocks, paper due, writtens, laundry boxes, choir practices, bills, long themes, and *exams*—etc. It hounds me doggedly and I think much too much about it and it makes me discouraged, and when I'm discouraged I can't do *anything*. This sounds so much worse than it is. I really shouldn't get discouraged. It is just because I can't see anything outside of college. It is so absorbing that it has loomed all out of proportion and I feel cut off from everything else.

But, Mother, in spite of this torrent of complaints, I love it—I really do—and I wouldn't stop for anything in the world. I've never had anything like it before. It is thrilling and absorbing and wonderful.

I'm not taking any writing course [next year]. Do you think that's awful? Of course there will be a good deal of writing in Eng. 19, and reports to make and write in the History. The reason I'm not taking it is that I won't have time to do them all as fully as I want to, if I do. Besides, I've learned from Miss Kirstein's course that (thrilling as she and it are) I really need more to think about and less to write about. Nothing I write has any backbone to it and it won't have until I absorb more. Do you think it's very silly?

[Northampton, October 10, 1925]
[Beginning of Sophomore year]

Mother, darling

I can't begin to describe the classes—the Renaissance History, the Elizabethan Literature course with *Miss Dunn!** *She* is taking it this year!! And she is *so* charming—her conversation so *rich* and so *stimulating*. It is the most glorious world—I feel like a Magellan! It is really a Renaissance course, too, and fits in *beautifully* with the History. Also Miss Lewis's† theme course, which is a "change" from Miss Kirstein's but so different that I think it will be very nice. Pure description, though, isn't half as intriguing as doing character sketches or criticism. It isn't going to be very easy for me—I *hate* describing country roads and approaches to houses. She is a charming hostess, a gracious lady in all her classes. She never talks louder than she has to, and that is so unusual here—a low, mellow, soothing voice that it is a delight to listen to. She smiles graciously too—the kind of smile that takes you by surprise. I can't describe it but that is what it does. She *suddenly* smiles, with her eyes first, and then—then all of a sudden her whole face is smiling, too. I don't believe she ever hurries, or that abrupt annoying things ever startle her. She is on an island. I have written one description for her. It was a frightful effort—I haven't it back yet.

Physics is going to be very hard. I am the slowest one in the class.

---

*Esther Cloudman Dunn, professor of English literature, and A. M. L.'s faculty adviser.

†Mary Delia Lewis, associate professor of English.

Psychology is like Hygiene, as yet, we haven't gotten to the interesting part.

The Music* is going to be *very* interesting. The man is *charming*.

I have to stop, but I have to tell you that the whole spirit of this place is better—it has entirely changed. I feel differently. Some powers have no hold on me as they seemed to have before—I feel like saying, "Let them not have dominion over me!" Then I am more apart. I've gotten out of things—hockey, and Students Christian Association. I feel as though my head were no longer down under the blankets at the bottom of the bed.

[Northampton, October 11, 1925]
Special delivery!

My darling Mother!
I have just finished this poem. I don't care whether it is good or not, but it just had to come, and I am crying for joy—it has been so long:

HEIGHT

When I was young I felt so small
And frightened, for the world was tall.

And even grasses seemed to me
A forest of immensity,

Until I learned that I could grow
A glance would leave them far below.

---

*Music Appreciation course given by Professor Roy D. Welch.

170

Spanning a tree's height with my eye,
Suddenly I soared as high;

And fixing on a star I grew,
I pushed my head against the blue!

Still, like a singing lark, I find
Rapture to leave the grass behind.

And sometimes standing in a crowd
My lips are cool against a cloud.

[Northampton, March 5, 1927]

(Please return theme)

Mother darling

Forgive me for writing you this right away but it was so exciting I wanted to tell you. You know how long—how terribly long—I work over themes: hours and hours and *hours*. I have been working for *weeks* on this paper about the B's, not trying to write down what happened but just trying to crystallize in some form, artificial or not, some kernel of the feeling I have about them. After writing pages and pages and rejecting them, after shaking it up and putting it in a thousand different molds, I finally reached this. It is not true at all—the form isn't, or the incident that happened to fit what I wanted— but I have at last to my own satisfaction at least crystallized something. Now I shall be *very* conceited about it: Miss Kirstein read it in class today. She said things about it that she has *never* before said about *anything* I have written! She said that it

171

was (it seems so crass to put this down) *very* difficult to do, that this was very successfully done, that
it shows a great deal of work (I'm glad it shows!)
and care, that she rarely came across anything that
was as well done as it could possibly be done apparently. And that, really, for *its kind*—for the kind of
thing it was—she had in the years she had been
teaching never had anything better and she noticed
all the threads in it that I had worked over and I
had *slaved* so over it. I am not as conceited as I
sound, I am just very happy. Praise like that is so
rare.

Then after class she called for me and said, "Really, Anne, this is *excellent*. I was really very excited
about it. I wish you would send it away. I think you
could send it to some magazine," etc. Of course I
wouldn't think of that but it was quite intoxicating,
and balances for my C in Miss Hanscom.

Oh, Mother, Mother, how heart-warming that
is—praise like that—even if it doesn't point to anything lasting, even if you know it "just happened"
and will not happen again.

Good night, darling. Do you feel this way when
they read your poems? But that happens so often!

Born in New York City in 1934, the daughter of immigrants from Grenada, **AUDRE LORDE** *has written about growing up in Harlem and Greenwich Village in* Zami: A New Spelling of My Name *(1982), the autobiography she calls a "biomythography." The excerpt that follows is taken from this volume in which the author's childhood and especially her mother are brought to life with the extraordinary power and sensuality of a majestic poet. The Grenadian mother's daughter grew up to become a well-known feminist, lesbian, and award-winning poet who is currently Poet-in-Residence and Professor of English at Hunter College of the City University of New York.*

Audre Lorde
from ZAMI
A NEW SPELLING OF MY NAME

Grenadians and Barbadians walk like African peoples. Trinidadians do not.

When I visited Grenada I saw the root of my mother's powers walking through the streets. I thought, this is the country of my foremothers, my forebearing mothers, those Black island women who defined themselves by what they did. "Island women make good wives; whatever happens, they've seen worse." There is a softer edge of African sharpness upon these women, and they swing through the rain-warm streets with an arrogant gentleness that I remember in strength and vulnerability.

My mother and father came to this country in 1924, when she was twenty-seven years old and he was twenty-six. They had been married a year. She lied about her age in immigration because her sisters who were here already had written her that americans wanted strong young women to work for them, and Linda was afraid she was too old to get work. Wasn't she already an old maid at home when she had finally gotten married?

My father got a job as a laborer in the old Waldorf Astoria, on the site where the Empire State Building now stands, and my mother worked there as a chambermaid. The hotel closed for demolition, and she went to work as a scullery maid in a teashop on Columbus Avenue and 99th Street. She went to work before dawn, and worked twelve hours a day, seven days a week, with no time off. The owner told my mother that she ought to be glad to have the job, since ordinarily the establishment didn't hire "spanish" girls. Had the owner known Linda was Black, she would never have been hired at all. In the winter of 1928, my mother developed pleurisy and almost died. While my mother was still sick, my father went to collect her uniforms from the teahouse to wash them. When the owner saw him, he realized my mother was Black and fired her on the spot.

In October 1929, the first baby came and the stockmarket fell, and my parents' dream of going home receded into the background. Little secret sparks of it were kept alive for years by my mother's search for tropical fruits "under the bridge," and her burning of kerosene lamps, by her treadle-machine and her fried bananas and her love of fish and the sea. Trapped. There was so little that she really knew about the stranger's country. How the electricity worked. The nearest church. Where the Free Milk Fund for Babies handouts occurred, and at what time—even though we were not allowed to drink charity.

She knew about bundling up against the wicked cold. She knew about Paradise Plums—hard, oval candies, cherry-red on one side, pineapple-yellow on the other. She knew which West Indian markets along Lenox Avenue carried them in tilt-back glass jars on the countertops. She knew how desirable Paradise Plums were to sweet-starved little children, and how important in maintaining discipline on long shopping journeys. She knew exactly how many of the imported goodies could be sucked and rolled around in the mouth before the wicked gum arabic with its acidic british teeth cut through the tongue's pink coat and raised little red pimples.

She knew about mixing oils for bruises and rashes, and about disposing of all toenail clippings and hair from the comb. About burning candles before All Souls Day to keep the soucoyants away, lest they suck the blood of her babies. She knew about blessing the food and yourself before eating, and about saying prayers before going to sleep.

She taught us one to the mother that I never learned in school.

Remember, oh most gracious Virgin Mary, that never was it known that anyone who fled to thy protection, implored thy help, or sought thy intercession, was ever left unaided. Inspired with this confidence I fly unto thee now, oh my sweet mother, to thee I come, before thee I stand, sinful and sorrowful. Oh mother of the word incarnate, despise not my petitions but in thy clemency and mercy oh hear and answer me now.

As a child, I remember often hearing my mother mouth these words softly, just below her breath, as she faced some new crisis or disaster—the icebox door breaking, the electricity being shut off, my sister gashing open her mouth on borrowed skates.

My child's ears heard the words and pondered the mysteries of this mother to whom my solid and austere mother could whisper such beautiful words.

And finally, my mother knew how to frighten children into behaving in public. She knew how to pretend that the only food left in the house was actually a meal of choice, carefully planned.

She knew how to make virtues out of necessities.

Linda missed the bashing of the waves against the sea-wall at the foot of Noel's Hill, the humped and mysterious slope of Marquis Island rising up from the water a half-mile off-shore. She missed the swift-flying bananaquits and the trees and the rank smell of the tree-ferns lining the road downhill into Grenville Town. She missed the music that did not have to be listened to because it was always around. Most of all, she missed the Sunday-long boat trips that took her to Aunt Anni's in Carriacou.

Everybody in Grenada had a song for everything. There was a song for the tobacco shop which was part of the general store, which Linda had managed from the time she was seventeen.

¾ of a cross
and a circle complete
2 semi-circles and a perpendicular meet . . .

A jingle serving to identify the store for those who could not read T O B A C C O.

The songs were all about, there was even one about them, the Belmar girls, who always carried their noses in the air. And you never talked your business too loud in the street, otherwise you were liable to hear your name broadcast in a song on the corner the very next day. At home, she learned from Sister Lou to disapprove of the endless casual song-making as a disreputable and common habit, beneath the notice of a decent girl.

But now, in this cold and raucous country called america, Linda missed the music. She even missed the annoyance of the early Saturday morning customers with their loose talk and slurred rhythms, warbling home from the rumshop.

She knew about food. But of what use was that to these crazy people she lived among, who cooked leg of lamb without washing the meat, and roasted even the toughest beef without water and a cover? Pumpkin was only a child's decoration to them, and they treated their husbands better than they cared for their children.

She did not know her way in and out of the galleries of the Museum of Natural History, but she did know that it was a good place to take children if you wanted them to grow up smart. It frightened her when she took her children there, and she would pinch each one of us girls on the fleshy part of our upper arms at one time or another all afternoon. Supposedly, it was because we wouldn't behave, but actually, it was because beneath the neat visor of the museum guard's cap, she could see pale blue eyes staring at her and her children as if we were a bad smell, and this frightened her. *This* was a situation she couldn't control.

What else did Linda know? She knew how to look into people's faces and tell what they were going to do before they did it. She knew which grapefruit was shaddock and pink, before it ripened, and what to do with the others, which was to throw them to the pigs. Except she had no pigs in Harlem, and sometimes those were the only grapefruit around to eat. She knew how to prevent infection in an open cut or wound by heating the black-elm leaf over a wood-fire until it wilted in the hand, rubbing the juice into the cut, and then laying the soft green now flabby fibers over the wound for a bandage.

But there was no black-elm in Harlem, no black oak leaves to be had in New York City. Ma-Mariah, her root-woman grandmother, had taught her well under the trees on Noel's Hill in Grenville, Grenada, overlooking the sea. Aunt Anni and Ma-Liz, Linda's mother, had carried it on. But there was no call for this knowledge now; and her husband Byron did not like to talk about home because it made him sad, and weakened his resolve to make a kingdom for himself in this new world.

She did not know if the stories about white slavers that she read in the *Daily News* were true or not, but she knew to forbid her children ever to set foot into any candystore. We were not even allowed to buy penny gumballs from the machines in the subway. Besides being a waste of precious money, the machines were slot machines and therefore evil, or at least suspect as connected with white slavery— *the most vicious kind*, she'd say ominously.

Linda knew green things were precious, and the peaceful, healing qualities of water. On Saturday afternoons, sometimes, after my mother finished cleaning the house, we would go looking for some park to sit in and watch the trees. Sometimes we went down to the edge of the Harlem River at 142nd Street to watch the water. Sometimes we took the D train and went to the sea. Whenever we were close to water, my mother grew quiet and soft and absent-minded. Then she would tell us wonderful stories about Noel's Hill in Grenville, Grenada, which overlooked the Caribbean. She told us stories about Carriacou, where she had been born, amid the heavy smell of limes. She told us about plants that healed and about plants that drove you crazy, and none of it made much sense to us children because we had never seen any of them. And she told us about the trees and fruits and flowers that grew outside the door of the house where she grew up and lived until she married.

Once *home* was a far way off, a place I had never been to but knew well out of my mother's mouth. She breathed exuded hummed the fruit smell of Noel's Hill morning fresh and noon hot, and I spun visions of sapadilla and mango as a net over my Harlem tenement cot in the snoring darkness rank with nightmare sweat. Made bearable because it was not all. This now, here, was a space, some temporary abode, never to be considered forever nor totally binding nor defining, no matter how much it commanded in energy and attention. For if we lived correctly and with frugality, looked both ways before crossing the street, then someday we would arrive back in the sweet place, back *home*.

We would walk the hills of Grenville, Grenada, and when the wind blew right smell the limetrees of Carriacou, spice island off the coast. Listen to the sea drum up on Kick'em Jenny, the reef whose loud voice split the night, when the sea-waves beat upon her sides. Carriacou, from where the Belmar twins set forth on inter-island schooners for the voyages that brought them, first and last, to Grenville town, and they married the Noel sisters there, mainlander girls.

The Noel girls. Ma-Liz's older sister, Anni, followed her Belmar back to Carriacou, arrived as sister-in-law and stayed to become her own woman. Remembered the root-truths taught her by their mother, Ma-Mariah. Learned other powers from the women of Carriacou. And in a house in the hills behind L'Esterre she birthed each of her sister Ma-Liz's seven daughters. My mother Linda was born between the waiting palms of her loving hands.

Here Aunt Anni lived among the other women who saw their men off on the sailing vessels, then tended the goats and groundnuts, planted grain and poured rum upon the earth to strengthen the corn's growing, built their women's houses and the rainwater catchments, harvested the limes, wove their lives and the lives of their children together. Women who survived the absence of their sea-faring men easily, because they came to love each other, past the men's returning.

Madivine. Friending. Zami. How Carriacou women

*love each other is legend in Grenada, and so is their
strength and their beauty.*

In the hills of Carriacou between L'Esterre and
Harvey Vale my mother was born, a Belmar woman.
Summered in Aunt Anni's house, picked limes with
the women. And she grew up dreaming of Carriacou
as someday I was to dream of Grenada.

Carriacou, a magic name like cinnamon, nutmeg,
mace, the delectable little squares of guava jelly
each lovingly wrapped in tiny bits of crazy-quilt
wax-paper cut precisely from bread wrappers, the
long sticks of dried vanilla and the sweet-smelling
tonka bean, chalky brown nuggets of pressed chocolate for cocoa-tea, all set on a bed of wild bay
laurel leaves, arriving every Christmas time in a
well-wrapped tea-tin.

Carriacou which was not listed in the index of the
Goode's School Atlas nor in the *Junior Americana
World Gazette* nor appeared on any map that I
could find, and so when I hunted for the magic
place during geography lessons or in free library
time, I never found it, and came to believe my
mother's geography was a fantasy or crazy or at
least too old-fashioned, and in reality maybe she
was talking about the place other people called
Curaçao, a Dutch possession on the other side of
the Antilles.

But underneath it all as I was growing up, *home*
was still a sweet place somewhere else which they
had not managed to capture yet on paper, nor to
throttle and bind up between the pages of a school-
book. It was our own, my truly private paradise of
blugoe and breadfruit hanging from the trees, of

nutmeg and lime and sapadilla, of tonka beans and red and yellow Paradise Plums.*

I have often wondered why the farthest-out position always feels so right to me; why extremes, although difficult and sometimes painful to maintain, are always more comfortable than one plan running straight down a line in the unruffled middle.

What I really understand is a particular kind of determination. It is stubborn, it is painful, it is infuriating, but it often works.

My mother was a very powerful woman. This was so in a time when that word-combination of *woman* and *powerful* was almost unexpressable in the white american common tongue, except or unless it was accompanied by some aberrant explaining adjective like blind, or hunchback, or crazy, or Black. Therefore when I was growing up, *powerful woman* equaled something else quite different from ordinary woman, from simply "woman." It certainly did not, on the other hand, equal "man." What then? What was the third designation?

As a child, I always knew my mother was different from the other women I knew, Black or white. I used to think it was because she was my mother. But different how? I was never quite sure. There were other West Indian women around, a lot in our neighborhood and church. There were also other

---

*Years later, as partial requirement for a degree in library science, I did a detailed comparison of atlases, their merits and particular strengths. I used, as one of the foci of my project, the isle of Carriacou. It appeared only once, in the *Atlas of the Encyclopedia Brittannica,* which has always prided itself upon the accurate cartology of its colonies. I was twenty-six years old before I found Carriacou upon a map.

Black women as light as she, particularly among the low-island women. *Red-bone*, they were called. *Different how?* I never knew. But that is why to this day I believe that there have always been Black dykes around—in the sense of powerful and women-oriented women—who would rather have died than use that name for themselves. And that includes my momma.

I've always thought that I learned some early ways I treated women from my father. But he certainly responded to my mother in a very different fashion. They shared decisions and the making of all policy, both in their business and in the family. Whenever anything had to be decided about any one of the three of us children, even about new coats, they would go into the bedroom and put their heads together for a little while. *Buzz buzz* would come through the closed door, sometimes in english, sometimes in patois, that Grenadian poly-language which was their lingua franca. Then the two of them would emerge and announce whatever decision had been arrived upon. They spoke all through my childhood with one unfragmentable and unappealable voice.

After the children came, my father went to real-estate school, and began to manage small rooming-houses in Harlem. When he came home from the office in the evening, he had one quick glass of brandy, standing in the kitchen, after we greeted him and before he took off his coat and hat. Then my mother and he would immediately retire into the bedroom where we would hear them discussing the day's events from behind closed doors, even if my mother had only left their office a few hours before.

If any of us children had transgressed against the rule, this was the time when we truly quaked in our orthopedic shoes, for we knew our fate was being discussed and the terms of punishment sealed behind those doors. When they opened, a mutual and irrefutable judgment would be delivered. If they spoke of anything important when we were around, Mother and Daddy immediately lapsed into patois.

Since my parents shared all making of policy and decision, in my child's eye, my mother must have been *other* than woman. Again, she was certainly not man. (The three of us children would not have tolerated that deprivation of womanliness for long at all; we'd have probably packed up our *kra* and gone back before the eighth day—an option open to all African child-souls who bumble into the wrong milieu.)

My mother was different from other women, and sometimes it gave me a sense of pleasure and specialness that was a positive aspect of feeling set apart. But sometimes it gave me pain and I fancied it the reason for so many of my childhood sorrows. *If my mother were like everybody else's maybe they would like me better*. But most often, her difference was like the season or a cold day or a steamy night in June. It just *was*, with no explanation or evocation necessary.

My mother and her two sisters were large and graceful women whose ample bodies seemed to underline the air of determination with which they moved through their lives in the strange world of Harlem and america. To me, my mother's physical substance and the presence and self-possession with which she carried herself were a large part of what made her *different*. Her public air of in-charge competence was quiet and effective. On the street people deferred to my mother over questions of taste, economy, opinion, quality, not to mention who had the right to the first available seat on the bus. I saw my mother fix her blue-grey-brown eyes upon a man scrambling for a seat on the Lenox Avenue bus, only to have him falter midway, grin abashedly, and, as if in the same movement, offer it to the old woman standing on the other side of him. I became aware, early on, that sometimes people would change their actions because of some opinion my mother never uttered, or even particularly cared about.

My mother was a very private woman, and actually quite shy, but with a very imposing, no-nonsense exterior. Full-bosomed, proud, and of no mean size, she would launch herself down the street like a ship under full sail, usually pulling me stumbling behind her. Not too many hardy souls dared cross her prow too closely.

Total strangers would turn to her in the meat market and ask what she thought about a cut of meat as to its freshness and appeal and suitability for such and such, and the butcher, impatient, would nonetheless wait for her to deliver her opinion, obviously quite a little put out but still deferential. Strangers counted upon my mother and I never knew why, but as a child it made me think she had a great deal more power than in fact she really had.

My mother was invested in this image of herself also, and took pains, I realize now, to hide from us as children the many instances of her powerlessness. Being Black and foreign and female in New York City in the twenties and thirties was not simple, particularly when she was quite light enough to pass for white, but her children weren't.

In 1936–1938, 125th Street between Lenox and Eighth Avenues, later to become the shopping mecca of Black Harlem, was still a racially mixed area, with control and patronage largely in the hands of white shopkeepers. There were stores into which Black people were not welcomed, and no Black salespersons worked in the shops at all. Where our money was taken, it was taken with reluctance; and often too much was asked. (It was these conditions which young Adam Clayton Powell, Jr., addressed in his boycott and picketing of Blumstein's and Weissbecker's market in 1939 in an attempt, successful, to bring Black employment to 125th Street.) Tensions on the street were high, as they always are in racially mixed zones of transition. As a very little girl, I remember shrinking from a particular sound, a hoarsely sharp, guttural rasp, because it often meant a nasty glob of grey spittle upon my coat or shoe an instant later. My mother wiped it off with the little pieces of newspaper she always carried in her purse. Sometimes she fussed about low-class people who had no better sense nor manners than to spit into the wind no matter where they went, impressing upon me that this humiliation was totally random. It never occurred to me to doubt her.

It was not until years later once in conversation I

said to her: "Have you noticed people don't spit into the wind so much the way they used to?" And the look on my mother's face told me that I had blundered into one of those secret places of pain that must never be spoken of again. But it was so typical of my mother when I was young that if she couldn't stop white people from spitting on her children because they were Black, she would insist it was something else. It was so often her approach to the world; to change reality. If you can't change reality, change your perceptions of it.

Both of my parents gave us to believe that they had the whole world in the palms of their hands for the most part, and if we three girls acted correctly—meaning working hard and doing as we were told—we could have the whole world in the palms of our hands also. It was a very confusing way to grow up, enhanced by the insularity of our family. Whatever went wrong in our lives was because our parents had decided that was best. Whatever went right was because our parents had decided that was the way it was going to be. Any doubts as to the reality of that situation were rapidly and summarily put down as small but intolerable rebellions against divine authority.

All our storybooks were about people who were very different from us. They were blond and white and lived in houses with trees around and had dogs named Spot. I didn't know people like that any more than I knew people like Cinderella who lived in castles. Nobody wrote stories about us, but still people always asked my mother for directions in a crowd.

It was this that made me decide as a child we must be rich, even when my mother did not have enough money to buy gloves for her chilblained hands, nor a proper winter coat. She would finish washing clothes and dress me hurriedly for the winter walk to pick up my sisters at school for lunch. By the time we got to St. Mark's School, seven blocks away, her beautiful long hands would be covered with ugly red splotches and welts. Later, I remember my mother rubbing her hands gingerly under cold water, and wringing them in pain. But when I asked, she brushed me off by telling me this was what they did for it at "home," and I still believed her when she said she hated to wear gloves.

At night, my father came home late from the office, or from a political meeting. After dinner, the three of us girls did our homework sitting around the kitchen table. Then my two sisters went off down the hall to their beds. My mother put down the cot for me in the front bedroom, and supervised my getting ready for bed.

She turned off all the electric lights, and I could see her from my bed, two rooms away, sitting at the same kitchen table, reading the *Daily News* by a kerosene lamp, and waiting for my father. She always said it was because the kerosene lamp reminded her of "home." When I was grown I realized she was trying to save a few pennies of electricity before my father came in and turned on the lights with "Lin, why you sitting in the dark so?" Sometimes I'd go to sleep with the soft chunk-a-ta-chink of her foot-pedal-powered Singer Sewing Machine, stitching up sheets and pillow-cases from unbleached muslin gotten on sale "under the bridge."

189

*   *   *

I only saw my mother crying twice when I was little. Once was when I was three, and sat on the step of her dental chair at the City Dental Clinic on 23rd Street, while a student dentist pulled out all the teeth on one side of her upper jaw. It was in a huge room full of dental chairs with other groaning people in them, and white-jacketed young men bending over open mouths. The sound of the many dental drills and instruments made the place sound like a street-corner excavation site.

Afterwards, my mother sat outside on a long wooden bench. I saw her lean her head against the back, her eyes closed. She did not respond to my pats and tugs at her coat. Climbing up upon the seat, I peered into my mother's face to see why she should be sleeping in the middle of the day. From under her closed eyelids, drops of tears were squeezing out and running down her cheek toward her ear. I touched the little drops of water on her high cheekbone in horror and amazement. The world was turning over. My mother was crying.

The other time I saw my mother cry was a few years later, one night, when I was supposed to be asleep in their bedroom. The door to the parlor was ajar, and I could see through the crack into the next room. I woke to hear my parents' voices in english. My father had just come home, and with liquor on his breath.

"I hoped I'd never live to see the day when you, Bee, stand up in some saloon and it's drink you drinking with some clubhouse woman."

"But Lin, what are you talking? It's not that way

190

a-tall, you know. In politics you must be friendly-friendly so. It doesn't mean a thing."

"And if you were to go before I did, I would never so much as look upon another man, and I would expect you to do the same."

My mother's voice was strangely muffled by her tears.

These were the years leading up to the Second World War, when Depression took such a terrible toll, and of Black people in particular.

Even though we children could be beaten for losing a penny coming home from the store, my mother fancied a piece of her role as lady bountiful, a role she would accuse me bitterly of playing years later in my life whenever I gave something to a friend. But one of my earlier memories of World War II was just before the beginning, with my mother splitting a one-pound tin of coffee between two old family friends who had come on an infrequent visit.

Although she always insisted that she had nothing to do with politics or government affairs, from somewhere my mother had heard the winds of war, and despite our poverty had set about consistently hoarding sugar and coffee in her secret closet under the sink. Long before Pearl Harbor, I recall opening each cloth five-pound sack of sugar which we purchased at the market and pouring a third of it into a scrubbed tin to store away under the sink, secure from mice. The same thing happened with coffee. We would buy Bokar Coffee at the A&P and have it ground and poured into bags, and then divide the bag between the coffee tin on the back of the stove, and the hidden ones under the sink. Not many people came to our house, ever, but no one left without at least a cupful of sugar or coffee during the war, when coffee and sugar were heavily rationed.

Meat and butter could not be hoarded, and throughout the early war, my mother's absolute refusal to accept butter substitutes (only "other people" used margarine, those same "other people" who fed their children peanut butter sandwiches for lunch, used sandwich spread instead of mayonnaise and ate pork chops and watermelon) had us on line in front of supermarkets all over the city on bitterly cold Saturday mornings, waiting for the store to open so we each could get first crack at buying our allotted quarter-pound of unrationed butter. Throughout the war, Mother kept a mental list of all the supermarkets reachable by one bus, frequently taking only me because I could ride free. She also noted which were friendly and which were not, and long after the war ended there were meat markets and stores we never shopped in because someone in them had crossed my mother during the war over some precious scarce commodity, and my mother never forgot and rarely forgave.

When I was five years old and still legally blind, I started school in a sight-conservation class in the local public school on 135th Street and Lenox Avenue. On the corner was a blue wooden booth where white women gave away free milk to Black mothers with children. I used to long for some Hearst Free Milk Fund milk, in those cute little bottles with their red and white tops, but my mother never allowed me to have any, because she said it was

192

charity, which was bad and demeaning, and besides the milk was warm and might make me sick.

The school was right across the avenue from the catholic school where my two older sisters went, and this public school had been used as a threat against them for as long as I could remember. If they didn't behave and get good marks in schoolwork and deportment, they could be "transferred." A "transfer" carried the same dire implications as "deportation" came to imply decades later.

Of course everybody knew that public school kids did nothing but "fight," and you could get "beaten up" every day after school, instead of being marched out of the schoolhouse door in two neat rows like little robots, silent but safe and unattacked, to the corner where the mothers waited.

But the catholic school had no kindergarten, and certainly not one for blind children.

Despite my nearsightedness, or maybe because of it, I learned to read at the same time I learned to talk, which was only about a year or so before I started school. Perhaps *learn* isn't the right word to use for my beginning to talk, because to this day I don't know if I didn't talk earlier because I didn't know how, or if I didn't talk because I had nothing to say that I would be allowed to say without punishment. Self-preservation starts very early in West Indian families.

I learned how to read from Mrs. Augusta Baker, the children's librarian at the old 135th Street branch library, which has just recently been torn down to make way for a new library building to house the Schomburg Collection on African-American History and Culture. If that was the only good deed that lady ever did in her life, may she rest in peace. Because that deed saved my life, if not sooner, then later, when sometimes the only thing I had to hold on to was knowing I could read, and that that could get me through.

My mother was pinching my ear off one bright afternoon, while I lay spreadeagled on the floor of the Children's Room like a furious little brown toad, screaming bloody murder and embarrassing my mother to death. I know it must have been spring or early fall, because without the protection of a heavy coat, I can still feel the stinging soreness in the flesh of my upper arm. There, where my mother's sharp fingers had already tried to pinch me into silence. To escape those inexorable fingers I had hurled myself to the floor, roaring with pain as I could see them advancing toward my ears again. We were waiting to pick up my two older sisters from story hour, held upstairs on another floor of the dry-smelling quiet library. My shrieks pierced the reverential stillness.

Suddenly, I looked up, and there was a library lady standing over me. My mother's hands had dropped to her sides. From the floor where I was lying, Mrs. Baker seemed like yet another mile-high woman about to do me in. She had immense, light, hooded eyes and a very quiet voice that said, not damnation for my noise, but "Would you like to hear a story, little girl?"

Part of my fury was because I had not been allowed to go to that secret feast called story hour since I was too young, and now here was this strange lady offering me my own story.

I didn't dare to look at my mother, half-afraid she might say no, I was too bad for stories. Still bewildered by this sudden change of events, I climbed up upon the stool which Mrs. Baker pulled over for me, and gave her my full attention. This was a new experience for me and I was insatiably curious.

Mrs. Baker read me *Madeline*, and *Horton Hatches the Egg*, both of which rhymed and had huge lovely pictures which I could see from behind my newly acquired eyeglasses, fastened around the back of my rambunctious head by a black elastic band running from earpiece to earpiece. She also read me another storybook about a bear named Herbert who ate up an entire family, one by one, starting with the parents. By the time she had finished that one, I was sold on reading for the rest of my life.

I took the books from Mrs. Baker's hands after she was finished reading, and traced the large black letters with my fingers, while I peered again at the beautiful bright colors of the pictures. Right then I decided I was going to find out how to do that myself. I pointed to the black marks which I could now distinguish as separate letters, different from my sisters' more grown-up books, whose smaller print made the pages only one grey blur for me. I said, quite loudly, for whoever was listening to hear, "I want to read."

My mother's surprised relief outweighed whatever annoyance she was still feeling at what she called my whelpish carryings-on. From the background where she had been hovering while Mrs.

Baker read, my mother moved forward quickly, mollified and impressed. I had spoken. She scooped me up from the low stool, and to my surprise, kissed me, right in front of everybody in the library, including Mrs. Baker.

This was an unprecedented and unusual display of affection in public, the cause of which I did not comprehend. But it was a warm and happy feeling. For once, obviously, I had done something right.

My mother set me back upon the stool and turned to Mrs. Baker, smiling.

"Will wonders never cease to perform!" Her excitement startled me back into cautious silence.

Not only had I been sitting still for longer than my mother would have thought possible, and sitting quietly. I had also spoken rather than screamed, something that my mother, after four years and a lot of worry, had despaired that I would ever do. Even one intelligible word was a very rare event for me. And although the doctors at the clinic had clipped the little membrane under my tongue so I was no longer tongue-tied, and had assured my mother that I was not retarded, she still had her terrors and her doubts. She was genuinely happy for any possible alternative to what she was afraid might be a dumb child. The ear-pinching was forgotten. My mother accepted the alphabet and picture books Mrs. Baker gave her for me, and I was on my way.

I sat at the kitchen table with my mother, tracing letters and calling their names. Soon she taught me how to say the alphabet forwards and backwards as it was done in Grenada. Although she had never gone beyond the seventh grade, she had been put in charge of teaching the first grade children their letters during her last year at Mr. Taylor's School in Grenville. She told me stories about his strictness as she taught me how to print my name.

I did not like the tail of the Y hanging down below the line in Audrey, and would always forget to put it on, which used to disturb my mother greatly. I used to love the evenness of AUDRE-LORDE at four years of age, but I remembered to put on the Y because it pleased my mother, and because, as she always insisted to me, that was the way it had to be because that was the way it was. No deviation was allowed from her interpretations of correct. . . .

How I Became a Poet

"Wherever the bird with no feet flew she found trees with no limbs."

When the strongest words for what I have to offer come out of me sounding like words I remember from my mother's mouth, then I either have to reassess the meaning of everything I have to say now, or re-examine the worth of her old words.

My mother had a special and secret relationship with words, taken for granted as language because it was always there. I did not speak until I was four. When I was three, the dazzling world of strange lights and fascinating shapes which I inhabited resolved itself in mundane definitions, and I learned another nature of things as seen through eyeglasses. This perception of things was less colorful and confusing but much more comfortable than the one native to my nearsighted and unevenly focused eyes.

I remember trundling along Lenox Avenue with my mother, on our way to school to pick up Phyllis and Helen for lunch. It was late spring because my legs felt light and real, unencumbered by bulky snowpants. I dawdled along the fence around the public playground, inside of which grew one stunted plane tree. Enthralled, I stared up at the sudden revelation of each single and particular leaf of green, precisely shaped and laced about with unmixed light. Before my glasses, I had known trees as tall brown pillars ending in fat puffy swirls of paling greens, much like the pictures of them I perused in my sisters' storybooks from which I learned so much of my visual world.

But out of my mother's mouth a world of comment came cascading when she felt at ease or in her element, full of picaresque constructions and surreal scenes.

We were never dressed too lightly, but rather "in next kin to nothing." *Neck skin to nothing?* Impassable and impossible distances were measured by the distance "from Hog to Kick 'em Jenny." *Hog? Kick 'em Jenny?* Who knew until I was sane and grown a poet with a mouthful of stars, that these were two little reefs in the Grenadines, between Grenada and Carriacou.

The euphemisms of body were equally puzzling, if no less colorful. A mild reprimand was accompanied not by a slap on the behind, but a "smack on the backass," or on the "bamsy." You sat on your "bam-bam," but anything between your hipbones and upper thighs was consigned to the "lower-region," a word I always imagined to have french origins, as in "Don't forget to wash your *l'oregión* before you go to bed." For more clinical and precise descriptions, there was always "between your legs"—whispered.

The sensual content of life was masked and cryptic, but attended in well-coded phrases. Somehow all the cousins knew that Uncle Cyril couldn't lift heavy things because of his "bam-bam-coo," and the lowered voice in which this hernia was spoken of warned us that it had something to do with "down there." And on the infrequent but magical occasions when mother performed her delicious laying on of hands for a crick in the neck or a pulled muscle, she didn't massage your backbone, she "raised your zandalee."

I never caught cold, but "got co-hum, co-hum," and then everything turned "cro-bo-so," topsy-turvy, or at least, a bit askew.

I am a reflection of my mother's secret poetry as well as of her hidden angers.

Sitting between my mother's spread legs, her strong knees gripping my shoulders tightly like some well-attended drum, my head in her lap, while she brushed and combed and oiled and braided. I feel my mother's strong, rough hands all up in my unruly hair, while I'm squirming around on a low stool or on a folded towel on the floor, my rebellious shoulders hunched and jerking against the inexorable sharp-toothed comb. After each springy portion is combed and braided, she pats it tenderly and proceeds to the next.

I hear the interjection of *sotto voce* admonitions that punctuated whatever discussion she and my father were having.

"Hold your back up, now! Deenie, keep still! Put your head so!" Scratch, scratch. "When last you wash your hair? Look the dandruff!" Scratch, scratch, the comb's truth setting my own teeth on edge. Yet, these were some of the moments I missed most sorely when our real wars began.

I remember the warm mother smell caught between her legs, and the intimacy of our physical touching nestled inside of the anxiety/pain like a nutmeg nestled inside its covering of mace.

The radio, the scratching comb, the smell of petroleum jelly, the grip of her knees and my stinging scalp all fall into—*the rhythms of a litany, the rituals of Black women combing their daughters' hair.*

Saturday morning. The one morning of the week my mother does not leap from bed to prepare me and my sisters for school or church. I wake in the cot in their bedroom, knowing only it is one of those lucky days when she is still in bed, and alone. My father is in the kitchen. The sound of pots and the slightly off-smell of frying bacon mixes with the smell of percolating Bokar coffee.

The click of her wedding ring against the wooden headboard. She is awake. I get up and go over and crawl into my mother's bed. Her smile. Her glycerine-flannel smell. The warmth. She reclines upon her back and side, one arm extended, the other flung across her forehead. A hot-water bottle wrapped in body-temperature flannel, which she used to quiet her gall-bladder pains during the night. Her large soft breasts beneath the buttoned flannel of her nightgown. Below, the rounded swell of her stomach, silent and inviting touch.

I crawl against her, playing with the enflanneled, warm, rubber bag, pummeling it, tossing it, sliding it down the roundness of her stomach to the warm sheet between the bend of her elbow and the curve of her waist below her breasts, flopping sideward inside the printed cloth. Under the covers, the morning smells soft and sunny and full of promise.

I frolic with the liquid-filled water bottle, patting and rubbing its firm giving softness. I shake it slowly, rocking it back and forth, lost in sudden tenderness, at the same time gently rubbing against my mother's quiet body. Warm milky smells of morning surround us.

Feeling the smooth deep firmness of her breasts against my shoulders, my pajama'd back, sometimes, more daringly, against my ears and the sides of my cheeks. Tossing, tumbling, the soft gurgle of the water within its rubber casing. Sometimes the thin sound of her ring against the bedstead as she moves her hand up over my head. Her arm comes down across me, holding me to her for a moment, then quiets my frisking.

"All right, now."

I nuzzle against her sweetness, pretending not to hear.

"All right, now, I said; stop it. It's time to get up

from this bed. Look lively, and mind you spill that water."

Before I can say anything she is gone in a great deliberate heave. The purposeful whip of her chenille robe over her warm flannel gown and the bed already growing cold beside me.

"Wherever the bird with no feet flew she found trees with no limbs."

PAULE MARSHALL *grew up in Brooklyn during the Depression, the daughter of immigrants from the West Indies, and graduated from Brooklyn College in 1953. She is the author of three novels,* Brown Girl, Brownstones *(1959),* The Chosen Place, *The* Timeless People *(1969), and* Praisesong for the Widow *(1983) as well as a book of novellas,* Soul Clap Hands and Sing *(1961). The* New Yorker *wrote of her fiction, "When Marshall writes about those she truly loves, she cannot be resisted. She brings to her characters an instinctive understanding, a generosity, and a free humor that combine to form a style remarkable for its courage, its color, and its natural control." In her much acclaimed autobiographical essay that follows here, "From the Poets in the Kitchen," originally published in* The New York Times Book Review's *series, "The Making of a Writer," Marshall celebrates her mother and her friends, the female equivalents of Ralph Ellison's invisible man, who gave the future writer the spoken word, the love of language, the legacy of "the wordshop of the kitchen."*

Paule Marshall
from
THE POETS IN THE KITCHEN

Some years ago, when I was teaching a graduate seminar in fiction at Columbia University, a well known male novelist visited my class to speak on his development as a writer. In discussing his formative years, he didn't realize it but he seriously endangered his life by remarking that women writers are luckier than those of his sex because they usually spend so much time as children around their mothers and their mothers' friends in the kitchen.

What did he say that for? The women students immediately forgot about being in awe of him and began readying their attack for the question and answer period later on. Even I bristled. There again was that awful image of women locked away from the world in the kitchen with only each other to talk to, and their daughters locked in with them.

But my guest wasn't really being sexist or trying to be provocative or even spoiling for a fight. What he meant—when he got around to explaining himself more fully—was that, given the way children are (or were) raised in our society, with little girls kept closer to home and their mothers, the woman writer stands a better chance of being exposed, while growing up, to the kind of talk that goes on among women, more often than not in the kitchen; and that this experience gives her an edge over her male counterpart by instilling in her an appreciation for ordinary speech.

It was clear that my guest lecturer attached great importance to this, which is understandable. Common speech and the plain, workaday words that make it up are, after all, the stock in trade of some of the best fiction writers. They are the principal means by which characters in a novel or story reveal themselves and give voice sometimes to profound feelings and complex ideas about themselves and the world. Perhaps the proper measure of a writer's talent is skill in rendering everyday speech—when it is appropriate to the story—as well as the ability to tap, to exploit the beauty, poetry and wisdom it often contains.

"If you say what's on your mind in the language that comes to you from your parents and your street and friends you'll probably say something beautiful." Grace Paley tells this, she says, to her students at the beginning of every writing course.

It's all a matter of exposure and a training of the ear for the would-be writer in those early years of apprenticeship. And, according to my guest lecturer, this training, the best of it, often takes place in as unglamorous a setting as the kitchen.

He didn't know it, but he was essentially describing my experience as a little girl. I grew up among poets. Now they didn't look like poets—whatever that breed is supposed to look like. Nothing about them suggested that poetry was their calling. They were just a group of ordinary housewives and mothers, my mother included, who dressed in a way (shapeless housedresses, dowdy felt hats and long, dark, solemn coats) that made it impossible for me to imagine they had ever been young.

Nor did they do what poets were supposed to do—spend their days in an attic room writing verses. They never put pen to paper except to write occasionally to their relatives in Barbados. "I take my pen in hand hoping these few lines will find you in health as they leave me fair for the time being," was the way their letters invariably began. Rather, their day was spent "scrubbing floor," as they described the work they did.

Several mornings a week these unknown bards would put an apron and a pair of old house shoes in a shopping bag and take the train or streetcar from our section of Brooklyn out to Flatbush. There, those who didn't have steady jobs would wait on certain designated corners for the white housewives in the neighborhood to come along and bargain with them over pay for a day's work cleaning their houses. This was the ritual even in the winter.

Later, armed with the few dollars they had earned, which in their vocabulary became "a few raw-mouth pennies," they made their way back to our neighborhood, where they would sometimes stop off to have a cup of tea or cocoa together before going home to cook dinner for their husbands and children.

The basement kitchen of the brownstone house where my family lived was the usual gathering place. Once inside the warm safety of its walls the women threw off the drab coats and hats, seated themselves at the large center table, drank their cups of tea or cocoa, and talked. While my sister and I sat at a smaller table over in a corner doing our homework, they talked—endlessly, passionately, poetically, and with impressive range. No subject was beyond them. True, they would indulge in the usual gossip: whose husband was running with whom, whose daughter looked slightly "in the way" (pregnant) under her bridal gown as she walked down the aisle. That sort of thing. But they also tackled the great issues of the time. They were always, for example, discussing the state of the economy. It was the mid and late 30's then, and the aftershock of the Depression, with its soup lines and suicides on Wall Street, was still being felt.

Some people, they declared, didn't know how to deal with adversity. They didn't know that you had to "tie up your belly" (hold in the pain, that is) when things got rough and go on with life. They took their image from the bellyband that is tied around the stomach of a newborn baby to keep the navel pressed in.

They talked politics. Roosevelt was their hero. He had come along and rescued the country with relief and jobs, and in gratitude they christened their sons Franklin and Delano and hoped they would live up to the names.

If F.D.R. was their hero, Marcus Garvey was their God. The name of the fiery, Jamaican-born black nationalist of the 20's was constantly invoked around the table. For he had been their leader when they first came to the United States from the

West Indies shortly after World War I. They had contributed to his organization, the United Negro Improvement Association (UNIA), out of their meager salaries, bought shares in his ill-fated Black Star Shipping Line, and at the height of the movement they had marched as members of his "nurses' brigade" in their white uniforms up Seventh Avenue in Harlem during the great Garvey Day parades. Garvey: He lived on through the power of their memories.

And their talk was of war and rumors of wars. They raged against World War II when it broke out in Europe, blaming it on the politicians. "It's these politicians. They're the ones always starting up all this lot of war. But what they care? It's the poor people got to suffer and mothers with their sons." If it was *their* sons, they swore they would keep them out of the Army by giving them soap to eat each day to make their hearts sound defective. Hitler? He was for them "the devil incarnate."

Then there was home. They reminisced often and at length about home. The old country. Barbados—or Bimshire, as they affectionately called it. The little Caribbean island in the sun they loved but had to leave. "Poor—poor but sweet" was the way they remembered it.

And naturally they discussed their adopted home. America came in for both good and bad marks. They lashed out at it for the racism they encountered. They took to task some of the people they worked for, especially those who gave them only a hard-boiled egg and a few spoonfuls of cottage cheese for lunch. "As if anybody can scrub floor on an egg and some cheese that don't have no taste to it!"

Yet although they caught H in "this man country," as they called America, it was nonetheless a place where "you could at least see your way to make a dollar." That much they acknowledged. They might even one day accumulate enough dollars, with both them and their husbands working, to buy the brownstone houses which, like my family, they were only leasing at that period. This was their consuming ambition: to "buy house" and to see the children through.

There was no way for me to understand it at the time, but the talk that filled the kitchen those afternoons was highly functional. It served as therapy, the cheapest kind available to my mother and her friends. Not only did it help them recover from the long wait on the corner that morning and the bargaining over their labor, it restored them to a sense of themselves and reaffirmed their self-worth. Through language they were able to overcome the humiliations of the work-day.

But more than therapy, that freewheeling, wide-ranging, exuberant talk functioned as an outlet for the tremendous creative energy they possessed. They were women in whom the need for self-expression was strong, and since language was the only vehicle readily available to them they made of it an art form that—in keeping with the African tradition in which art and life are one—was an integral part of their lives.

And their talk was a refuge. They never really ceased being baffled and overwhelmed by America—its vastness, complexity and power. Its strange customs and laws. At a level beyond words they remained fearful and in awe. Their uneasiness and fear were even reflected in their attitude toward the children they had given birth to in this country. They referred to those like myself, the little Brooklyn-born Bajans (Barbadians), as "these New York children" and complained that they couldn't discipline us properly because of the laws here. "You can't beat these children as you would like, you know, because the authorities in this place will dash you in jail for them. After all, these is New York children." Not only were we different, American, we had, as they saw it, escaped their ultimate authority.

Confronted therefore by a world they could not encompass, which even limited their rights as parents, and at the same time finding themselves permanently separated from the world they had known, they took refuge in language. "Language is the only homeland," Czeslaw Milosz, the emigré Polish writer and Nobel Laureate, has said. This is what it became for the women at the kitchen table.

It served another purpose also, I suspect. My mother and her friends were after all the female counterpart of Ralph Ellison's invisible man. Indeed, you might say they suffered a triple invisibility, being black, female and foreigners. They really didn't count in American society except as a source of cheap labor. But given the kind of women they were, they couldn't tolerate the fact of their invisibility, their powerlessness. And they fought back, using the only weapon at their command: the spoken word.

Those late afternoon conversations on a wide range of topics were a way for them to feel they exercised some measure of control over their lives and the events that shaped them. "Soully-gal, talk yuh talk!" they were always exhorting each other. "In this man world you got to take yuh mouth and make a gun!" They were in control, if only verbally and if only for the two hours or so that they remained in our house.

For me, sitting over in the corner, being seen but not heard, which was the rule for children in those days, it wasn't only what the women talked about—the content—but the way they put things—their style. The insight, irony, wit and humor they brought to their stories and discussions and their poet's inventiveness and daring with language—which of course I could only sense but not define back then.

They had taken the standard English taught them in the primary schools of Barbados and transformed it into an idiom, an instrument that more adequately described them—changing around the syntax and imposing their own rhythm and accent so that the sentences were more pleasing to their ears. They added the few African sounds and words that had survived, such as the derisive suck-teeth sound and the word "yam," meaning to eat. And to make it more vivid, more in keeping with their expressive quality, they brought to bear a raft of metaphors, parables, Biblical quotations, sayings and the like:

"The sea ain' got no back door," they would say, meaning that it wasn't like a house where if there was a fire you could run out the back. Meaning that it was not to be trifled with. And meaning perhaps in a larger sense that man should treat all of nature with caution and respect.

"I has read hell by heart and called every generation blessed!" They sometimes went in for hyperbole.

A woman expecting a baby was never said to be pregnant. They never used that word. Rather, she was "in the way" or, better yet, "tumbling big." "Guess who I butt up on in the market the other day tumbling big again!"

And a woman with a reputation of being too free with her sexual favors was known in their book as a "thoroughfare"—the sense of men like a steady stream of cars moving up and down the road of her life. Or she might be dubbed "a free-bee," which was my favorite of the two. I liked the image it conjured up of a woman scandalous perhaps but independent, who flitted from one flower to another in a garden of male beauties, sampling their nectar, taking her pleasure at will, the roles reversed.

And nothing, no matter how beautiful, was ever described as simply beautiful. It was always "beautiful-ugly": the beautiful-ugly dress, the beautiful-ugly house, the beautiful-ugly car. Why the word "ugly," I used to wonder, when the thing they were referring to was beautiful, and they knew it. Why the antonym, the contradiction, the linking of opposites? It used to puzzle me greatly as a child.

There is the theory in linguistics which states that the idiom of a people, the way they use language, reflects not only the most fundamental views they hold of themselves and the world but their very conception of reality. Perhaps in using the term "beautiful-ugly" to describe nearly everything, my mother and her friends were expressing what they believed to be a fundamental dualism in life: the idea that a thing is at the same time its opposite, and that these opposites, these contradictions make up the whole. But theirs was not a Manichaean brand of dualism that sees matter, flesh, the body, as inherently evil, because they constantly addressed each other as "soully-gal"—soul: spirit; gal: the body, flesh, the visible self. And it was clear from their tone that they gave one as much weight and importance as the other. They had never heard of the mind/body split.

As for God, they summed up His essential attitude in a phrase. "God," they would say, "don' love ugly and He ain' stuck on pretty."

Using everyday speech, the simple commonplace words—but always with imagination and skill—they gave voice to the most complex ideas. Flannery O'Connor would have approved of how they made ordinary language work, as she put it, "doubletime," stretching, shading, deepening its meaning. Like Joseph Conrad they were always trying to infuse new life in the "old old words worn thin . . . by . . . careless usage." And the goals of their oral art were the same as his: "to make you hear, to make you feel . . . to make you *see*." This was their guiding esthetic.

By the time I was 8 or 9, I graduated from the corner of the kitchen to the neighborhood library, and thus from the spoken to the written word. The Macon Street Branch of the Brooklyn Public Library was an imposing half block long edifice of heavy gray masonry, with glass-paneled doors at the front and two tall metal torches symbolizing the light that comes of learning flanking the wide steps outside.

The inside was just as impressive. More steps—of pale marble with gleaming brass railings at the center and sides—led up to the circulation desk, and a great pendulum clock gazed down from the balcony stacks that faced the entrance. Usually stationed at the top of the steps like the guards outside Buckingham Palace was the custodian, a stern-faced West Indian type who for years, until I was old enough to obtain an adult card, would immediately shoo me with one hand into the Children's Room and with the other threaten me into silence, a finger to his lips. You would have thought he was the chief librarian and not just someone whose job it was to keep the brass polished and the clock wound. I put him in a story called "Barbados" years later and had terrible things happen to him at the end.

I sheltered from the storm of adolescence in the Macon Street library, reading voraciously, indiscriminately, everything from Jane Austen to Zane Grey, but with a special passion for the long, full-blown, richly detailed 18th- and 19th-century picaresque tales: "Tom Jones," "Great Expectations," "Vanity Fair."

But although I loved nearly everything I read and would enter fully into the lives of the characters—indeed, would cease being myself and become them—I sensed a lack after a time. Something I couldn't quite define was missing. And then one day, browsing in the poetry section, I came across a book by someone called Paul Laurence Dunbar, and opening it I found the photograph of a wistful, sad-eyed poet who to my surprise was black. I turned to a poem at random. "Little brown-baby wif spa'klin' / eyes / Come to yo' pappy an' set on his knee." Although I had a little difficulty at first with the words in dialect, the poem spoke to me as nothing I had read before of the closeness, the special relationship I had had with my father, who by then had become an ardent believer in Father Divine and gone to live in Father's "kingdom" in Harlem. Reading it helped to ease somewhat the tight knot of sorrow and longing I carried around in my chest that refused to go away. I read another poem. " 'Lias! 'Lias! Bless de Lawd! / Don' you know de day's / erbroad? / Ef you don' get up, you scamp / Dey'll be trouble in dis camp." I laughed. It reminded me of the way my mother sometimes yelled at my sister and me to get out of bed in the mornings.

And another: "Seen my lady home las' night / Jump back, honey, jump back. / Hel' huh han' an' sque'z it tight . . ." About love between a black man and a black woman. I had never seen that written about before and it roused in me all kinds of delicious feelings and hopes.

And I began to search then for books and stories and poems about "The Race" (as it was put back then), about my people. While not abandoning Thackeray, Fielding, Dickens and the others, I started asking the reference librarian, who was white, for books by Negro writers, although I must admit I did so at first with a feeling of shame—the shame I and many others used to experience in those days whenever the word "Negro" or "colored" came up.

No grade school literature teacher of mine had ever mentioned Dunbar or James Weldon Johnson or Langston Hughes. I didn't know that Zora Neale Hurston existed and was busy writing and being published during those years. Nor was I made aware of people like Frederick Douglass and Harriet Tubman—their spirit and example—or the great 19th-century abolitionist and feminist Sojourner Truth. There wasn't even Negro History Week when I attended P.S. 35 on Decatur Street!

What I needed, what all the kids—West Indian and native black American alike—with whom I grew up needed, was an equivalent of the Jewish shul, someplace where we could go after school—the schools that were shortchanging us—and read works by those like ourselves and learn about our history.

It was around that time also that I began harboring the dangerous thought of someday trying to write myself. Perhaps a poem about an apple tree, although I had never seen one. Or the story of a girl who could magically transplant herself to wherever she wanted to be in the world—such as Father Divine's kingdom in Harlem. Dunbar—his dark, eloquent face, his large volume of poems—permitted me to dream that I might someday write, and with something of the power with words my mother and her friends possessed.

When people at readings and writers' conferences ask me who my major influences were, they are sometimes a little disappointed when I don't immediately name the usual literary giants. True, I am indebted to those writers, white and black, whom I read during my formative years and still read for instruction and pleasure. But they were preceded in my life by another set of giants whom I always acknowledge before all others: the group of women around the table long ago. They taught me my first lessons in the narrative art. They trained my ear. They set a standard of excellence. This is why the best of my work must be attributed to them; it stands as testimony to the rich legacy of language and culture they so freely passed on to me in the wordshop of the kitchen.

MARGARET MEAD *was born in Philadelphia in 1901 and educated at Barnard and Columbia University. A renowned anthropologist, ethnologist, writer, teacher, and lecturer, her many books include* Coming of Age in Samoa *(1928),* Growing Up in New Guinea *(1930),* Sex and Temperament in Three Primitive Societies *(1935),* And Keep Your Powder Dry *(1942), and* Male and Female *(1949). The mother of Mary Catherine Bateson Kassarjian by her second husband, Gregory Bateson, Dr. Mead published the personal story behind her remarkable experiences and their effects on her as a woman in the form of an autobiography,* Blackberry Winter: My Earlier Years *(1972) from which the following passage about her mother is taken. Jane Howard, reviewing the book in* The New York Times Book Review, *called it "a hymn to her own family in particular and the idea of families in general."*

Margaret Mead
The Original Punk

I was a first child, wanted and loved.

When I was fifteen, I asked my mother whether she had planned her children. She answered, "Goodness, no! There are some things that are best left to the Lord!" In fact, "the Lord" was only a figure of speech. She did not believe in a personal God, but she had an abiding trust in a generally benevolent providence.

Before my birth, my mother kept a little notebook in which she jotted down, among other things, quotations from William James about developing all of a child's senses, as well as the titles of articles on which she was working for various encyclopedias, and here she wrote, "When I knew baby was coming I was anxious to do the best for it."

Pictures of me as a baby show me in the arms of my mother or grandmother, with their hair down and wearing wrappers, dressed in a way I have no memory of seeing either of them. Only now, after so many years, I realize that it was for her chil-

From *Blackberry Winter: My Earlier Years*.

dren's sake that my mother pinned up her hair so
carefully every morning as soon as she got up. Earlier, when I was too young to notice, she let it fall
softly around her face—but later, never. In turn,
the first thing I do in the morning is to comb my
hair, and when my daughter was young I put on
something pretty—as I still do when I am staying in
a house where there are children.

Another picture shows me, a three-month-old
baby, prone and head up, in a Morris chair. Years
later we still had the Morris chair, and by the time I
could think about it, I knew both that the chair
represented some kind of revolution in furniture
design and that it was somehow a good thing to
have slept in a Morris chair instead of a crib, like
other babies.

I was the first baby born in a new hospital, so
Mother had the attention of the entire staff. She
made a modern choice, but when I began to read
school poetry—including "I remember, I remember
the house where I was born" and "Over the river
and through the woods,/To grandfather's house we'll
go"—I felt somewhat aggrieved that I had no house
where I was born and no grandfather's house to go
on Thanksgiving Day, because both my grandfa-
thers were dead and my paternal grandmother lived
with us in our house.

These two views of my childhood, our houses,
and my unusual upbringing persisted all through my
early years. I took pride in being unlike other children and in living in a household that was itself
unique. But at the same time I longed to share in
every culturally normal experience. I wished that I

had been born in a house. I wanted to have a locket, like other little girls, and to wear a hat with ribbons and fluffy petticoats instead of the sensible bloomers that very advanced mothers put on their little daughters so they could climb trees. The prevailing cultural style, as it was expressed in stories, poems, aphorisms, and the behavior of our neighbors, fascinated me in every smallest detail. I longed to live out every bit of it. But I also wanted to be very sure that I would always be recognized as myself.

My father called me, very affectionately, "Punk." Then, when my brother was born two years later, I was called "the original punk" and Dick was known as "the boy-punk," a reversal of the usual pattern, according to which the girl is only a female version of the true human being, the boy.

Before Dick was born, my parents made the common mistake of promising me a playmate in the new baby. As a result I found his newborn ineptitude very exasperating. I have been told that I once got him, as a toddler, behind a door and furiously demanded, "Can't you say anything but 'da da da' all the time?"

I was a sturdy child and had no ailments. But my brother was fragile, always—it seemed to me—ill and a worry to my parents. I early learned to expect that any disasters that occurred would happen to Dick and I even conveniently displaced onto him frightening memories, like being locked up in a dark cupboard by a German governess, who lasted no more than a week in our household. When I told the story later, I believed that it had happened not to me but to my brother, as I also recalled, mistakenly, that it was he, not I, who had been bitten by a rabbit in the zoo. Even today I have some difficulty in keeping in mind unpleasant things that have happened to me. So I learned long ago to check my memories very carefully and to write down what I found out, but I still tend to erase small misfortunes from my mind. Later other people have to recall them to me.

My father was six feet tall, which was very tall in 1901. He called my mother, who was just five feet tall, "Tiny Wife," and that was what I called her, too, when I first learned to talk. She was slight and had very blue eyes and golden hair, and I delighted in her gentle beauty. However, she seldom allowed herself to enjoy pretty clothes or elaborately dressed hair. Life was real, life was earnest—it was too serious for trivial things. She had babies to care for and a house to manage. She also felt it was important to continue her own intellectual life and to be a responsible citizen in a world in which there were many wrongs—wrongs to the poor and the downtrodden, to foreigners, to Negroes, to women—that had to be set right. Long afterward, near the end of her life, when she was recovering from a stroke and allowed herself to take pleasure in pretty bed jackets, she confided in her son-in-law, Leo Rosten, "Margaret wanted a little rosebud mother." When she died, we dressed her in pale blue with a spray of sweetheart roses. Then, for those last hours, my father felt that his young wife had been given back to him.

Gotthard Booth, who is very much interested in

223

inheritance in family lines, gave the Rorschach test to both my parents when they were in their seventies. I spent one of the pleasantest hours of my life discussing with him my mother's Rorschach, in which she discerned, disentangled from the chiaroscuro shadows, rare and tiny images, tinkling brooks and kissing children. Out of my own earliest memories I could bring back the poetry that evoked these images:

> Hast thou seen, with flash incessant,
> Bubbles gliding under ice,
> Bodied forth and evanescent,
> No one knows by what device?

and

> When all at once I saw a crowd,
> A host, of golden daffodils;
> Beside the lake, beneath the trees,
> Fluttering and dancing in the breeze;
> . . .
> And then my heart with pleasure fills
> and dances with the daffodils.

My mother grew up on the shores of Lake Michigan. Her Chicago childhood was so real to her that I, too, thought of the past as "before the Fire"—in 1871—from which my grandfather's house on the North Side just escaped destruction, or "before the Fair"—the Chicago World's Fair in 1893. One of my treasures, as a child, was a miniature can of Van Houten's cocoa that came from the Fair. For years I kept it carefully on my prayer desk—the prie-dieu my mother had bought at a sale, not realizing what it was. "Someday," I thought, "someday I will open that little can and actually taste the essence of the World's Fair contained in it." Meanwhile, since this could be done only once, I kept the can standing next to a miniature jar made from the clay of the Holy Land.

For all her slightness and delicate beauty, my mother had been a determined and impetuous young girl. She told us stories of how she had led the whole high school out on the streets to celebrate the election of Grover Cleveland and how she had refused to kiss a boy, who was later lost on an expedition to the interior of China, because, instead of kissing her, he had said, "Emily, I am going to kiss you!"—and so, of course, she had said he couldn't. Father countered with the story of how he saw Mother sitting in the front row of a class at the University of Chicago and sat down beside her, announcing (probably only to himself, but we never knew for sure), "I am going to marry you." Fifty years later, an elderly lady, the mother of a colleague, came up to me after a lecture and announced in a menacing voice, "I am responsible for your existence. I introduced your father to your mother."

Mother wore a wedding ring, but she never had another ring until, thirty years after their marriage, Father gave her a turquoise ring. Turquoise is my birthstone, and as a small child I learned to say, "December's child shall live to bless the turquoise that ensures success." But I didn't find out about being a Sagittarian—someone who goes as far as anyone else and shoots a little farther—until I was sixteen, when we learned about astrology from the physicist husband of one of my mother's college friends.

It was always difficult to give Mother a present. She felt that the money would be better spent on a good cause. Once Father, in a fit of remorse, I suspect, about some fancied infidelity and remembering how Mother had often said she would like a string of blue beads, went to Tiffany in New York, where he bought her a lapis lazuli necklace for ninety dollars. Mother reacted to this flamboyant gesture with horror and insisted that the necklace be taken back. The credit was given to me to use when I got married. And so, ten years later three undergraduate friends and I rode down from Barnard on the top deck of a Fifth Avenue bus to pick out Tiffany teaspoons and coffee spoons and an unappreciated gravy spoon that was not shaped like a ladle.

Whenever a question arose about how money was to be spent—should we buy a new rug or give the money to the fellowship fund of the American Association of University Women?—my mother always tried to capture the money for the more worthy purpose. Between the quotations of sheer delight, from Wordsworth and Browning, that came so readily to her lips, there were also the stern phrases of her American forebears and the impassioned declarations of early feminists, for example, about freeing women from the ignominy of being classified along with criminals and imbeciles, as incapable of voting.

Mother's vehemence was reserved for the causes she supported and her fury was directed at impersonal institutions, such as political machines—the Vares of Philadelphia or Tammany Hall—the Telephone Company, Standard Oil, or the Chicago Stockyards. As a matter of principle, she never wore furs; and feathers, except for ostrich plumes, were forbidden. Long before I had an idea what they were, I learned that aigrettes represented a murder of the innocents. There were types of people, too, for whom she had no use—anti-suffragettes (women who probably kept poodles) or "the kind of woman who comes down at ten in the morning wearing a boudoir cap and who takes headache powders." But these were never people whom she knew.

For actual, living people she had only gentleness and generosity and a radiant smile that lives on in the memory of those who knew her and of everyone who turned to her for help. Her vehemence was wholly disinterested, and so she could argue with an intensity that upset my grandmother, who had been used to quieter family meals.

The lack of any contradiction between my mother's ardent support of good principles and her fury at injustice, on the one hand, and her deep personal gentleness, on the other, came out clearly in her response to the advice given mothers in a baby book that was published just about the time I was born. The author, L. E. Holt, was an advocate of the kind of regimen, such as schedules for bottle-fed babies, that ever since has bedeviled our child-rearing practices. She read the book, but she nursed her babies. She accepted the admonition about never picking up a crying child unless it was in pain. But she said her babies were good babies who would cry only if something was wrong, and so she picked them up. Believing that she was living by the principles of the most modern child-rearing practices, she quite contentedly adapted what she was told about children in the abstract to the living reality of her own children.

All her life she kept a kind of innocence that we all too readily interpreted as an inability to appreciate humor. Once, on Groundhog Day, she reported that she had seen in Doylestown a barrel with a sign on it that read, "Ground hog, just caught." When she looked inside the barrel, she found that it contained sausage. "Why sausage?" she asked, very puzzled. Or quite seriously, she would make some intellectual conversion, as when she transformed "pep" into a lament. "This horse has no pepper!" By putting the promptings of the senses and of the unconscious at a distance, she also distantiated humor.

In fact, she had no gift for play and very little for pleasure or comfort. She saw to it that we had wholesome food, but it was always very plain. It was only toward the end of her life that I began to suspect that both the plainness of our food and, in some measure, her own fastidiousness were due to a sensory deficiency of smell and taste.

She herself conscientiously filled the eighteen lamps we needed in our house in Bucks County, but she let me arrange the flowers. Indeed, she gave far less attention to the flower garden than to the vegetable garden. Changes in style—giving up tablecloths for doilies—were made not for the sake of fashion, but to save work for servants. Her two younger sisters were far more pleasure-loving and often criticized my mother for her austerity. But she easily accorded to her sister Fanny McMaster a sense of beauty and style which she felt she herself lacked. Yet any room in which she lived, filled with books and papers, had lamps that were good for the eyes and an air of welcome. It never gave one the sense that here were things among which children had to walk warily. The few precious things we had—the Wedgwood coffee service and the Meissen "onion pattern" china, which everyone in my mother's family was given by Great-aunt Fanny Howe—were always used and only briefly regretted when a piece was broken or lost in one of our many moves from one house to another. My mother did, however, reserve a little impersonal rage for the unfair way long-dead ancestors had distributed the family silver.

As she had no real gift for play, she also could neither tell nor make up stories, and there was always a touch of duty in the parties and games she planned for us. By the time I was eight, I had taken over the preparations for festivities. I made the table decorations and the place cards, filled the stockings, and trimmed the Christmas tree while Mother sat up half the night finishing the tie for Father's Christmas present. She could neither cook nor sew, although intermittently she did a little cross-stitch embroidery or some enjoined knitting. What household skills she had were primarily managerial—providing a safe and comfortable home in which children were fed nutritionally, book salesmen and nuns collecting for charity were invited to lunch, other people's children were welcomed and treated as people, and in which there were rooms large enough for committees to meet.

In many ways she shared the intellectual snobbishness of the tradition that was so characteristic of families of New England origin, Unitarian or once Unitarian, college-bred, readers of serious novels and deeply imbued with the attitudes and imagery of the nineteenth-century essayists and poets, especially Robert Browning. The world, as she saw it, was divided into "people with some background"—a charitable phrase which accorded neither credit nor blame, but somehow divested them of privilege—"ordinary people," and a special group of "fine people"—a term that was most often applied to "fine women."

Ordinary people let their children chew gum, read girls' and boys' books, drink ice cream sodas, and go to Coney Island or Willow Grove, where they mingled with "the common herd"—a phrase we never let Mother forget she had used. They also read cheap paperback novels and were riddled by prejudice—prejudice against Labor, against foreigners, against Negroes, against Catholics and Jews.

In contrast, fine people were highly literate and had taste and sophistication. Even more important, they engaged actively in efforts to make this a better world. They fought for causes and organized community efforts. Mother believed strongly in the community, in knowing her neighbors and in treating servants as individuals with dignity and rights. In fact, by insisting on their rights, she often alienated servants who might well have responded more easily to expressions of warm but capricious affection.

Her involvement in causes carried with it a fixed belief in the value of walking. She gave walking as her main avocation in her listing in *American Women*. For years she was famous in Bucks County because, during the summer we moved there, she walked to Plumsteadville to attend a sale and back home again, a journey of some fifteen miles, and also because she herself painted the kitchen ceiling—two strange and, in local terms, unfeminine activities. It was a kind of criticism she did not mind.

All these things were part of my consciousness of my mother, but for me she had two outstanding characteristics. One was her unfailing and ungrudging generosity. In my life I realized every one of her unrealized ambitions, and she was unambivalently delighted. The other was that she was absolutely trustworthy. I know that if I had ever written to her to say, "Please go and wait for me on the corner of Thirteenth and Chestnut Streets," she would have stayed there until I came or she dropped from sheer fatigue.

. . . I, as the eldest—the original punk, the child who was always told, "There's no one like Margaret" —had the clearest sense of what she was.

MARY CATHERINE BATESON, *the daughter of Margaret Mead and Gregory Bateson, lives in Cambridge, Massachusetts, with her husband and daughter, and commutes to Amherst where she is professor of anthropology at Amherst College. She received her undergraduate degree from Radcliffe in 1960 and a Ph.D. from Harvard in 1963. Her parents were legends in their own lifetimes. The selection that follows is taken from her memoir of both of them,* With a Daughter's Eye. *Central in her memory is "the quality time" her busy mother Margaret planned for mother and daughter whose schedules kept them apart a great deal. The daughter remembers in fascinating detail these "times of delight." Her book is a tribute to the conscientious and creative mothering of a most original and loving woman.*

Mary Catherine Bateson
from
WITH A DAUGHTER'S EYE: A MEMOIR OF MARGARET MEAD AND GREGORY BATESON

"Once upon a time," my mother would narrate as the sun moved higher in the sky, "in the kingdom between the grass stems, there lived a king and a queen who had three daughters. The eldest was tall and golden-haired and laughing, the second was bold and raven-haired. But the youngest was gray-eyed and gentle, walking apart and dreaming." The story varies but the pattern remains the same, woven from the grass of the meadow and the fears and longings of generations. For this king and queen lived in no anarchic world, but in a world of rhythm and just symmetries. Their labors, quests, and loves grew out of each other with the same elegance that connects the parts of a flowering plant and its cycles of growth. At their court, as at the fairies' banquets, crystal goblets and courtly etiquette reflected a social order. Prince and princess find one another in a world of due peril and challenge and happiness ever after. The flower is pollinated, seed is formed, scattered, and germinated. Look! The silk in the milkweed pods is what the fairies use to stuff their mattresses. Blow on the dandelion down to make a wish, anticipating the wind. Pause in the middle of fantasy to see the natural world as fragile and precious, threatened as well as caressed by human dreaming.

Worlds can be found by a child and an adult bending down and looking together under the grass stems or at the skittering crabs in a tidal pool. They can be spun from the stuff of fantasy and tradition. And they can be handled and changed, created in little from all sorts of materials. On a coffee table in the center of our living room, which often held toys and projects of mine, I constructed a series of worlds on trays. One of these was meant to depict a natural landscape, built up from rocks and soil, with colored sand and tinted strawflowers set into it. Another was inspired by a book my father had read to me in which a child constructs a city with cups, dishes, and utensils from the kitchen and then visits it in his dreams. My mother, in that same period, was fascinated by the World Test of Margaret Lowenfeld, an English child analyst. This projective test consists of a tray of moist sand and a vast array of miniatures: people and animals, trees and houses and vehicles. In using the test, one molds the soil and handles the objects, arranging and changing them, and then weaves narratives within the world one has created, so that the creation of a microcosm becomes the expression of an inner, psychic world, a world that embodies pain and perplexity as well as symmetry. . . .

Through my mother's writing echoes the question "What kind of world can we *build* for our children?" She thought in terms of building. She set out to create a community for me to grow up in, she threw herself wholeheartedly into the planning and governance of my elementary school, and she built and sustained a network of relationships around herself, at once the shelter in which I rested and the matrix of her work and thought. . . .

All my mother's arrangements, the choice of a nurse like the choice of a name, had the complicated quality of that kind of lacework that begins with a woven fabric from which threads are drawn and gathered, over which an embroidery is then laid, still without losing the integrity of the original weave. Thus, the choice of my nurse was both a solution to the problems of child care that would permit her her own professional life and an attempt to build a bridge between two cultural traditions and two styles of child rearing. At the same time, it was also a reference back to strategies developed by her own mother, who hired as domestics women with illegitimate children, allowing them to keep the children with them instead of being separated. Nanny, whose husband was long gone from the scene, had an adolescent daughter who lived with us and helped "amuse the baby." . . .

When Margaret added a detail to the pattern or made some innovation in the arrangement of life, she was expressing her awareness of how the details of any stable human way of life are linked, interacting in meeting needs and also resonating aesthetically. In a lifetime of rapid change and borrowing of cultural traits from one place to another, a lifetime in which there were continual rents opened in the fabric she worked with, she engaged in constant careful needlework in which repair and elaboration were indistinguishable. . . .

When Margaret planned for my care and feeding, she set out to combine the generosity of most primitive mothers, who nurse their infants when they cry and remain with them constantly, with the resource of civilization, the clock, and this too meant recording. She would record the hours at which I demanded feeding and then, by analyzing these times, construct a schedule from the order immanent in my own body's rhythms which would make the process predictable enough so she could schedule her classes and meetings and know when she should be home to feed me. I have the notebook that records these feeding times and other observations, as I also have the notebook in which my grandmother recorded her observations of the infant Margaret and the one in which I recorded my observations of my daughter, Vanni, while I went off between feedings to teach a seminar and analyze films of the interactions of other mothers with their children.

Margaret's ideas influenced the rearing of countless children, not only through her own writings but through the writings of Benjamin Spock, who was my pediatrician and for whom I was the first breastfed and "self-demand" baby he had encountered. If the weight of early experience is as great as we believe it to be, I belong to a generation that is chronologically some five years younger than I, psychologically one of the postwar babies although I was born in 1939. What Spock finally wrote about "self-demand" after the war, however, was not quite the same as the method Margaret developed, for

Spock advised mothers not to enforce a schedule immediately but to wait and shift infants gradually into the classic feeding times, rather than assuming they would develop and retain individual rhythms. . . .

I have wondered sometimes about her assurance, since she was doing things that were widely believed to be wrong or unhealthy for infants, calmly planning how to bully doctors and vamp nurses into allowing all sorts of irregularities at a time when most women find themselves easily bullied by those who represent medical authority. When Vanni* was born, I was enriched by my mother's confidence, becoming able in my turn to reject the kinds of advice that undermine breast-feeding and invade the intimacy of mother and child. It was splendid, for instance, to have Margaret robustly declare that it was rubbish that I should never nurse Vanni in bed for fear of dozing off and suffocating her, as all the nurses insisted. All around the world mothers and infants sleep side by side and the danger of suffocation arises mainly when mothers are drunk or sick, not under normal circumstances—it is the American habit of leaving an infant alone in a crib in a separate room that is at odds with the normal range of human behavior.

Some of her assurance came from having seen alternative ways of doing things, healthy mothers and infants thriving within a variety of different patterns. This range gave her a sense, behind the diversity, of what was essential, different from the assurance of those who take tradition as their only

*The author's daughter

base. She had been raised in a context of educational experimentation and she was working in a time of newly vivid awareness of the damage that could be done by Western and "modern" forms of child care, of the burdens of neurosis carried by members of her own generation. Indeed, she selected Spock as a pediatrician because he had been psychoanalyzed.

Nevertheless, she would have known that there were risks in her innovations. Details of infant care are helpful or harmful depending on the way they fit into the rest of experience. She often told stories of incongruous or incomplete cultural borrowing—a change in patterns of food preparation that leaves out an essential nutrient, or the way that many Western mothers, imitating other methods of child rearing, carry their infants on the right hip, making themselves unable to work and depriving the infant of their heartbeat. There is always the risk of crippling some basic biological capacity, as has been demonstrated in experiments with distortions of the infant experiences of monkeys or birds, which then grow up unable to mate or unable to care for their young. The more important risk was that some changed constellation of infant experience would set me at odds with my own society in subtle ways or leave me unable to adjust to later challenges, to fall in love, to care for a child, to function in relation to contemporaries whose early experiences were profoundly different from my own. I was inordinately proud, as a child, of having been a "self-demand baby," but in other periods I puzzled about whether I was different and whether there was something in my childhood that made it seem so difficult for me as an adolescent to blend in and be like everyone else.

It seems to me in retrospect that Margaret's willingness to make innovations came out of a certainty of her own love, a sense that she had been loved and could trust herself to love in turn, with a continuity of spontaneous feeling even where she was introducing variation. She was prepared to take responsibility because she did not suspect herself of buried ambivalence either toward me or toward her own parents. Indeed, in a life lived in an era of introspection and self-doubt, her conviction of undivided motives was distinctive, an innocence that leaves me sometimes skeptical and sometimes awed. Just as all of her commentaries about American culture and suggestions for alternative arrangements must be read against her general affirmation of the American tradition, so her sense of choosing her own style in child rearing was secured by her appreciation of her own childhood and her desire for motherhood, for she believed that these would protect her from destructive choices. She drew an immense freedom from her conviction that she had no inherent temptation to destruction and that the arrangements that best served her professional life, given her ingenuity, were in no inherent conflict with my welfare. Over the years this attitude was contrasted with cultural styles that depend upon a suspicion of one's own cruel or evil impulses, as English children are taught to be kind to animals because of the temptation of cruelty.

My mother and I used to discuss sometimes which

parts of her approach to child rearing seemed right in retrospect and which needed to be thought through again. Both of us felt comfortable about self-demand feeding and I followed her version with Vanni, but there were areas where more or less pattern seemed to me necessary. I argued with her, for instance, that pleasant as it is to have an unroutinized body in a society where others are dogged with concerns about "regularity," a little more routine would be useful—some points should be fixed in the day, if only so that one could, if necessary, remember to take medication on schedule. Thus, she never insisted that I brush my teeth because she had found the process unpleasant and painful as a child, so this was a routine I had to establish on my own, that required attention at a stage when most of my contemporaries did it automatically—but then, I don't suffer when some hitch in arrangements separates me from my toothbrush for twenty-four hours. Another area that we debated was sleep and how to arrive at a balance between a child's sense of her own needs and the patterns of the day. I resisted sleep all through my childhood, giving Vanni in turn much more leeway to find her own rhythms, and I teased Margaret at her inconsistency in not applying the concept of self-demand to sleep as well.

Margaret's childhood experience had made her different from others, but generally in ways that she found rewarding rather than alienating, and this was something she wanted to pass on. She spoke, for instance, of having been brought up by parents who were genuinely not racist and thus of not sharing in the residual guilt that others use to mobilize commitment. Similarly, I sometimes wish I could share more in the feminist anger of my contemporaries; but even though anger and guilt are useful in many situations, they carry great costs. There is no way finally that I can evaluate the extent of my own difference or how much this is related to infant experience. For it seems to me that all of us share to some degree in the experience of unintelligibility, sometimes feeling less than we might have been, or uncomfortable in our own skins and alien from those around us. I have always tended to look to the special circumstances of my childhood whenever I felt unhappy or lacking in confidence, and yet it is not reasonable to attribute a degree of estrangement that is part of the general human condition to a particular idiosyncratic experience. There is no form of human child rearing that does not leave an occasional residue of fear and yearning; these are part of a common inheritance matched in the wider culture by at least partial forms of solace, with as many forms of psychotherapy as there are forms of ritual and belief. In this country, too, difference is part of what we share. . . .

In relation to religion Margaret did not present me with a set of doctrines in which to believe, but set out to make sure that I knew what it would feel like to believe, for the great gap between those for whom faith is a living force and those for whom it is an irrelevance is not a disagreement about fact but an incommensurate way of experiencing.

When I think about the ways in which she chose to pass on her own deep commitment to Christianity in my childhood, I am struck by the fact that she rarely talked about either doctrine or personal prayer. We shared the narratives and poetry of religion: the stories of Jesus' life, reading the nativity narrative aloud each year from the Gospel of St. Luke, a child's book of psalms that she gave me for my birthday, called *Small Rain*, and mementos from her childhood like *A Child's Book of Saints and Friendly Beasts*, full of legends, mostly Irish, of saints in friendship with animals, weaned away from wildness. She arranged for me to spend many weekends with Aunt Marie, who took me with her to the Episcopal church and taught me the Lord's Prayer at bedtime without addressing the very complex relationship of participant and observer, metaphor and conviction that Margaret preferred not to try to spell out in her own faith.

She bought me beautiful postcard reproductions of Renaissance paintings of the gospels so that I could look at them rather than being bored during sermons, and as I grew older arranged that I sing in a children's choir instead of being bored during Sunday school. I think this was based on the conviction that much of religion is distorted by a misapprehension of the absolute seriousness and truth of metaphor as metaphor. The wordiness of sermon and Sunday school would both carry a distorted message, as if only prose could be true, a message she avoided for herself by dozing through sermons or by going to early morning services, since, in the Episcopal church, the early service has neither homily nor sermon. I went to church with her on the days of high drama, Good Friday and Easter and midnight mass at Christmas.

The Christian tradition was passed on to me as a great rich mixture, a bouillabaisse of human imagination and wonder brewed from the richness of individual lives, reduced down to a meager and tasteless minimum. She had a St. Christopher's medal on her key ring and preferred those Episcopal churches where the bent knee of genuflection and the hand moving in the sign of the cross would bridge doubt and separation. She never said, this is true, but instead, this is something I care about and enjoy, and taught me to follow the intricacies prescribed by tradition. She had, for example, a book of Holy Week services that had been given to her by her godmother, and on Good Friday we would go to the highest of high-church Episcopal parishes in New York. This was St. Mary the Virgin, which Luther Cressman's seminary classmates used to call "Smoky Mary's," saying that the bishop kept a car with the motor running outside his office so he could dash down and stop them from implementing some new detail of Anglo-Catholic ritual. It seems to me that she felt no deep necessity to comply in detail with tradition, but valued its completeness so that the mystery of the Passion was expressed in an aesthetic whole. The detailed wholeness of tradition mirrored a wholeness of commitment and confidence that she held at some deep and unarticulated level where care and communion were abiding certainties.

She had a confidence that the essential would be most likely to occur when it was embedded in rich human elaboration. The grace of that elaboration, the fact that it expressed aesthetic judgment as well as playfulness, in forms shaped and shared over time, would guarantee a certain integrity. She believed that decent and caring human relationships are sustained by courtesy. Thus, in talking about sexuality and about the functions of the human body, she clearly wanted me to be both proper—respectful of external forms—and free to play, pleased to be woman and unconstrained by gender. Being a female was fun. At the same time that I was taught that there were no limits to what women of intelligence and determination could achieve, I was taught to value being a woman, to value the scope that femininity gave for play and elaboration and to look forward to motherhood. I asked her once, as a small child, passing the General Theological Seminary, whether girls could be priests, and when she said no, I comfortably said, "Well, by the time I grow up they'll have invented girls being priests too." . . .

Margaret's approach to teaching about sex involved a certain balance that kept sexuality from becoming a pervasive concern. That was a period when some psychoanalytically "enlightened" parents were pressing children into an early and tense sense of sexual possibility. She wanted to avoid this. When Americans first read *Coming of Age in Samoa*, they read it as a description of a society characterized by complete permissiveness and free love, and one reviewer described Samoan behavior—with approval?—as almost promiscuous. But no one who rereads the book now, in the 1980s, should come away with that impression. Instead, you find what she describes in an unused section of draft manuscript for *Blackberry Winter* as "a certain degree of sexual permissiveness but not too much, for enjoined active sexuality may be as stressful as enjoined chastity; a willingness to let children and young people develop as slowly as they wished. . . ." The adolescents in Samoa say *Laititi a'u*, "I am but young," when pressed toward some form of precocity, sexual or otherwise. Against that background, the young Samoan girls who remained virgins were as much beneficiaries of the lack of pressure to make choices as those who formed liaisons.

One of the things Margaret emphasized was that the young girls were free to go out or not to amorous rendezvous. She cited this freedom as a possible explanation for the low rate of premarital pregnancy, suggesting that perhaps the young girls, free in their sense of their own bodies, knew when they were liable to become pregnant and simply did not go down to the shore. This choice might have freed them from the pressure to comply with the rhythms of male desire that for many American girls shapes their participation in adolescent social life. Even saying this, she was not able to say how the young girls would have known when they could safely go, but we know now that reproduction can largely be controlled through the "ovulation method" that depends not on calendars and thermometers but on women's willingness to note variations in the texture of their own vaginal secretions—and their option, rarer perhaps, to say no, not tonight.

Margaret was determined that I should grow up

with a feeling of friendliness toward my body, and particularly that I should have no negative feelings about menstruation. She was convinced that whole populations do not suffer from dysmenorrhea, or at least that in some groups the physical sensations associated with the beginning of a menstrual period are not normally identified as discomfort. She set out with considerable success to strike a consistently positive note, so she must have been deeply disappointed when I telephoned from California, where I was staying after my father's remarriage, to say that I had had my first period. I remember being mildly perplexed when his new wife, Betty, asked me whether I felt all right, whether I had any pains or nausea, and whether I really felt comfortable about proceeding on a planned camping trip with my father—wasn't I supposed to feel well? And for the first time I heard menstruation called "the curse."

By the next month when I joined my mother for the trip that took us to Australia for six months, she was able to pick up on her agenda. She labored in Hawaii to teach me to use tampons for she had found the invention of tampons tremendously liberating, hoping to bypass entirely the worries, embarrassments, and clumsiness of pads. Then I remember a day of sunshine somewhere in the country in Australia, with that lovely feeling of lightness that often comes two or three days into a menstrual period, and I skipped through the garden, saying how happy I felt, and she talked about feeling a possibility of love and birth and growth, all as kinds of giving, and about feeling a communion with nature in shared biological process. I remember thinking, "She's trying too hard," and feeling that my particular happiness was cheerful rather than mystical.

There is always the problem, in talking to children about sex, of making knowledge available without burdening them. She puzzled me, that day, by using a lot of imagery about other zones of the body, about how it feels to defecate and the pleasures of eating and kissing, which seemed simply irrelevant. It is curious to be able to look at that moment from two vantage points, myself as I was then and myself as I am now. I am sure that I responded politely, tolerant of what she was trying to do, but almost certainly she would have felt the lack of response in me as a withdrawal. At the same time, the moment remains in my memory and there seems to be a direct connection between what she said then and the conviction I have felt since that the menstrual cycle as experienced by women—and, secondhand, by men—might be one of the things that can shape our consciousness toward a sensitivity to the rhythms of natural systems.

I think there were two important underlying ideas in the way she talked about sex and the body. One was an effort to be clear and honest, using the proper scientific terms and avoiding that recurrent problem of sex education that goes round and round the central issue and leaves children wondering what in fact happens. The other was to keep a sense of romance, a warm positive glow touched with awe for the wonders of the human body and the varieties of pleasure it can give. . . .

She loathed the fact that the familiar set of four-letter words are used to express anger, so that she would speak of intercourse as making love rather than as fucking, not as a euphemism but as a precision. Indeed, able to be frank and explicit about sexual behavior as an anthropologist must be, and with no thrill of emancipation such as many people felt and still feel about blasphemy or four-letter words, she avoided ever using them casually. She taught me as I have tried to teach my daughter not to develop habits of language that might slip out automatically in a situation in which they would be felt as offensive. How we understand our bodies, and the ways in which human beings have tried to understand the universe, are simply too important to be littered through our conversations, ugly and out of place as beer bottles in the wilderness.

I grew up well informed but rather solemn about sex, going off with my girl friends to share information and heap scorn on the sniggering little boys who told the silly dirty jokes children tell, who were so immature about such a serious and important matter. Over the years as I grew up, it never occurred to me that sex had any continuing place in my mother's life, since she was not living with a husband, and I think the discretion she wished to preserve put everything at a distance and meant that little was actually conveyed of sex as playful. When I was a teen-ager she would make comments by which she was trying, it seemed to me, to make sure that I knew it was all right to enjoy sexuality in a variety of ways. By that time I had read enough books not to bother to pick up the bait—after all, questions of sexuality and gender were one of the main topics of the household and I browsed in prepublication copies of the Kinsey reports. Good taste was equally important, however, and that included a certain reticence.

FAYE MOSKOWITZ's A Leak in the Heart: Tales from a Woman's Life, *the source of the following selection, consists of twenty-four autobiographical story-essays about growing up part of an unassimilated Jewish Orthodox family in small-town Jackson, Michigan, in the 1930s and '40s. Faye Moskowitz's mother—indeed, all the matriarchs in the author's life—appear in these pieces as tough, infuriating, and loving forces who shape the author's sensibility in her roles as young mother, activist, college student, teacher, and wonderful writer. Some of these essays began as "Hers" columns in* The New York Times. *Moskowitz lives in Washington, D.C., with her husband, where they have raised four children. When* A Leak in the Heart *was published in 1985, Russell Baker called it "a lovely book, beautifully written, the kind that makes you want to grab your friends, say Hey, listen to this, and start reading aloud."*

Faye Moskowitz
from
A LEAK IN THE HEART

My mother came to America in the twenties in the last of the hopeful waves of immigrants. If she ever felt oppressed in her role as a female, she never communicated it to me. I think she was far too busy adapting to the ways of her adopted country to bother with any such ideas.

When I was a child, the mothers of my friends, like my own mother, stayed home and kept house. It was hard enough for men to find work during the Depression. Married women coped with their husband's shrunken paychecks—or often no paycheck at all. They put up and let down pant cuffs and hems until the material fell apart, stretched the stew until finding the meat became a game, and sent us to school so well-scrubbed we squeaked.

No matter how little we had, my mother refused to allow us to consider ourselves in want. I remember vividly a visit to an aunt's house when I was about five years old. We all sat in the summer kitchen while my mother and her sister chattered endlessly about things that didn't interest me, and I whined and whined, complaining that I was hungry.

252

I couldn't understand why I was offered nothing to eat or why my mother kept motioning me to be quiet. Finally my aunt said, "Sweetheart, how about some bread and milk?"

By this time I really was hungry, and angry too, and I shouted, "Only poor people eat bread and milk."

I'll never forget my mother's face and how fiercely she said to me, "Don't you ever call us poor. We are not poor. Only people who have no hope are poor."

No, my mother would not consider us poor. Wasn't this the Promised Land? In spite of everything, she would make certain the promise was kept. She perceived America as a land where both men and women were capable of unlimited goals. Barriers were everywhere for her, yet she always found a way, if not through them, then around them.

Even though she was having her own crisis of faith, she doggedly insisted that I be proud of my religion in a little town where to profess my Judaism was to mark myself as different from everybody else. At a time in my life when I would have sold my soul in exchange for being 'Piscopalian like my friend Eileen, my mother coaxed me into carrying a box of matzo to school so I could give my classmates an explanation of Passover.

The year I was in sixth grade, one of my teachers decided to put together a school program on the concept of "America as the Melting Pot." She pounced on me eagerly, of course. "Won't you contribute something to the program?" she asked.

My stomach lurched in misery. I didn't want to be different, no matter what my mother believed.

I received no sympathy at home. My mother stared at me incredulously when I told her of my reluctance to be singled out. "For five thousand years the Jews have been persecuted because of their faith, and you want to hide your heritage," she scolded. "Go to school and sing them Hatikvoh and be proud of what you are."

"Mama," I said. "What if I sing off key? You know what happens when I get nervous."

She looked at me for a long moment and then she laughed. "How many people in your school know the Hebrew National Anthem?"

"No one," I said.

Triumphantly she pushed the bangs off my worried forehead. "Then who will know if you sing off key?"

Amateur psychology it certainly was, but it worked. Some weeks later, fortified by my mother's advice, I stood in the little assembly room of the T. A. Wilson School while my heart stopped thumping long enough for me to hear the stirring anthem— absolutely on key—ring out over the heads of my schoolmates sitting cross-legged on the floor to their mothers sitting behind them on wooden folding chairs. But my mother, hands clasped in her lap, eyes shining, was the only person I saw.

My mother died in 1948 without ever having seen a television set. My daughter, who was born two years later, watched men walk on the moon while she brushed her teeth one morning. If she has difficulty conceiving of my mother's world, how could my mother ever have conceived of hers?

Yet my mother's life provides me with a good road map into the next generation, if for no other reason than that the detours and dead ends are marked for me. She taught me to hold America to its promise. She had great expectations and no intention of letting her adopted country off the hook. But she also taught me what any Jewish mother knows: a country, just like a child, needs a shove in the right direction sometimes.

DERVLA MURPHY *was born in Ireland in 1931, of Dublin parents. Her father was the County Waterford librarian, and when she had to leave school at fourteen to keep house and nurse her invalid mother, she was not at all upset. Her ambitions had always been to write and travel, so she continued her education by reading, with occasional breaks to explore the Continent on a bicycle. Her mother's death left her free to go farther afield and in 1963 she cycled to India. There she worked with Tibetan refugee children, before returning home for a year to write her first two books. She has cycled extensively through India, Nepal, and the Andes, now in the company of her own daughter. Her books include* Full Tilt: Ireland to India with a Bicycle, A Place Apart, *for which she received the Christopher Ewart-Biggs Memorial Prize in 1978, and the source of the following selection,* Wheels Within Wheels, *a memoir of her first thirty years. Benedict Kiely called it "a book to give strength to the weakest of us and courage to the most timid." As much as anything, this book celebrates the courage and spunky individuality of the writer's mother; and in her own life and in her writing, the daughter has lived up to her legacy.*

Dervla Murphy
from
WHEELS WITHIN WHEELS

At 7.45 on the morning of November 28, 1931, a young woman in the first stage of labour was handed by her husband into Lismore's only hackney-car. The couple were slowly driven east to Cappoquin along a narrow road, in those days potholed and muddy. It was a mild, still, moist morning. During the journey a pale dawn spread over the Blackwater valley, a place as lovely in winter as in summer—a good place to be born.

The woman had waist-length chestnut hair, wavy, glossy and thick. Her features were classically regular, her wide-set eyes dark blue, her complexion had never known—or needed—cosmetics. She had an athletic build, with shoulders too broad for feminine grace. On the previous day, impatient because the baby was a week late, she had walked fifteen miles. . . .

Although my mother's recovery was rapid we were not allowed home until December 12. Then my first journey took me through countryside that had scarcely changed since Thackeray described it in 1842: 'Beyond Cappoquin, the beautiful Black-

258

water river suddenly opened before us, and driving along it for three miles through some of the most beautiful rich country ever seen, we came to Lismore. Nothing certainly can be more magnificent than this drive. Parks and rocks covered with the grandest foliage; rich handsome seats of gentlemen in the midst of fair lawns and beautiful bright plantations and shrubberies; and at the end, the graceful spire of Lismore church, the prettiest I have seen in or, I think, out of Ireland. Nor in any country that I have visited have I seen a view more noble—it is too rich and peaceful to be what is called romantic, but lofty, large and *generous*, if the term may be used; the river and banks as fine as the Rhine; the castle not as large but as noble and picturesque as Warwick. As you pass the bridge, the banks stretch away on either side in amazing verdure, and the castle walks remind one somewhat of the dear old terrace of St Germains, with its groves, and long, grave avenues of trees.' . . .

During the first year of my life the steep climb up to Ballinaspic was among my mother's favourite walks. ("Sure the creature must be mad entirely to be pushin' a pram up there!") Yet by November 1932 she could push me no further than the Main Street. Suddenly she had been attacked again by that rheumatoid arthritis which had first threatened her at the age of twenty. By my first birthday she could no longer walk without the aid of a stick and by my second she could no longer walk at all. On the 29th of that December she was twenty-six.

There was of course no cure. But doctors in various countries were doggedly experimenting and, escorted by her favourite brother, my mother went to England, Italy and Czechoslovakia for six months, pretending to hope yet sure, inwardly, that she would never walk again. She spent the whole of 1934 either abroad or in Dublin, leaving me to be looked after by Nora under the vague supervision of my father. In theory this abrupt and inexplicable disappearance of an adored mother, when I was at the crucial age of two years, should have damaged me for life. Perhaps it has, but I am never troubled by the scars. I was by nature adaptable, my routine was unbroken, Nora was devoted and sensible and my father was attentive in his didactic way. (A family legend, possibly apocryphal but very revealing, tells of his bewildered grief when I failed, at the age of two and a half, to assimilate the rules governing the solar system.)

In December 1934 my mother returned to Lismore as a complete cripple, unable even to walk from the sitting-room to the downstairs lavatory, or to wash or dress herself, or to brush her hair. Between them, my father and the steadfast Nora cared for her and for me.

Now there were major money worries. My mother's search for a cure had cost a great deal and my father was heavily in debt to numerous relatives. Both my parents found this deeply humiliating, innocent though they were of any imprudence or extravagance. My father was almost panic-stricken and it was my mother who calmly took up the challenge. Probably a practical crisis, and the discovery of her own unsuspected ability to manage money, helped her at this stage. She soon began to enjoy poundstretching; I still have some of the little account books in which she neatly entered every penny spent on food, fuel, clothes, rent and so on. My father then happily returned to his natural money-ignoring state and for the rest of their married life my mother held the purse-strings.

By this time my parents had realised that they could have no more children, which for devout Roman Catholics meant resigning themselves to an unnaturally restricted marriage. In our sex-centred world, this may seem like the setting for a life-long nightmare. Having been thoroughly addled by popular pseudo-Freudian theories about libidos, repressions and fixations, we tend to forget that human beings are not animals. It would be ridiculous to suggest that the ending of their sexual relationship imposed no strain on my parents, but they certainly found it a lighter burden than we might think. Religious beliefs strong enough to make sexual taboos seem acceptable, as 'God's will', do not have to be merely negative; faith of that quality can generate the fortitude necessary for the contented observance of such taboos. Restrictions of personal liberty are destructive if accepted only through superstitious fear, but to both my parents the obeying of God's laws, as interpreted by the Holy Roman Catholic Church, was part of a rich and vigorous spiritual life. This area of their experience—I felt later on—put them in a mental and emotional world remote from my own, where they were equipped with an altogether different set of strengths and weaknesses.

Not long before her death, my mother told me that after getting into bed on their wedding night neither of my parents had known quite what to do next. So they went to sleep. In the 1970s it is hard to believe that two healthy, intelligent human beings, who were very much in love, could have devoted their wedding night exclusively to sleep. But perhaps they were not exceptional among their breed and generation. My mother had been curtly informed by her mother—who had borne seven children and endured countless miscarriages—that sexual intercourse was at all times painful and distasteful. And my father would certainly have considered any investigation of the subject, even in theory, to be grossly improper before marriage.

Sex apart, an inability to have more children was agonising for someone as intensely maternal as my mother. It also put me, at once, in danger. All the emotion and interest that should have been shared among half-a-dozen became mine only. By the time I was five most people considered me a peculiarly nasty child and mistook the reason why. In fact my mother was such a strict disciplinarian that throughout childhood and adolescence I remained healthily afraid of arousing her anger. But what she could not avoid—my being the sole object of her maternal concern—was the encouragement of a ruthless egotism. However, this trait was no doubt useful at the time as insulation against the adult suffering around me. Elizabeth Bowen once wrote, 'Perhaps children are sterner than grown-up people in their refusal to suffer, in their refusal, even, to feel at all.' My mother—reading *Bowen's Court*—once drew my attention to that remark. She did not comment on it, but I have since wondered if she meant it to comfort me. During childhood, I never stopped to sympathise with my parents' situation. Indeed, only when I became a mother myself did I appreciate how my own mother must have felt when she found herself unable to pick me up and hug me, and brush my hair, and tuck me up in bed.

After my parents' deaths I came upon the letters they had written to each other, almost daily, during their six-month engagement. On the whole these might have been written by any happy young couple to whom marriage promised nothing but fulfilment. My father hoped to found a model county library service and write novels; with my mother to inspire him he felt certain these must be masterpieces. For relaxation he looked forward to some deep-sea fishing and an expanding record collection. My mother hoped to have six children at two-year intervals (three of each, if possible, though she conceded this might be difficult to arrange) and to use them—one gathered, reading between the lines—as guinea-pigs on which to test her various theories about physical and mental health. She also hoped to find time to study in depth, under my father's guidance, the early schisms within the Christian Church—a subject of ineffable tedium to which she remained addicted all her life. She felt, too, that in her role as county librarian's wife she should initiate a Literary Debating Society (she had not yet visited the town) and perhaps a Music Society. For relaxation she looked forward to walking tours in West Cork and Kerry, presumably on her own while my father deep-sea fished and their systematically increasing offspring were being looked after by some capable Treasure. This correspondence had just one surprising feature. Neither of my penniless parents ever mentioned money, or promotion, or buying a house or a motor-car, or in any way planning financially for the future. Both seemed to assume that they would spend the rest of their lives in Lismore—my father wrote ecstatic descriptions of the surrounding countryside—and judging by these letters they were utterly without material ambition. . . .

In November 1936 my father at last found a house to rent at a price we could afford. It was on the South Mall, Lismore's most respectable street, but the dwelling itself was so irreparably decrepit that no modern squatter would stay there overnight. Short of a leaking roof, it suffered from every defect buildings are heir to and, for the next twenty-one years, it decayed—usually quietly, but occasionally dramatically—about our ears. Dating from the 1820s, it was two-storeyed, semi-detached and covered in Virginia creeper. The fanlight and wooden porch were attractive, a pair of romantic stone urns graced the front garden and overgrown fuchsia-bushes billowed on either side of the hall door. The well-proportioned rooms had good marble mantelpieces and mock-Adam ceilings and the wide hall was tiled in cream and dull red—pleasant, old-fashioned, indestructible tiles. However, some past tenant with execrable taste had left the whole place superficially hideous. The hall was painted a dead laurel green, only relieved by irregular patches of yellow-grey mildew where the plaster had fallen off. (For years I was fascinated by those patches, seeing them as maps of undiscovered countries.) The staircase was covered with cracked red and blue linoleum which ill-matched the magnificent mahogany banisters. Upstairs were five rooms: three large bedrooms, a boxroom which became my playroom and another large room, complete with fireplace, which at some remote period had been converted into a bathroom. The bath stood on four gigantic iron lion's paws and resembled a modern child's swimming-pool. It was patriotically stained green and orange and had a shower-device, of considerable antiquarian interest, near the ceiling. This had become viciously perverted and it sprayed, with tremendous force, only onto the opposite wall. When my father had forgotten to warn three successive guests he put up a notice saying 'Please do not touch'. The lavatory also had its notice, to explain that the chain needed three morse-like pulls: long–short–long. The wash-basin could almost have been used as a bath and was without a plug: apparently none to fit it had been manufactured since the turn of the century. Had my father exerted himself he could, at the cost of a few pence, have remedied this and many other defects. But the idea of personally improvising a wash-basin plug—or anything else—would never have entered his mind and he judged our numerous discomforts too trivial to warrant expensive expert attention.

Throughout the house we found peeling beige woodwork and wallpaper that had faded to a uniform grey-brown. Everywhere the paper was coming unstuck and in the dining-room rats had eaten through it at several points, thus demonstrating the fragility of the basic structure. Dry-rot afflicted the floor boards and some other sort of rot caused the ground-floor ceilings to snow gently if anyone walked about too vigorously overhead. This perhaps explains why I have always moved rather lightly for one of my build.

At the end of the hall a semi-glazed door led to a narrow, dark, flagged passage with ominously bulging henna-distempered walls. Having passed a storeroom, a pantry and a larder one entered the kitchen. Here sly draughts sneaked up from damp non-foundations through gaps between ancient flags, and blatant draughts whined through the slits between rotting window frames and rattling panes. The roughly plastered walls were an evil shade of green and a temperamental coal-range stood in an alcove. A row of discoloured pewter bells hung high above the door; in our day these never responded to the relevant buttons being pushed but they emitted ghostly chimes when gales blew. A dozen iron hooks suspended from the rafters—"The better to hang yourself on my dear," observed my mother as she toured her new home. In one corner a steep ladder-stairs led through a trap-door to an attic where the servants would have slept in the Bad Old Days. An adult could stand upright only in the middle of the attic room and this retreat soon became one of my Private Paradises.

Behind the house were several collapsing stables and, beyond a wide cobbled yard, stood Lismore's recently opened cinema, the property of our landlord, who lived next door. It was enormous and no one could tell us what purpose it had originally served; it may have been a series of barns whose internal walls had been demolished. Mercifully our landlord did not prosper as a film-wallah and within a few years the local doctor had built a new 'Palladium'. Then the old cinema became another of my Private Paradises; in semi-darkness I leapt from row to row of moth-eaten red plush seats, being pursued by imaginary cannibals and collecting swarms of real fleas. These were not found tolerable by my mother, even when identified by me as rare tropical insects picked up while exploring in New Guinea.

Beyond the cinema were our garden and orchard, half an acre of wilderness which, despite consistent neglect, provided us for many years with an abundance of loganberries, gooseberries, apples and pears. At intervals my mother would remark on the advantages of growing one's own vegetables. Then my father would borrow some implements and might on the following Saturday be observed reclining beside a minute pile of cut brambles reading Plato's *Theaetetus* or the latest Dorothy Sayers. Like myself, he lacked the urge to cultivate. Our genes have perhaps resisted change since the Age of the Gatherers.

Although our new home was very nearly a ruin we tolerated it for the next twenty-one years. My mother must have abhorred these slum-like surroundings but she refrained, as always, from complaining about the inevitable. For a rent of ten shillings a week one couldn't, even in Lismore in the 1930s, expect very much.

The rent was so low not only because of the house's dilapidation but because of the previous tenant's suicide in the dining-room. This snag considerably influenced my destiny since it made it far harder to engage local maid-servants, or to persuade those who came from a distance to remain in residence. It was not that any ghost operated—at least to our knowledge—but the neighbourhood vociferously believed that a suicide without a consequent haunting was against nature.

As a child I always knew there was nothing to spare for non-essentials. But I was never hungry or cold so it did not occur to me to interpret this condition as poverty. Nor did I ever long for the unobtainable, with one spectacular exception—a pony of my own. And since that desire so clearly belonged to the realm of fantasy it caused me no discontent. In Dublin I enjoyed the luxury toys of my cousins—rocking-horses, tricycles, pedal motor-cars and the like—yet I never asked or even wished for such things. They belonged to another sort of person who lived in another sort of world. And it was not a world I should have cared to inhabit permanently. It had no rivers, fields, woods, moors and mountains. . . .

As I seem always to have known the facts of life I assume they were simply absorbed from my mother during that phase of obsessional questioning when everything in nature arouses a child's curiosity. I therefore find it hard to understand the difficulties that even in this explicit age are said to surround basic sex instruction by parents. It is far easier to explain to a three-year-old how babies are made than to explain the processes whereby bread or sugar appear on the table.

By the age of six I was a proficient and dedicated masturbator and someone—probably Old Brigid—had infected me with an acute guilt complex about this hobby. So I consulted my mother, who said the activity in question was certainly not a matter to worry about. It was a babyish habit and quite soon I would grow out of it—just as I had grown out of wetting my bed. These remarks must have had the intended effect. Guilt evaporated and in time the 'babyish' habit was superseded by more cerebral sexual interests centred on scientific investigations of the male anatomy.

I was about seven when an outraged neighbour complained to my mother that I had been seen, on the public street, removing a little boy's shorts and examining him from every angle. All I can now remember is the colour and texture of this four-year-old's shorts. They had been knitted from coarse burgundy-coloured wool and as he wore no under-pants I pitied him, reasoning that he must feel miserably scratchy.

The fact that this scene took place on the Main Street—"in broad daylight", as our neighbour several times emphasised unconsciously implying that had it taken place in a dark corner it would have been less culpable—the fact that this could have happened shows how well my parents had thus far protected me from Irish puritanism. But there are limits. The time had come to risk unhealthy repression and my mother told me that never again must I do such a thing because little boys are very sensitive to the cold around that area, and could get a bad chill if stripped in the open air. I was not, of course, deceived. I had got the message that the relevant area merited special treatment and indeed was, for some utterly incomprehensible reason, Taboo. This

new awareness gave the physiological differences
between boys and girls an extra fascination; but my
investigations, from now on, were more discreet.

Soon Providence favoured me; newcomers took
the house opposite and within hours it became ap-
parent that their eight-year-old son was a professional exhibitionist. He had perfected a variety of
ingenious urinating techniques and his penis was
public property. We were an ideally suited couple.
He performed, I admired, and it occurred to neither of us that his penis could be put to other uses.
Almost certainly he was ignorant of the mechanics
of reproduction, as he was without curiosity about
the female anatomy (he had five sisters). And it
would no more have occurred to me to initiate an
experiment than to smoke a cigarette. In my mind a
clear line was drawn between the activities of grown-
ups and children, and for all my defiance I was
never tempted to cross this line prematurely. The
world was organised in a certain way. There was a
pattern and one felt no impulse to disarrange it. . . .

The neighbours quite often found Murphy standards unacceptable. I was seven when three small
girls—sisters—were forbidden to play with me because I had assured them that every night a lion
slunk across the rooftops of Lismore, hunting the
crows which nested in the chimneys, roaring at the
stars just to show he was very fierce and fighting
with an orang-utan who lived in the cathedral bel-
fry. Nightmares resulted and the parish priest received a formal complaint about my pernicious
untruthfulness. When Father Power relayed this complaint to my parents they made no attempt to con-

ceal their amusement. But my mother cautioned me against further terrorising of my contemporaries and advised me to write such stories down in future instead of telling them, as it were, in the market-place.

Thus began an enduring custom; every year I wrote long stories for my parents' birthday and Christmas presents. Only one of these survives, written when I was eight. In about three thousand mis-spelt words it describes the adventures of two boys in a jungle that, judging by the available fauna, extended from Peru to Siberia. Having throttled a sabre-toothed tiger with their bare hands, rescued a shepherd's baby from a condor and killed an ana-conda with a poisoned dart my heroes returned to Ireland by an unspecified route and lived happily ever after.

In a letter to her father-in-law my mother re-ported that when I was four—not yet able to read—I picked up a Little Grey Rabbit book and pointing to the author's name on the title-page said, "When I'm grown up I'm going to write books and have my name there." My mother commented, "I think she means it. She is a very decided and determined child." This comment was probably regarded as the typical effusion of a doting mother, but it was cor-rect. I did mean it. And I went on meaning it though none of my literary efforts, during child-hood or adolescence, showed any trace of promise.

I preferred not to discuss my ambition with anyone—it was tacitly understood between my par-ents and myself—and from the age of about twelve I was well aware that I might follow in my father's and grandfather's footsteps and be a failed writer. But this did not deter me. I was not thinking in terms of success or failure, prosperity or poverty, fame or obscurity. To me writing was not a career but a necessity. And so it remains, though I am now, technically, a professional writer. The strength of this inborn desire to write has always baffled me. It is understandable that the really gifted should feel an overwhelming urge to use their gift; but a strong urge with only a slight gift seems almost a genetic mistake.

My parents naturally approved of these literary ambitions. Yet to have encouraged me too enthusiastically, in the absence of any discernible talent, would have been irresponsible. Fortunately my mother enjoyed nothing more than being a literary critic. Everything she read was dissected and an ill-written book, endured for the sake of the subject matter, made her look quite haggard. An aspiring writer could ask for no more suitable mother and after a tactful interval—never look a gift story in the syntax—my parents' Christmas and birthday presents would reappear to be torn phrase from phrase. During these sessions I sat beside my mother like the most docile of Victorian daughters, attentively absorbing her every suggestion. This was the one area in which I did not spurn adult advice. . . .

At about this time I was suddenly afflicted by an irrational terror of darkness. Electricity had not yet come to Lismore; at dusk the lamp-lighter went up and down the South Mall and Old Brigid lit the oil lamps and closed and barred the shutters and drew the curtains and, when I had been put to bed at seven o'clock, darkness was, officially, final. However, for reading illicitly I had a secret supply of candles and matches and my new terror was revealed to myself when I forgot, one evening, to smuggle these in from my playroom. The playroom door was a mere three steps away, across the landing, yet I felt sick with fear at the thought of venturing out into the total, silent blackness. Inevitably I then saw myself as a most despicable coward, a craven sissy, a lily-livered, weak-kneed, spineless rotter.

This terror quickly became a phobia that dominated all my waking hours. Sometimes I was tempted to confide in my mother, but pride inhibited me. As the days passed my dread of bedtime increased; this had become my regular test of courage and always I failed it. At breakfast-time I might have successfully persuaded myself that, that very evening, I would do what had to be done. Yet when the moment came, when Old Brigid and my father had said good-night and kissed me and gone, I simply lay listening to the mealtime noises in the dining-room below while little shivers of shame ran through my body. Night after night, I told myself that within minutes this torment could be ended—if I found the necessary courage.

Then one very cold evening I did find it. I slipped out of bed, tip-toed to the door and began a deliberately slow tour of the whole of the first floor—including the airing cupboard and attic, which to many seemed quite spooky even by daylight. I moved silently through the dense blackness, my hands outstretched to guide me, and the thudding of my heart seemed to hurt my ribs. Something odd happened to my sense of time and the ordeal seemed to be taking place outside the normal framework of hours and minutes. But it was worth it. When I got back to my bedroom my self-respect was restored and all fear of darkness exorcised forever.

On most issues, at this period, I did confide in my mother. Yet already my attitude towards her was habitually guarded; while half of me needed comfort and guidance the other half was suspicious of interference. From my father I had inherited a certain shyness or gaucherie or tendency towards self-effacement—to this day I am not sure of the exact nature of the trait—and this was aggravated by observation of a woman who always seemed at ease in every sort of situation. Unwittingly, my mother gave me an inferiority complex I was never to outgrow. I recognised and took for granted the fact that in looks, intelligence and poise she set a standard I could never hope to reach and for years I heroine-worshipped her. Yet I may also have unconsciously envied her capacity to inspire such devotion—not only in myself but in many others. 'A magnetic personality' is the stock phrase. And as a child I expended a disproportionate amount of energy on testing myself against the power of that magnet.

SYLVIA TOWNSEND WARNER, *the celebrated English author, was born in Middlesex, England, in 1893. Her first novel,* Lolly Willowes, *published in 1926, was the first selection of the newly founded Book-of-the-Month Club. Miss Warner is perhaps best known as a short-story writer, and many of her stories in the past four decades have appeared in* The New Yorker. *At the time of her death, in 1978, she had published eight collections of short stories, seven novels, six volumes of poetry, and a biography of the novelist T. H. White. In her long career she never wrote a memoir; from the 1930s to the 1970s, however, she did contribute a series of short reminiscences to* The New Yorker, *which eventually became the full-length book* Scenes of Childhood. *The selection that follows is, in style and content, a comic tribute to a mother's pluck and persistence against a background of worldwide stupidity. The implication is, of course, that had the author's mother been in charge during those catastrophic years of 1914–1918 such monumental waste and inefficiency would never have occurred.*

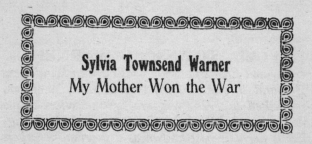

Sylvia Townsend Warner
My Mother Won the War

I think it is pretty generally admitted that my mother
won the last war.* By generally admitted I do not
mean officially recognized. Offical recognition would
have involved many difficulties. Admirals and Field-
Marshals, for instance, who had spent their lives in
the study of warfare, and panted into their sixties
towards the happy day when those studies might be
let loose in practice, might well have been piqued if
the honours had been unpinned from them and
fastened on a middle-aged civilian lady of the upper
middle-classes. There were the Allied Nations to
consider, too. And though my mother would have
been quite prepared to become a second Helen of
Troy, getting along with it in her spare time when
she wasn't busy with her rock garden, her ward-
robe, her housekeeping, and her water colours, it
was thought best to leave things as they were.

It always seems to me a convincing testimony to
my mother's part in the last war that the legend that
the last war was won by somebody's mother is so

*From *Scenes of Childhood*. The author is of course referring to the
Great War of 1914–1918.

276

widespread. I have met any amount of familes with the same belief. They believe it about their mothers, not mine. But legend is like that. A truth is spread around, then it gets corrupted. And the great truth that my mother won the last war passed in this manner into the larger rumour that the last war was won by somebody's mother. The fact that people get the mother wrong does not invalidate the archetypal truth.

My mother won the last war in November, 1914. There was a British Red Cross depot in our town, where ladies met to scrape lint, roll bandages, pick over moss for stomach-wound dressings, and make shirts and pyjamas. The lady in charge was a Mrs. Moss-Henry, and when my mother offered her services, Mrs. Moss-Henry set her to cutting out pyjama trousers.

There was a pattern, supplied by the Red Cross authorities, and though it wasn't as good as my mother could have made it, still, it wasn't too bad, and my mother followed it. Maybe she introduced a few improvements, but she didn't win the war on these, so I won't waste time over them.

The next time she went, my mother was surprised when the pyjama trousers she had cut out and handed over to the seamstresses were returned to her. She inquired the reason for this from a fellow-worker who was cutting out pyjama jackets.

'Mrs. Moss-Henry asked me to ask you if you would mind marking where the button and buttonhole are to be.'

'Button?' exclaimed my mother. 'Buttonhole? Ridiculous! The woman's a fool!'

My mother has a decisive mind, a mind that goes straight to essentials. She realized at once that, as the pyjama trousers were made to be fastened by a cord passing through a slot, the addition of a button and buttonhole halfway down the opening was redundant. The other cutter, one of those dull, faithful souls who can only do as they are told, repeated, 'That's what Mrs. Moss-Henry said.'

My mother brooded for a while, but not for long. Five minutes or so. Then, gathering up the pyjama trousers, she rushed from the room in search of Mrs. Moss-Henry.

'I'm not going to mark these trousers for buttons,' she declared. 'It's totally unnecessary.'

Mrs. Moss-Henry, in a very autocratic manner, said that she would be glad if my mother marked the trousers for buttons. It would enable the seamstresses, she said, to know where to sew them on.

My mother explained, clearly, why buttons were redundant. There were no buttons on the pattern which she had been supplied by the Red Cross, she said.

Mrs. Moss-Henry said that it was a paper pattern, unsuited for supporting buttons under hard usage. But buttons had been specified, and must be affixed.

My mother again and categorically registered her protest, and was going on with some good reasons when Mrs. Moss-Henry pretended to hear the telephone bell, and left the room. My mother remained a while with the moss-pickers, amplifying her position. Was it not an outrage, she asked, that our fighting men, who had gone so cheerfully and gallantly to the defence of their country, should,

when they came all glorious with wounds into the
Red Cross hospitals, be insulted by being buttoned
into their pyjama trousers like little boys? Had they
not suffered enough for their country and their dear
ones left behind? Must they, weak and in pain, be
teased with buttoning and unbuttoning themselves?
Many of them, she added, would be too weak to do
up buttons, anyway.

Some of the moss-pickers agreed with my mother,
some sided with Mrs. Moss-Henry. But none were
indifferent; they realized that this was a crucial matter. My mother pursued Mrs. Moss-Henry into the
bandage-room, and again attacked her.

This time Mrs. Moss-Henry was positively rude
to my mother. She said, with a falsely sweet air,
that perhaps my mother, as a civilian, was accus-
tomed to civilian pyjamas. Mrs. Moss-Henry's husband had been an Army man, and this enabled
Mrs. Moss-Henry to assure my mother that buttons
were in order.

The blood of her uncle, who was a brigadier
general in the Sudan, boiled in my mother's veins.
It was one of those moments when deeds speak
louder than words and tearing the pyjama trousers
from Mrs. Moss-Henry's grasp she flapped them to
and fro in her face.

Mrs. Moss-Henry again retreated. My mother
stayed a while with the bandage-rollers, pointing
out that even though Mrs. Moss-Henry had passed
so much of her life on a baggage wagon, that did
not warrant her trying to boss everything and everybody. Some more arguments then occurred to her,
and she went off after Mrs. Moss-Henry.

This running battle continued through the morning. Finally Mrs. Moss-Henry locked herself in the lavatory. My mother, careless of the ridicule to which the position exposed her, stood outside the lavatory haranguing Mrs. Moss-Henry through the door, and the other Red Cross ladies stood around, some silently supporting my mother, some silently supporting Mrs. Moss-Henry. At last the combatants dispersed for lunch.

On the morrow my mother, after a sleepless night, returned to the struggle. She found a new force to contend with. Mrs. Moss-Henry, while refusing to give battle, had set up a peculiarly insidious propaganda, designed to belittle my mother's achievements, tarnish her laurels, and undermine any future advance. This propaganda took the form of suggesting that it was not really all that important whether the pyjama trousers had buttons or no; and a specious plea was made that the output of the workers would suffer if my mother continued to make such a fuss about nothing. During the previous morning, it was alleged, the Red Cross ladies had either done no work at all or worked less well than usual. Their attention had been distracted. Mrs. Cory, for instance, had sewn sleeves into the necks of pyjama jackets instead of into the armholes; and the garments in question were produced, with striped-flannel factory chimneys extending where turn-down collars should have been, as an example of the sort of thing which might be looked for unless my mother gave up attacking Mrs. Moss-Henry.

My mother instantly saw through these misrepresentations. Sleeves in the wrong place, she said,

were no worse than buttons where no buttons need
be. If output was so important, then time was important, too. Nothing wasted time more than em-
broidering needless buttonholes to corroborate
buttons that were perfectly unnecessary. For her
part, she would never grudge time devoted to our
splendid soldiers; it was on their behalf, and for
their comfort, that she had joined issue with Mrs.
Moss-Henry over the buttons, and she considered it
time well spent.

When one of the Moss-Henry minions squirmingly
alleged that, after all, the buttons need not incom-
mode the wounded soldiers, for if they found it
tiresome to button their pyjama trousers they could
leave them unbuttoned, my mother demolished this
in an instant. If the buttons were there, regulations
to enforce buttoning would be there too. Everyone
knew that military-hospital discipline was like that.

Mrs. Moss-Henry entered the room.

'Not still talking about buttons, surely?'

Her tone was sarcastic. My mother replied with
firmness, 'I am.'

Mrs. Moss-Henry feigned a yawn.

'I really don't think we want to hear any more
about them.'

'You will!' riposted my mother. 'This afternoon I
am going to Devonshire House.'

Such words struck awe into every hearer. Devonshire House was the Ark of the Covenant, and the
Lion's Jaws. It was the headquarters of the British
Red Cross, it was in Piccadilly, and it had been lent
to the Red Cross by a duke.

Naturally, my mother put on her best clothes. At

the station she was surprised to see Mrs. Moss-Henry, who had put on her best clothes also. Two other ladies—one apiece—completed the deputation. The suburban train took half an hour to get them into London. It was crowded and the four ladies were obliged to travel together, though in silence. Sometimes Mrs. Moss-Henry consulted the papers which she carried in a large portfolio.

My mother had no papers to consult. Instead, she gazed at Mrs. Moss-Henry's hat with an annoying air of unconcern.

The marble hall of Devonshire House was crowded with people waiting for interviews. There was a terrific air of splendour and organization. Secretaries darted to and fro. The two supporters of the deputation began, after a while, to stare about them and whisper, identifying among the waiting throng many stately profiles of England which they had seen in the society papers. Mrs. Moss-Henry behaved as though the aristocracy were nothing to her. So did my mother.

After an hour or so, they were summoned into a large room with desks all round it. Behind each desk was a lady, and each lady was rustling papers. It was as though one stood on some majestic seashore. Their allotted lady gave them a gracious smile, and told them that they were from the Mutton Hill depot. They agreed to this.

As an act of courtesy to the Red Cross organization which had, however misguidedly, placed Mrs. Moss-Henry at the head of the Mutton Hill depot, my mother allowed her to speak first. She spoke next.

The lady behind the desk looked grave; it was obvious that my mother's fearless eloquence had made an impression on her. She said she thought she had better fetch someone else who was more of a specialist. The lady she fetched told them they were from the Mutton Hill depot, and that it was a matter of pyjamas. They answered that it was so.

Mrs. Moss-Henry and my mother restated their positions, exactly, circumstantially, and emphatically. They made it clear (my mother made it clearest) that this was something that must be settled at once, and settled for all time.

The lady who was more of a specialist kept her eyes fixed on the offical trouser pattern, as though a button in invisible ink might be lurking there. At last she said, 'Thank you so much. We quite appreciate your difficulties, and we will write to you shortly.' And she gave them a little dismissing bow.

They were moving away when my mother, with a great surge of indignation and another argument, which had just occurred to her, turned back towards the desk. The lady saw her coming, and held up her hand.

'For the present perhaps you had better leave the buttons off,' she said.

That evening Mrs. Moss-Henry resigned. No letter came from Devonshire House to the Mutton Hill Red Cross depot. After a while my mother resigned, too. There was no need to go on. She had won the war.

EUDORA WELTY *was born in 1909 in Jackson, Mississippi, where she still lives in her father's house. In* One Writer's Beginnings, *the source of the following excerpt, she sketches her autobiography and tells us how her family—and in this passage, especially her mother—shaped her personality and her writing. The origin of this award-winning book is the set of three lectures the writer delivered at Harvard University in 1983 at the invitation of the graduate program in the History of American Civilization. This work of nonfiction contains the wisdom that Miss Welty expresses in her novel,* Delta Wedding: *"How deep were the complexities of the everyday, of the family, what caves were in the mountains, what blocked chambers and what crystal rivers that had not yet seen light." Her many literary honors include the Pulitzer Prize, the American Book Award for fiction, and the Gold Medal for the Novel, given by the American Academy and Institute of Arts and Letters for her entire work in fiction.*

Eudora Welty
Listening

I learned from the age of two or three that any room in our house, at any time of day, was there to read in, or to be read to. My mother read to me. She'd read to me in the big bedroom in the mornings, when we were in her rocker together, which ticked in rhythm as we rocked, as though we had a cricket accompanying the story. She'd read to me in the diningroom on winter afternoons in front of the coal fire, with our cuckoo clock ending the story with "Cuckoo," and at night when I'd got in my own bed. I must have given her no peace. Sometimes she read to me in the kitchen while she sat churning, and the churning sobbed along with *any* story. It was my ambition to have her read to me while *I* churned; once she granted my wish, but she read off my story before I brought her butter. She was an expressive reader. When she was reading "Puss in Boots," for instance, it was impossible not to know that she distrusted *all* cats.

It had been startling and disappointing to me to

From *One Writer's Beginnings*.

find out that story books had been written by *people*, that books were not natural wonders, coming up of themselves like grass. Yet regardless of where they came from, I cannot remember a time when I was not in love with them—with the books themselves, cover and binding and the paper they were printed on, with their smell and their weight and with their possession in my arms, captured and carried off to myself. Still illiterate, I was ready for them, committed to all the reading I could give them.

Neither of my parents had come from homes that could afford to buy many books, but though it must have been something of a strain on his salary, as the youngest officer in a young insurance company, my father was all the while carefully selecting and ordering away for what he and Mother thought we children should grow up with. They bought first for the future.

Besides the bookcase in the livingroom, which was always called "the library," there were the encyclopedia tables and dictionary stand under windows in our diningroom. Here to help us grow up arguing around the diningroom table were the Unabridged Webster, the Columbia Encyclopedia, Compton's Pictured Encyclopedia, the Lincoln Library of Information, and later the Book of Knowledge. And the year we moved into our new house, there was room to celebrate it with the new 1925 edition of the Britannica, which my father, his face always deliberately turned toward the future, was of course disposed to think better than any previous edition.

In "the library," inside the mission-style bookcase with its three diamond-latticed glass doors, with my father's Morris chair and the glass-shaded lamp on its table beside it, were books I could soon begin on—and I did, reading them all alike and as they came, straight down their rows, top shelf to bottom. There was the set of Stoddard's Lectures, in all its late nineteenth-century vocabulary and vignettes of peasant life and quaint beliefs and customs, with matching halftone illustrations: Vesuvius erupting, Venice by moonlight, gypsies glimpsed by their campfires. I didn't know then the clue they were to my father's longing to see the rest of the world. I read straight through his other love-from-afar: the Victrola Book of the Opera, with opera after opera in synopsis, with portraits in costume of Melba, Caruso, Galli-Curci, and Geraldine Farrar, some of whose voices we could listen to on our Red Seal records.

My mother read secondarily for information; she sank as a hedonist into novels. She read Dickens in the spirit in which she would have eloped with him. The novels of her girlhood that had stayed on in her imagination, besides those of Dickens and Scott and Robert Louis Stevenson, were *Jane Eyre*, *Trilby*, *The Woman in White*, *Green Mansions*, *King Solomon's Mines*. Marie Corelli's name would crop up but I understood she had gone out of favor with my mother, who had only kept *Ardath* out of loyalty. In time she absorbed herself in Galsworthy, Edith Wharton, above all in Thomas Mann of the *Joseph* volumes.

St. Elmo was not in our house; I saw it often in

other houses. This wildly popular Southern novel is where all the Edna Earles in our population started coming from. They're all named for the heroine, who succeeded in bringing a dissolute, sinning roué and atheist of a lover (St. Elmo) to his knees. My mother was able to forgo it. But she remembered the classic advice given to rose growers on how to water their bushes long enough: "Take a chair and *St. Elmo.*" . . .

My mother had brought from West Virginia that set of Dickens; those books looked sad, too—they had been through fire and water before I was born, she told me, and there they were, lined up—as I later realized, waiting for *me*.

I was presented, from as early as I can remember, with books of my own, which appeared on my birthday and Christmas morning. Indeed, my parents could not give me books enough. They must have sacrificed to give me on my sixth or seventh birthday—it was after I became a reader for myself— the ten-volume set of Our Wonder World. These were beautifully made, heavy books I would lie down with on the floor in front of the diningroom hearth, and more often than the rest volume 5, *Every Child's Story Book,* was under my eyes. There were the fairy tales—Grimm, Andersen, the English, the French, "Ali Baba and the Forty Thieves"; and there was Aesop and Reynard the Fox; there were the myths and legends, Robin Hood, King Arthur, and St. George and the Dragon, even the history of Joan of Arc; a whack of *Pilgrim's Progress* and a long piece of *Gulliver.* They all carried their classic illustrations. I located myself in these pages and could go straight to the stories and pictures I loved; very often "The Yellow Dwarf" was first choice, with Walter Crane's Yellow Dwarf in full color making his terrifying appearance flanked by turkeys. Now that volume is as worn and backless and hanging apart as my father's poor *Sanford and Merton*. The precious page with Edward Lear's "Jumblies" on it has been in danger of slipping out for all these years. One measure of my love for Our Wonder World was that for a long time I wondered if I would go through fire and water for it as my mother had done for Charles Dickens; and the only comfort was to think I could ask my mother to do it for me.

I believe I'm the only child I know of who grew up with this treasure in the house. I used to ask others, "Did you have Our Wonder World?" I'd have to tell them The Book of Knowledge could not hold a candle to it.

I live in gratitude to my parents for initiating me—and as early as I begged for it, without keeping me waiting—into knowledge of the word, into reading and spelling, by way of the alphabet. They taught it to me at home in time for me to begin to read before starting to school. I believe the alphabet is no longer considered an essential piece of equipment for traveling through life. In my day it was the keystone to knowledge. You learned the alphabet as you learned to count to ten, as you learned "Now I lay me" and the Lord's Prayer and your father's and mother's name and address and telephone number, all in case you were lost.

My love for the alphabet, which endures, grew

out of reciting it but, before that, out of seeing the letters on the page. In my own story books, before I could read them for myself, I fell in love with various winding, enchanted-looking initials drawn by Walter Crane at the heads of fairy tales. In "Once upon a time," an "O" had a rabbit running it as a treadmill, his feet upon flowers. When the day came, years later, for me to see the Book of Kells, all the wizardry of letter, initial, and word swept over me a thousand times over, and the illumination, the gold, seemed a part of the world's beauty and holiness that had been there from the start. . . .

My mother always sang to her children. Her voice came out just a little bit in the minor key. "Wee Willie Winkie's" song was wonderfully sad when she sang the lullabies.

"Oh, but now there's a record. She could have her own record to listen to," my father would have said. For there came a Victrola record of "Bobby Shafftoe" and "Rock-a-Bye Baby", all of Mother's lullabies, which could be played to take her place. Soon I was able to play her my own lullabies all day long.

Our Victrola stood in the diningroom. I was allowed to climb onto the seat of a diningroom chair to wind it, start the record turning, and set the needle playing. In a second I'd jumped to the floor, to spin or march around the table as the music called for—now there were all the other records I could play too. I skinned back onto the chair just in time to lift the needle at the end, stop the record and turn it over, then change the needle. That brass receptacle with a hole in the lid gave off a metallic smell like human sweat, from all the hot needles that were fed it. Winding up, dancing, being cocked to start and stop the record, was of course all in one the act of *listening*—to "Overture to *Daughter of the Regiment*," "Selections from *The Fortune Teller*," "Kiss Me Again," "Gypsy Dance from *Carmen*," "Stars and Stripes Forever," "When the Midnight Choo-Choo Leaves for Alabam," or whatever came next. Movement must be at the very heart of listening.

Ever since I was first read to, then started reading to myself, there has never been a line read that I didn't *hear*. As my eyes followed the sentence, a voice was saying it silently to me. It isn't my mother's voice, or the voice of any person I can identify, certainly not my own. It is human, but inward, and it is inwardly that I listen to it. It is to me the voice of the story or the poem itself. The cadence, whatever it is that asks you to believe, the feeling that resides in the printed word, reaches me through the reader-voice. I have supposed, but never found out, that this is the case with all readers—to read as listeners—and with all writers, to write as listeners. It may be part of the desire to write. The sound of what falls on the page begins the process of testing it for truth, for me. Whether I am right to trust so far I don't know. By now I don't know whether I could do either one, reading or writing, without the other.

My own words, when I am at work on a story, I hear too as they go, in the same voice that I hear when I read in books. When I write and the sound of it comes back to my ears, then I act to make my changes. I have always trusted this voice. . . .

It was when my mother came out onto the sleeping porch to tell me goodnight that her trial came. The sudden silence in the double bed meant my younger brothers had both keeled over in sleep, and I in the single bed at my end of the porch would be lying electrified, waiting for this to be the night when she'd tell me what she'd promised for so long. Just as she bent to kiss me I grabbed her and asked: "Where do babies come from?"

My poor mother! But something saved her every time. Almost any night I put the baby question to her, suddenly, as if the whole outdoors exploded, Professor Holt would start to sing. The Holts lived next door; he taught penmanship (the Palmer Method), typing, bookkeeping and shorthand at the high school. His excitable voice traveled out of their dining-room windows across the two driveways between our houses, and up to our upstairs sleeping porch. His wife, usually so quiet and gentle, was his uncannily spirited accompanist at the piano. "High-ho! Come to the Fair!" he'd sing, unless he sang "Oho ye oho ye, who's bound for the ferry, the briar's in bud and the sun's going down!"

"Dear, this isn't a very good time for you to hear Mother, is it?"

She couldn't get started. As soon as she'd whisper something, Professor Holt galloped into the chorus, "And 'tis but a penny to Twickenham town!" "Isn't that enough?" she'd ask me. She'd told me that the mother and the father had to both *want* the baby. This couldn't be enough. I knew she was not trying to fib to me, for she never did fib, but also I could not help but know she was not really *telling* me. And more than that, I was afraid of what I was going to hear next. This was partly because she wanted to tell me in the dark. I thought *she* might be afraid. In something like childish hopelessness I thought she probably *couldn't* tell, just as she *couldn't* lie.

On the night we came the closest to having it over with, she started to tell me without being asked, and I ruined it by yelling, "Mother, look at the lightning bugs!"

In those days, the dark was dark. And all the dark out there was filled with the soft, near lights of lightning bugs. They were everywhere, flashing on the slow, horizontal move, on the upswings, rising and subsiding in the soundless dark. Lightning bugs signaled and answered back without a stop, from down below all the way to the top of our sycamore tree. My mother just gave me a businesslike kiss and went on back to Daddy in their room at the front of the house. Distracted by lightning bugs, I had missed my chance. The fact is she never did tell me.

I doubt that any child I knew ever was told by her mother any more than I was about babies. In fact, I doubt that her own mother ever told her any more than she told me, though there were five brothers who were born after Mother, one after the other, and she was taking care of babies all her childhood.

Not being able to bring herself to open that door

to reveal its secret, one of those days, she opened another door.

In my mother's bottom bureau drawer in her bedroom she kept treasures of hers in boxes, and had given me permission to play with one of them—a switch of her own chestnut-colored hair, kept in a heavy bright braid that coiled around like a snake inside a cardboard box. I hung it from her door-knob and unplaited it; it fell in ripples nearly to the floor, and it satisfied the Rapunzel in me to comb it out. But one day I noticed in the same drawer a small white cardboard box such as her engraved calling cards came in from the printing house. It was tightly closed, but I opened it, to find to my puzzlement and covetousness two polished buffalo nickels, embedded in white cotton. I rushed with this opened box to my mother and asked if I could run out and spend the nickels.

"No!" she exclaimed in a most passionate way. She seized the box into her own hands. I begged her; somehow I had started to cry. Then she sat down, drew me to her, and told me that I had had a little brother who had come before I did, and who had died as a baby before I was born. And these two nickels that I'd wanted to claim as my find were his. They had lain on his eyelids, for a purpose untold and unimaginable. "He was a fine little baby, my first baby, and he shouldn't have died. But he did. It was because your mother almost died at the same time," she told me. "In looking after me, they too nearly forgot about the little baby."

She'd told me the wrong secret—not how babies

could come but how they could die, how they could be forgotten about.

I wondered in after years: how could my mother have kept those two coins? Yet how could someone like herself have disposed of them in any way at all? She suffered from a morbid streak which in all the life of the family reached out on occasions—the worst occasions—and touched us, clung around us, making it worse for her; her unbearable moments could find nowhere to go.

The future story writer in the child I was must have taken unconscious note and stored it away then: one secret is liable to be revealed in the place of another that is harder to tell, and the substitute secret when nakedly exposed is often the more appalling.

Perhaps telling me what she did was made easier for my mother by the two secrets, told and still not told, being connected in her deepest feeling, more intimately than anyone ever knew, perhaps even herself. So far as I remember now, this is the only time this baby was ever mentioned in my presence. So far as I can remember, and I've tried, he was never mentioned in the presence of my father, for whom he had been named. I am only certain that my father, who could never bear pain very well, would not have been able to bear it.

It was my father (my mother told me at some later date) who saved her own life, after that baby was born. She had in fact been given up by the doctor, as she had long been unable to take any nourishment. (That was the illness when they'd cut her hair, which formed the switch in the same bureau drawer.) What had struck her was septicemia, in those days nearly always fatal. What my father did was to try champagne.

I once wondered where he, who'd come not very long before from an Ohio farm, had ever heard of such a remedy, such a measure. Or perhaps as far as he was concerned he invented it, out of the strength of desperation. It would have been desperation augmented because champagne couldn't be bought in Jackson. But somehow he knew what to do about that too. He telephoned to Canton, forty miles north, to an Italian orchard grower, Mr. Trolio, told him the necessity, and asked, begged, that he put a bottle of his wine on Number 3, which was due in a few minutes to stop in Canton to "take on water" (my father knew everything about train schedules). My father would be waiting to meet the train in Jackson. Mr. Trolio did—he sent the bottle in a bucket of ice and my father snatched it off the baggage car. He offered my mother a glass of chilled champagne and she drank it and kept it down. She was to live, after all.

Now, her hair was long again, it would reach in a braid down her back, and now I was her child. She hadn't died. And when I came, I hadn't died either. Would she ever? Would I ever? I couldn't face *ever*. I must have rushed into her lap, demanding her like a baby. And she had to put her first-born aside again, for me.

Of course it's easy to see why they both overprotected me, why my father, before I could wear a new pair of shoes for the first time, made me wait while he took out his thin silver pocket knife and with the point of the blade scored the polished soles all over, carefully, in a diamond pattern, to prevent me from sliding on the polished floor when I ran.

As I was to learn over and over again, my mother's mind was a mass of associations. Whatever happened would be forever paired for her with something that had happened before it, to one of us or to her. It became a private anniversary. Every time any possible harm came near me, she thought of how she lost her first child. When a Roman candle at Christmas backfired up my sleeve, she rushed to smother the blaze with the first thing she could grab, which was a dish towel hanging in the kitchen, and the burn on my arm became infected. I was nothing but proud of my sling, for I could wear it to school, and her repeated blaming of herself—for even my sling—puzzled and troubled me.

When my mother would tell me that she wanted me to have something because she as a child had never had it, I wanted, or I partly wanted, to give it back. All my life I continued to feel that bliss for me would have to imply my mother's deprivation or sacrifice. I don't think it would have occurred to her what a double emotion I felt, and indeed I know that it was being unfair to her, for what she said was simply the truth.

"I'm going to let you go to the Century Theatre with your father tonight on my ticket. I'd rather you saw *Blossom Time* than go myself."

In the Century first-row balcony, where their seats always were, I'd be sitting beside my father at this hour beyond my bedtime carried totally away by the performance, and then suddenly the thought of my mother staying home with my sleeping younger brothers, missing the spectacle at this moment before my eyes, and doing without all the excitement and wonder that filled my being, would arrest me and I could hardly bear my pleasure for my guilt.

Jackson's Carnegie Library was on the same street where our house was, on the other side of the State Capitol. "Through the Capitol" was the way to go to the Library. You could glide through it on your bicycle or even coast through on roller skates, though without family permission.

I never knew anyone who'd grown up in Jackson without being afraid of Mrs. Calloway, our librarian. She ran the Library absolutely by herself, from the desk where she sat with her back to the books and facing the stairs, her dragon eye on the front door, where who knew what kind of person might come in from the public? SILENCE in big black letters was on signs tacked up everywhere. She herself spoke in her normally commanding voice; every word could be heard all over the Library above a steady seething sound coming from her electric fan; it was the only fan in the Library and stood on her desk, turned directly onto her streaming face.

As you came in from the bright outside, if you were a girl, she sent her strong eyes down the stairway to test you; if she could see through your skirt she sent you straight back home: you could just put on another petticoat if you wanted a book that badly from the public library. I was willing; I would do anything to read.

My mother was not afraid of Mrs. Calloway. She

wished me to have my own library card to check out books for myself. She took me in to introduce me and I saw I had met a witch. "Eudora is nine years old and has my permission to read any book she wants from the shelves, children or adult," Mother said. "With the exception of *Elsie Dinsmore*," she added. Later she explained to me that she'd made this rule because Elsie the heroine, being made by her father to practice too long and hard at the piano, fainted and fell off the piano stool. "You're too impressionable, dear," she told me. "You'd read that and the very first thing you'd do, you'd fall off the piano stool." "Impressionable" was a new word. I never hear it yet without the image that comes with it of falling straight off the piano stool.

Mrs. Calloway made her own rules about books. You could not take back a book to the Library on the same day you'd taken it out; it made no difference to her that you'd read every word in it and needed another to start. You could take out two books at a time and two only; this applied as long as you were a child and also for the rest of your life, to my mother as severely as to me. So two by two, I read library books as fast as I could go, rushing them home in the basket of my bicycle. From the minute I reached our house, I started to read. Every book I seized on, from *Bunny Brown and His Sister Sue at Camp Rest-a-While* to *Twenty Thousand Leagues under the Sea,* stood for the devouring wish to read being instantly granted. I knew this was bliss, knew it at the time. Taste isn't nearly so important; it comes in its own time. I wanted to read *immediately*. The only fear was that of books coming to an end.

My mother was very sharing of this feeling of insatiability. Now, I think of her as reading so much of the time while doing something else. In my mind's eye *The Origin of Species* is lying on the shelf in the pantry under a light dusting of flour—my mother was a bread maker; she'd pick it up, sit by the kitchen window and find her place, with one eye on the oven. I remember her picking up *The Man in Lower Ten* while my hair got dry enough to unroll from a load of kid curlers trying to make me like my idol, Mary Pickford. A generation later, when my brother Walter was away in the Navy and his two little girls often spent the day in our house, I remember Mother reading the new issue of *Time* magazine while taking the part of the Wolf in a game of "Little red Riding Hood" with the children. She'd just look up at the right time, long enough to answer—in character—"The better to eat you with, my dear," and go back to her place in the war news. . . .

Even as we grew up, my mother could not help imposing herself between her children and whatever it was they might take it in mind to reach out for in the world. For she would get it for them, if it was good enough for them—she would have to be very sure—and give it to them, at whatever cost to herself: valiance was in her very fibre. She stood always prepared in herself to challenge the world in our place. She did indeed tend to make the world look dangerous, and so it had been to her. A way had to be found around her love sometimes, without challenging *that,* and at the same time cherishing it in its unassailable strength. Each of us children did, sooner or later, in part at least, solve this in a different, respectful, complicated way.

But I think she was relieved when I chose to be a writer of stories, for she thought writing was safe.

"Especially in . . . 'A Sketch of the Past' . . . we have, I think, the single most moving and beautiful thing that **VIRGINIA WOOLF** *ever wrote about her own life." So wrote Hilton Kramer in* The New York Times *when the five essay-length memoirs that appear in* Moments of Being *were first published in 1976. These autobiographical writings, called "The Monks House Papers," belonged to Leonard Woolf. After his death the essays, which were unrevised and had never been intended for publication, were published. In the opinion of the estate of Virginia Woolf, this material so richly illuminates the sensibility of one of the greatest writers in the history of English literature that it constitutes a tribute to the writer's memory and an extremely important contribution to our literature. A wise opinion, and the decision to publish was equally so. For in a strange way, the excerpt that follows, from "A Sketch of the Past," brings Virginia Woolf closer to her readers than she has ever been.*

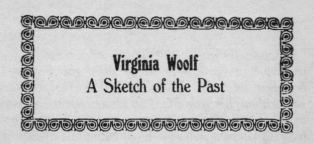

Virginia Woolf
A Sketch of the Past

Two days ago—Sunday 16th April 1939 to be precise—Nessa said that if I did not start writing my memoirs I should soon be too old. I should be eighty-five, and should have forgotten—witness the unhappy case of Lady Strachey.* As it happens that I am sick of writing Roger's life, perhaps I will spend two or three mornings making a sketch.† There are several difficulties. In the first place, the enormous number of things I can remember; in the second, the number of different ways in which memoirs can be written. As a great memoir reader, I know many different ways. But if I begin to go through them and to analyse them and their merits and faults, the mornings—I cannot take more than two or three at most—will be gone. So without

---

From *Moments of Being*.
*Lady Strachey, mother of Lytton, died at the age of eighty-nine, in 1928. In old age she wrote "Some Recollections of a Long Life" which were very short—less than a dozen pages in *Nation and Athenaeum*. This may indicate, as Michael Holroyd has suggested, that by the early 1920s she had forgotten more than she remembered.
†VW was at work on *Roger Fry: A Biography* (The Hogarth Press; London, 1940).

stopping to choose my way, in the sure and certain knowledge that it will find itself—or if not it will not matter—I begin: the first memory.

This was of red and purple flowers on a black ground—my mother's dress; and she was sitting either in a train or in an omnibus, and I was on her lap. I therefore saw the flowers she was wearing very close; and can still see purple and red and blue, I think, against the black; they must have been anemones, I suppose. Perhaps we were going to St Ives; more probably, for from the light it must have been evening, we were coming back to London. But it is more convenient artistically to suppose that we were going to St Ives, for that will lead to my other memory, which also seems to be my first memory, and in fact it is the most important of all my memories. If life has a base that it stands upon, if it is a bowl that one fills and fills and fills—then my bowl without a doubt stands upon this memory. It is of lying half asleep, half awake, in bed in the nursery at St Ives. It is of hearing the waves breaking, one, two, one, two, and sending a splash of water over the beach; and then breaking, one, two, one, two, behind a yellow blind. It is of hearing the blind draw its little acorn across the floor as the wind blew the blind out. It is of lying and hearing this splash and seeing this light, and feeling, it is almost impossible that I should be here; of feeling the purest ecstasy I can conceive.

I could spend hours trying to write that as it should be written, in order to give the feeling which is even at this moment very strong in me. But I should fail (unless I had some wonderful luck); I dare say I should only succeed in having the luck if I had begun by describing Virginia herself.

Here I come to one of the memoir writer's difficulties—one of the reasons why, though I read so many, so many are failures. They leave out the person to whom things happened. The reason is that it is so difficult to describe any human being. So they say: "This is what happened"; but they do not say what the person was like to whom it happened. And the events mean very little unless we know first to whom they happened. Who was I then? Adeline Virginia Stephen, the second daughter of Leslie and Julia Prinsep Stephen, born on 25th January 1882, descended from a great many people, some famous, others obscure; born into a large connection, born not of rich parents, but of well-to-do parents, born into a very communicative, literate, letter writing, visiting, articulate, late nineteenth century world; so that I could if I liked to take the trouble, write a great deal here not only about my mother and father but about uncles and aunts, cousins and friends. But I do not know how much of this, or what part of this, made me feel what I felt in the nursery at St Ives. I do not know how far I differ from other people. This is another memoir writer's difficulty. Yet to describe oneself truly one must have some standard of comparison; was I clever, stupid, good looking, ugly, passionate, cold—? Owing partly to the fact that I was never at school, never competed in any way with children of my own age, I have never been able to compare my gifts and defects with other people's. But of course there was one external reason for the intensity of this first impression: the impression of the waves and the acorn on the blind; the feeling, as I describe it sometimes to myself, of lying in a grape and seeing through a film of semi-transparent yellow—it was due partly to the many months we spent in London. The change of nursery was a great change. And there was the long train journey; and the excitement. I remember the dark; the lights; the stir of the going up to bed.

But to fix my mind upon the nursery—it had a balcony; there was a partition, but it joined the balcony of my father's and mother's bedroom. My mother would come out onto her balcony in a white dressing gown. There were passion flowers growing on the wall; they were great starry blossoms, with purple streaks, and large green buds, part empty, part full.

If I were a painter I should paint these first impressions in pale yellow, silver, and green. There was the pale yellow blind; the green sea; and the silver of the passion flowers. I should make a picture that was globular; semi-transparent. I should make a picture of curved petals; of shells; of things that were semi-transparent; I should make curved shapes, showing the light through, but not giving a clear outline. Everything would be large and dim; and what was seen would at the same time be heard; sounds would come through this petal or leaf—sounds indistinguishable from sights. Sound and sight seem to make equal parts of these first impressions. When I think of the early morning in bed I also hear the caw of rooks falling from a great height. The sound seems to fall through an elastic, gummy air; which holds it up; which prevents it from being sharp and distinct.* The quality of the air above Talland House seemed to suspend sound, to let it sink down slowly, as if it were caught in a blue gummy veil. The rooks cawing is part of the waves breaking—one, two, one, two—and the splash as the wave drew back and then it gathered again, and I lay there half awake, half asleep, drawing in such ecstasy as I cannot describe.

The next memory—all these colour-and-sound memories hang together at St Ives—was much more robust; it was highly sensual. It was later. It still makes me feel warm; as if everything were ripe; humming; sunny; smelling so many smells at once; and all making a whole that even now makes me stop—as I stopped then going down to the beach; I stopped at the top to look down at the gardens. They were sunk beneath the road. The apples were on a level with one's head. The gardens gave off a murmur of bees; the apples were red and gold; there were also pink flowers; and grey and silver leaves. The buzz, the croon, the smell, all seemed to press voluptuously against some membrane; not to burst it; but to hum round one such a complete rapture of pleasure that I stopped, smelt; looked. But again I cannot describe that rapture. It was rapture rather than ecstasy.

The strength of these pictures—but sight was always then so much mixed with sound that picture is not the right word—the strength anyhow of these

---

*VW has written 'made it seem to fall from a great height' above 'prevents . . . distinct.'

impressions makes me again digress. Those moments
—in the nursery, on the road to the beach—can still
be more real than the present moment. This I have
just tested. For I got up and crossed the garden.
Percy was digging the asparagus bed; Louie was
shaking a mat in front of the bedroom door.* But I
was seeing them through the sight I saw here—the
nursery and the road to the beach. At times I can
go back to St Ives more completely than I can this
morning. I can reach a state where I seem to be
watching things happen as if I were there. That is, I
suppose, that my memory supplies what I had forgotten, so that it seems as if it were happening
independently, though I am really making it happen. In certain favourable moods, memories—what
one has forgotten—come to the top. Now if this is
so, is it not possible—I often wonder—that things
we have felt with great intensity have an existence
independent of our minds; are in fact still in existence? And if so, will it not be possible, in time,
that some device will be invented by which we can
tap them? I see it—the past—as an avenue lying
behind; a long ribbon of scenes, emotions. There at
the end of the avenue still, are the garden and the
nursery. Instead of remembering here a scene and
there a sound, I shall fit a plug into the wall; and
listen in to the past. I shall turn up August 1890. I
feel that strong emotion must leave its trace; and it
is only a question of discovering how we can get

*The gardener and daily help, respectively, at Monks House, the
country home of the Woolfs in Rodmell, Sussex from 1919.

ourselves again attached to it, so that we shall be able to live our lives through from the start.

But the peculiarity of these two strong memories is that each was very simple. I am hardly aware of myself, but only of the sensation. I am only the container of the feeling of ecstasy, of the feeling of rapture. Perhaps this is characteristic of all childhood memories; perhaps it accounts for their strength. Later we add to feelings much that makes them more complex; and therefore less strong; or if not less strong, less isolated, less complete. . . .

Many bright colours; many distinct sounds; some human beings, caricatures; comic; several violent moments of being, always including a circle of the scene which they cut out: and all surrounded by a vast space—that is a rough visual description of childhood. This is how I shape it; and how I see myself as a child, roaming about, in that space of time which lasted from 1882 to 1895. A great hall I could liken it to; with windows letting in strange lights; and murmurs and spaces of deep silence. But somehow into that picture must be brought, too, the sense of movement and change. Nothing remained stable long. One must get the feeling of everything approaching and then disappearing, getting large, getting small, passing at different rates of speed past the little creature; one must get the feeling that made her press on, the little creature driven on as she was by growth of her legs and arms, driven without her being able to stop it, or to change it, driven as a plant is driven up out of the earth, up until the stalk grows, the leaf grows, buds swell. That is what is indescribable, that is what makes all images too static, for no sooner has one said this was so, than it was past and altered. How immense must be the force of life which turns a baby, who can just distinguish a great blot of blue and purple on a black background, into the child who thirteen years later can feel all that I felt on May 5th 1895—now almost exactly to a day, forty-four years ago—when my mother died.

This shows that among the innumerable things left out in my sketch I have left out the most important—those instincts, affections, passions, attachments—there is no single word for them, for they changed month by month—which bound me, I suppose, from the first moment of consciousness to other people. If it were true, as I said above, that the things that ceased in childhood, are easy to describe because they are complete, then it should be easy to say what I felt for my mother, who died when I was thirteen. Thus I should be able to see her completely undisturbed by later impressions, as I saw Mr Gibbs and C. B. Clarke. But the theory, though true of them, breaks down completely with her. It breaks down in a curious way, which I will explain, for perhaps it may help to explain why I find it now so curiously difficult to describe both my feeling for her, and her herself.

Until I was in the forties—I could settle the date by seeing when I wrote *To the Lighthouse*, but am too casual here to bother to do it—the presence of my mother obsessed me.* I could hear her voice,

---

To the Lighthouse was begun in 1925 and published in 1927 when VW was forty-five.

see her, imagine what she would do or say as I went about my day's doings. She was one of the invisible presences who after all play so important a part in every life. This influence, by which I mean the consciousness of other groups impinging upon ourselves; public opinion; what other people say and think; all those magnets which attract us this way to be like that, or repel us the other and make us different from that; has never been analysed in any of those Lives which I so much enjoy reading, or very superficially.

Yet it is by such invisible presences that the "subject of this memoir" is tugged this way and that every day of his life; it is they that keep him in position. Consider what immense forces society brings to play upon each of us, how that society changes from decade to decade; and also from class to class; well, if we cannot analyse these invisible presences, we know very little of the subject of the memoir; and again how futile life-writing becomes. I see myself as a fish in a stream; deflected; held in place; but cannot describe the stream.

To return to the particular instance which should be more definite and more capable of description than for example the influence on me of the Cambridge Apostles,* or the influence of the Galsworthy, Bennett, Wells school of fiction, or the influence of the Vote, or of the War—that is, the influence

*The popular name for the semi-secret 'Cambridge Conversazione Society' which was founded in the 1820s. All the young men who formed the nucleus of 'old Bloomsbury' belonged to it, except Clive Bell and Thoby Stephen.

of my mother. It is perfectly true that she obsessed me, in spite of the fact that she died when I was thirteen, until I was forty-four. Then one day walking round Tavistock Square I made up, as I sometimes make up my books, *To the Lighthouse*; in a great, apparently involuntary, rush.* One thing burst into another. Blowing bubbles out of a pipe gives the feeling of the rapid crowd of ideas and scenes which blew out of my mind, so that my lips seemed syllabling of their own accord as I walked. What blew the bubbles? Why then? I have no notion. But I wrote the book very quickly; and when it was written, I ceased to be obsessed by my mother. I no longer hear her voice; I do not see her.

I suppose that I did for myself what psycho-analysts do for their patients. I expressed some very long felt and deeply felt emotion. And in expressing it I explained it and then laid it to rest. But what is the meaning of "explained" it? Why, because I described her and my feeling for her in that book, should my vision of her and my feeling for her become so much dimmer and weaker? Perhaps one of these days I shall hit on the reason; and if so, I will give it, but at the moment I will go on, describing what I can remember, for it may be true that what I remember of her now will weaken still further. (This note is made provisionally, in order to explain in part why it is now so difficult to give any clear description of her.)

---

*52 Tavistock Square was the London home of the Woolfs from 1924 to 1939.

Certainly there she was, in the very centre of that great Cathedral space which was childhood; there she was from the very first. My first memory is of her lap; the scratch of some beads on her dress comes back to me as I pressed my cheek against it. Then I see her in her white dressing gown on the balcony; and the passion flower with the purple star on its petals. Her voice is still faintly in my ears—decided, quick; and in particular the little drops with which her laugh ended—three diminishing ahs . . . "Ah—ah—ah . . ." I sometimes end a laugh that way myself. And I see her hands, like Adrian's, with the very individual square-tipped fingers, each finger with a waist to it, and the nail broadening out. (My own are the same size all the way, so that I can slip a ring over my thumb.) She had three rings; a diamond ring, an emerald ring, and an opal ring. My eyes used to fix themselves upon the lights in the opal as it moved across the page of the lesson book when she taught us, and I was glad that she left it to me (I gave it to Leonard). Also I hear the tinkle of her bracelets, made of twisted silver, given her by Mr Lowell, as she went about the house; especially as she came up at night to see if we were asleep, holding a candle shaded; this is a distinct memory, for, like all children, I lay awake sometimes and longed for her to come. Then she told me to think of all the lovely things I could imagine. Rainbows and bells . . . But besides these minute separate details, how did I first become conscious of what was always there—her astonishing beauty? Perhaps I never became conscious of it; I think I accepted her beauty as the natural quality that a mother—she seemed typical, universal, yet our own in particular—had by virtue of being our mother. It was part of her calling. I do not think that I separated her face from that general being; or from her whole body. Certainly I have a vision of her now, as she came up the path by the lawn at St Ives; slight, shapely—she held herself very straight. I was playing. I stopped, about to speak to her. But she half turned from us, and lowered her eyes. From that indescribably sad gesture I knew that Philips, the man who had been crushed on the line and whom she had been visiting, was dead. It's over, she seemed to say. I knew, and was awed by the thought of death. At the same time I felt that her gesture as a whole was lovely. Very early, through nurses or casual visitors, I must have known that she was thought very beautiful. But that pride was snobbish, not a pure and private feeling: it was mixed with pride in other people's admiration. It was related to the more definitely snobbish pride caused in me by the nurses who said one night talking together while we ate our supper: "They're very well connected. . . ."

But apart from her beauty, if the two can be separated, what was she herself like? Very quick; very direct; practical; and amusing, I say at once offhand. She could be sharp, she disliked affectation. "If you put your head on one side like that, you shan't come to the party," I remember she said to me as we drew up in a carriage in front of some house. Severe; with a background of knowledge that made her sad. She had her own sorrow waiting behind her to dip into privately. Once when she had set us to write exercises I looked up from mine and watched her reading—the Bible perhaps; and, struck by the gravity of her face, told myself that her first husband had been a clergyman and that she was thinking, as she read what he had read, of him. This was a fable on my part; but it shows that she looked very sad when she was not talking.

But can I get any closer to her without drawing upon all those descriptions and anecdotes which after she was dead imposed themselves upon my view of her? Very quick; very definite; very upright; and behind the active, the sad, the silent. And of course she was central. I suspect the word "central" gets closest to the general feeling I had of living so completely in her atmosphere that one never got far enough away from her to see her as a person. (That is one reason why I see the Gibbses and the Beadles and the Clarkes so much more distinctly.) She was the whole thing; Talland House was full of her; Hyde Park Gate was full of her. I see now, though the sentence is hasty, feeble and inexpressive, why it was that it was impossible for her to leave a very private and particular impression upon a child. She was keeping what I call in my shorthand the panoply of life—that which we all lived in common—in being. I see now that she was living on such an extended surface that she had not time, nor strength, to concentrate, except for a moment if one were ill or in some child's crisis, upon me, or upon anyone—unless it were Adrian. Him she cherished separately; she called him 'My Joy'. The later view, the understanding that I now have of her position must have its say; and it shows me that a woman of forty with seven children, some

of them needing grown-up attention, and four still
in the nursery; and an eighth, Laura, an idiot, yet
living with us; and a husband fifteen years her elder, difficult, exacting, dependent on her; I see now
that a woman who had to keep all this in being and
under control must have been a general presence
rather than a particular person to a child of seven or
eight. Can I remember ever being alone with her
for more than a few minutes? Someone was always
interrupting. When I think of her spontaneously she
is always in a room full of people; Stella, George
and Gerald are there; my father, sitting reading
with one leg curled round the other, twisting his
lock of hair; "Go and take the crumb out of his
beard," she whispers to me; and off I trot. There
are visitors, young men like Jack Hills who is in
love with Stella; many young men, Cambridge friends
of George's and Gerald's; old men, sitting round
the tea table talking—father's friends, Henry James,
Symonds,* (I see him peering up at me on the
broad staircase at St Ives with his drawn yellow face
and a tie made of a yellow cord with two plush balls
on it); Stella's friends—the Lushingtons, the Still-
mans; I see her at the head of the table underneath
the engraving of Beatrice given her by an old governess and painted blue; I hear jokes; laughter; the
clatter of voices; I am teased; I say something funny;
she laughs; I am pleased; I blush furiously; she
observes; someone laughs at Nessa for saying that
Ida Milman is her B.F.; Mother says soothingly,

*John Addington Symonds, man of letters, was the father of Kath-
erine who married the artist Charles Fuse and Margaret (Madge)
who married William Wyamar Vaughan.

tenderly, "Best friend, that means." I see her going
to the town with her basket; and Arthur Davies
goes with her; I see her knitting on the hall step
while we play cricket; I see her stretching her arms
out to Mrs Williams when the bailiffs took possession of their house and the Captain stood at the
window bawling and shying jugs, basins, chamber
pots onto the gravel—"Come to us, Mrs. Williams";
"No, Mrs Stephen," sobbed Mrs Williams, "I will
not leave my husband."—I see her writing at her
table in London and the silver candlesticks, and the
high carved chair with the claws and the pink seat;
and the three-cornered brass ink pot; I wait in agony peeping surreptitiously behind the blind for her
to come down the street, when she has been out
late the lamps are lit and I am sure that she has
been run over. (Once my father found me peeping;
questioned me; and said rather anxiously but re-
provingly, "You shouldn't be so nervous, Jinny.")
And there is my last sight of her; she was dying; I
came to kiss her and as I crept out of the room she
said: "Hold yourself straight, my little Goat." . . .
What a jumble of things I can remember, if I let
my mind run, about my mother; but they are all of
her in company; of her surrounded; of her gen-
eralised; dispersed, omnipresent, of her as the creator of that crowded merry world which spun so
gaily in the centre of my childhood. It is true that I
enclosed that world in another made by my own
temperament; it is true that from the beginning I
had many adventures outside that world; and often
went far from it; and kept much back from it; but
there it always was, the common life of the family,

very merry, very stirring, crowded with people; and she was the centre; it was herself. This was proved on May 5th 1895. For after that day there was nothing left of it. I leant out of the nursery window the morning she died. It was about six, I suppose. I saw Dr Seton walk away up the street with his head bent and his hands clasped behind his back. I saw the pigeons floating and settling. I got a feeling of calm, sadness, and finality. It was a beautiful blue spring morning, and very still. That brings back the feeling that everything had come to an end.

May 15th 1939. The drudgery of making a coherent life of Roger has once more become intolerable, and so I turn for a few day's respite to May 1895. The little platform of present time on which I stand is, so far as the weather is concerned, damp and chilly. I look up at my skylight—over the litter of *Athenaeum* articles, Fry letters—all strewn with the sand that comes from the house that is being pulled down next door—I look up and see, as if reflecting it, a sky the colour of dirty water. And the inner landscape is much of a piece. Last night Mark Gertler* dined here and denounced the vulgarity, the inferiority of what he called "literature"; compared with the integrity of painting. "For it always deals with Mr and Mrs Brown,"—he said—with the personal, the trivial, that is; a criticism which has its sting and its chill, like the May sky. Yet if one could give a sense of my mother's personality one would have to be an artist. It would be as difficult to do that, as it should be done, as to paint a Cézanne.

---

*The artist who committed suicide in this same year, 23 June 1939.

One of the few things that is certain about her is that she married two very different men. If one looks at her not as a child, of seven or eight, but as a woman now older than she was when she died, there is something to take hold of in that fact. She was not so rubbed out and featureless, not so dominated by the beauty of her own face, as she has since become—and inevitably. For what reality can remain real of a person who died forty-four years ago* at the age of forty-nine, without leaving a book, or a picture, or any piece of work—apart from the three children who now survive and the memory of her that remains in their minds? There is the memory; but there is nothing to check that memory by; nothing to bring it to ground with.

There are however these two marriages; and they show that she was capable of falling in love with two very different men; one, to put it in a nutshell, the pink of propriety; the other, the pink of intellectuality. She could span them both. This must serve me by way of foot rule, in trying to measure her character.

The elements of that character, though, are formed in twilight. She was born, I think, in 1848;† I think in India; the daughter of Dr Jackson and his half-French wife. Not very much education came her way. An old governess—was she Mademoiselle Rose? did she give her the picture of Beatrice that hung in the dining room at Talland House?—taught her French, which she spoke with a very good accent;

---

*VW mistakenly typed '43 years ago'.
†Julia was born in 1846, not in 1848.

and she could play the piano and was musical. I remember that she kept De Quincey's *Opium Eater* on her table, one of her favourite books; and for a birthday present she chose all the works of Scott which her father gave her in the first edition—some remain; others are lost. For Scott she had a passion. She had an instinctive, not a trained mind. But her instinct, for books at least, seems to me to have been strong, and I liked it, for she gave a jump, I remember, when reading *Hamlet* aloud to her I misread 'sliver' 'silver'—she jumped as my father jumped at a false quantity when we read Virgil with him. She was her mother's favourite daughter of the three; and as her mother was an invalid even as a child she was used to nursing; to waiting on a sick bed. They had a house at Well Walk during the Crimean War; for there was an anecdote about watching the soldiers drill on the Heath. But her beauty at once came to the fore, even as a little girl; for there was another anecdote—how she could never be sent out alone, but must have Mary with her, to protect her from admiring looks: to keep her unconscious of that beauty—and she was, my father said, very little conscious of it. It was due to this beauty, I suspect, that she had that training which was much more important than any she had from governesses—the training of life at Little Holland House. She was a great deal at Little Holland House as a child, partly, I imagine, because she was acceptable to the painters, and the Prinseps—Aunt Sara and Uncle Thoby must have been proud of her.*

---

*Julia's Aunt Sara, one of the seven Pattle sisters, married Thoby Prinsep. They settled in Little Holland House, Kensington, where

Little Holland House was her world then. But what was that world like? I think of it as a summer afternoon world. To my thinking Little Holland House is an old white country house, standing in a large garden. Long windows open onto the lawn. Through them comes a stream of ladies in crinolines and little straw hats; they are attended by gentlemen in peg-top trousers and whiskers. The date is round about 1860. It is a hot summer day. Tea tables with great bowls of strawberries and cream are scattered about the lawn. They are "presided over" by some of the six lovely sisters;* who do not wear crinolines, but are robed in splendid Venetian draperies; they sit enthroned, and talk with foreign emphatic gestures—my mother too gesticulated, throwing her hands out—to the eminent men (afterwards to be made fun of by Lytton);† rulers of India, statesmen, poets, painters. My mother comes out of the window wearing that striped silk dress buttoned at the throat with a flowing skirt that appears in the photograph.‡ She is of course "a vision" as they used to say; and there she stands, silent, with her plate of strawberries and cream; or perhaps is told to take a party across the garden to

they entertained in a highly eccentric fashion an aristocracy of intellect in which the painters—Holman Hunt, Burne-Jones and above all, G. F. Watts who was long a resident—played a dominant role.

*Although there were seven Pattle sisters, no one ever spoke of Julia (Cameron) as beautiful. However, F. W. Maitland in *The Life and Letters of Leslie Stephen* (London, 1906) makes the same error when referring to Maria Pattle as "one of six sisters" (p. 317n).
†Strachey.
‡Efforts to trace this photograph have been unsuccessful.

Signior's studio.* The sound of music also comes
from those long low rooms where the great Watts
pictures hang; Joachim playing the violin; also the
sound of a voice reading poetry—Uncle Thoby would
read his translations from the Persian poets. How
easy it is to fill in the picture with set pieces that I
have gathered from memoirs—to bring in Tennyson
in his wideawake; Watts in his smock frock; Ellen
Terry dressed as a boy; Garibaldi in his red shirt—
and Henry Taylor turned from him to my mother—
"the face of one fair girl was more to me"—so he
says in a poem. But if I turn to my mother, how
difficult it is to single her out as she really was; to
imagine what she was thinking, to put a single sentence into her mouth! I dream; I make up pictures
of a summer's afternoon.

But the dream is based upon one fact. Once
when we were children, my mother took us to
Melbury road; and when we came to the street that
had been built on the old garden she gave a little
spring forward, clapped her hands, and cried "That
was where it was!" as if a fairyland had disap-
peared. Thus I think it is true that Little Holland
House was a summer afternoon world to her. As a
fact too I know that she adored her Uncle Thoby.
His walking stick, with a hole in the top through
which a tassel must have hung, a beautiful eighteenth-
century looking cane, always stood at the head of
her bed at Hyde Park Gate. She was a hero wor-
shipper, simple, uncritical, enthusiastic. She felt for
Uncle Thoby, my father said, much more than she

*The studio of G. F. Watts.

323

felt for her own father—"old Dr Jackson"; "respectable"; but, for all his good looks and the amazing mane of white hair that stood out like a three-cornered hat round his head, he was a commonplace prosaic old man; boring people with his stories of a famous poison case in Calcutta; excluded from this poetical fairyland; and no doubt out of temper with it. My mother had no romance about him; but she derived from him, I suspect, the practicality, the shrewdness, which were among her qualities.

Little Holland House then was her education. She was taught there to take such part as girls did then in the lives of distinguished men; to pour out tea; to hand them their strawberries and cream; to listen devoutly, reverently to their wisdom; to accept the fact that Watts was the great painter; Tennyson the great poet; and to dance with the Prince of Wales. For the sisters, with the exception of my grandmother who was devout and spiritual, were worldly in the thoroughgoing Victorian way. Aunt Virginia, it is plain, put her own daughters, my mother's first cousins, through tortures compared with which the boot or the Chinese shoe is negligible, in order to marry one to the Duke of Bedford, the other to Lord Henry Somerset. (That is how we came to be, as the nurses said, so "well connected".) But here again I am dipping into memoirs, and leaving Julia Jackson, the real person, on one side. The only certainties I can lay hands on in those early years are that two men proposed to her (or to her parents on her behalf); one was Holman Hunt;

the other Woolner, a sculptor.* Both proposals were made and refused when she was scarcely out of the nursery. I know too that she went once wearing a hat with grey feathers to a river party where Anny Thackeray† was; and Nun (that is Aunt Caroline, father's sister) saw her standing alone; and was amazed that she was not the centre of a bevy of admirers; "Where are they?" she asked Anny Thackeray; who said, "Oh they don't happen to be here today"—a little scene which makes me suspect that Julia aged seventeen or eighteen was aloof; and shed a certain silence round her by her very beauty.

That little scene is dated; she cannot have been more than eighteen; because she married when she was nineteen.‡ She was in Venice; met Herbert Duckworth; fell head over ears in love with him, he with her, and so they married. That is all I know, perhaps all that anyone now knows, of the most important thing that ever happened to her. How important it was is proved by the fact that when he died four years later she was "as unhappy as it is possible for a human being to be". That was her own saying; it came to me from Kitty Maxse. "I have been as unhappy and as happy as it is possible for a human being to be." Kitty remembered it, because though she was very intimate with my mother, this was the only time in all their friendship

*Hunt and Thomas Woolner were founder members of the Pre-Raphaelite Brotherhood.
†Anne Thackeray was the elder daughter of the novelist W. M. Thackeray and sister of Leslie Stephen's first wife. She married her cousin, Richmond Ritchie.
‡She was twenty-one when she married Herbert Duckworth.

that she ever spoke of what she had felt for Herbert
Duckworth.

What my mother was like when she was as happy
as anyone can be, I have no notion. Not a sound or
a scene has survived from those four years. They
were well off; lived in Bryanston Square; he prac-
tised not very seriously at the Bar; (once they went
on circuit; and a friend said to him, "I spent the
whole morning in Court looking at a beautiful face"
—Herbert's wife); George was born; then Stella;
and Gerald was about to be born when Herbert
Duckworth died. They were staying with the Vaughans at Upton;* he stretched to pick a fig for my
mother; an abscess burst; and he died in a few
hours. Those are the only facts I know about those
four happy years.
If it were possible to know what Herbert himself
was like, some ray of light might fall from him upon
my mother. But, like all very handsome men who
die tragically, he left not so much a character behind him as a legend. Youth and death shed a halo
through which it is difficult to see a real face—a
face one might see today in the street or here in my
studio. To Aunt Mary—my mother's sister, likely
thus to share some of her feelings —he was "Oh
darling, a beam of light . . . like no one I have ever
met . . . When Herbert Duckworth smiled . . . when
Herbert Duckworth came into the room . . ." here
she broke off, shook her head quickly from side to

---

*Julia's sister, Adeline, married Henry Halford Vaughan. Upton
Castle, in Pembrokeshire, was rented by the Vaughans.

side and screwed her face up, as if he were ineffable; no words could describe him. And in this spasmodic way she gave an echo of what must have been my mother's feeling; only hers was much deeper, and stronger. He must have been to her the perfect man; heroic; handsome; magnanimous; "the great Achilles, whom we knew"—it seems natural to quote Tennyson—and also genial, lovable, simple, and also her husband; and her children's father. It was thus natural to her when she was a girl to love the simple, the genial, the normal ordinary type of man, in preference to the queer, the uncouth artistic, the intellectual, whom she had met and who had wished to marry her. Herbert was the perfect type of public school boy and English gentleman, my father said. She chose him; and how completely he satisfied her is proved by the collapse, the complete collapse into which she fell when he died. All her gaiety, all her sociability left her. She was as unhappy as it is possible for anyone to be. There is very little known of the years that were thus stamped. Only that saying, and Stella once told me that she used to lie upon his grave at Orchardleigh. As she was undemonstrative that seems a superlative expression of her grief.

What is known, and is much more remarkable, is that during those eight years spent, so far as she had time over from her children and house, 'doing good', nursing, visiting the poor, she lost her faith. This hurt her mother, a deeply religious woman, to whom she was devoted, and thus must have been a genuine conviction; something arrived at as the result of solitary and independent thinking. It proves that there was more in her than simplicity; enthusiasm; romance; and thus makes sense of her two incongruous choices: Herbert and my father. There was a complexity in her; great simplicity and directness combined with a sceptical, a serious spirit. Probably it was that combination that accounted for the great impression she made on people; the positive impression. Her character was sharpened by the mixture of simplicity and scepticism. She was sociable yet severe; very amusing; but very serious; extremely practical but with a depth in her . . . "She was a mixture of the Madonna and a woman of the world," is Miss Robins's description.*

The certain fact at any rate is that when at last she was left alone—"Oh the torture of never being left alone!" is a saying of hers, reported I forget by whom, that refers to her widowhood, and the fuss that friends and family made—when she was alone at last in Hyde Park Gate, she began to think out her position; and for this reason perhaps read something my father had written. She liked it (he says in the 'Mausoleum Book'), when she was not sure that she liked him. It is thus permissible to think of her sitting in the creeper-shaded drawing room at Hyde Park Gate in her widow's dress, alone, when the children had gone to bed, with a copy of the *Fortnightly*, trying to reason out the case for agnosticism. From that she would go on to think of Leslie Stephen, the gaunt bearded man who lived up the street, married to Minny Thackeray. He was in every way the opposite of Herbert Duckworth; but

*Elizabeth Robins, the actress, had been a friend of Julia's.

there was something in his mind that interested her. One evening she called on the Leslie Stephens, [and] found them sitting over the fire together; a happy married pair, with one child in the nursery, and another to be born soon. She sat talking; and then went home, envying them their happiness and comparing it with her own loneliness. Next day Minny died suddenly. And about two years later she married the gaunt bearded widower.*

"How did father ask you to marry him?" I once asked her, with my arm slipped in hers as we went down the twisted stairs into the dining room. She gave her little laugh, half surprised, half shocked. She did not answer. He asked her in a letter; and she refused him. Then one night when he had given up all thought of it, and had been dining with her, and asking her advice about a governess for Laura, she followed him to the door and said "I will try to be a good wife to you."

Perhaps there was pity in her love; certainly there was devout admiration for his mind; and so she spanned the two marriages with the two different men; and emerged from that corridor of the eight silent years to live fifteen years more;† to bear four children; and [to] die early on the morning of the 5th of May 1895. George took us down to say goodbye. My father staggered from the bedroom as we came. I stretched out my arms to stop him, but he brushed past me, crying out something I could

---

*Minny died in 1875; Leslie Stephen married Julia in 1878.
†After her marriage to Leslie Stephen, Julia lived seventeen years.

not catch; distraught. And George led me in to kiss my mother, who had just died.

May 28th 1939. Led by George with towels wrapped round us and given each a drop of brandy in warm milk to drink, we were taken into the bedroom. I think candles were burning; and I think the sun was coming in. At any rate I remember the long looking-glass; with the drawers on either side; and the washstand; and the great bed on which my mother lay. I remember very clearly how even as I was taken to the bedside I noticed that one nurse was sobbing, and a desire to laugh came over me, and I said to myself as I have often done at moments of crisis since, "I feel nothing whatever". Then I stooped and kissed my mother's face. It was still warm. She [had] only died a moment before. Then we went upstairs into the day nursery.

Perhaps it was the next evening that Stella took me into the bedroom to kiss mother for the last time. She had been lying on her side before. Now she was lying straight in the middle of her pillows. Her face looked immeasurably distant, hollow and stern. When I kissed her, it was like kissing cold iron. Whenever I touch cold iron the feeling comes back to me—the feeling of my mother's face, iron cold, and granulated. I started back. Then Stella stroked her cheek, and undid a button on her nightgown. "She always liked to have it like that," she said. When she came up to the nursery later she said to me, "Forgive me. I saw you were afraid." She had noticed that I had started. When Stella asked me to forgive her for having given me that shock, I cried—we had been crying off and on all day—and said, "When I see mother, I see a man sitting with her." Stella looked at me as if I had frightened her. Did I say that in order to attract attention to myself? Or was it true? I cannot be sure, for certainly I had a great wish to draw attention to myself. But certainly it was true that when she said: "Forgive me," and thus made me visualize my mother, I seemed to see a man sitting bent on the edge of the bed.

"It's nice that she shouldn't be alone", Stella said after a moment's pause.

Of course the atmosphere of those three or four days before the funeral was so melodramatic, histrionic and unreal that any hallucination was possible. We lived through them in hush, in artificial light. Rooms were shut. People were creeping in and out. People were coming to the door all the time. We were all sitting in the drawing room round father's chair sobbing. The hall reeked of flowers. They were piled on the hall table. The scent still brings back those days of astonishing intensity.